HOST

Russ Capasso

Book Cover Design & Art by Kasey Regan

ebook ISBN: 979-8-9886256-2-9

Paperback ISBN: 979-8-9886256-0-5

Hardcover ISBN: 979-8-9886256-1-2

1st edition 2023

To friends and family for their support.

Contents

Chapter 1

It didn't take long for panic to set in.

Elliot Bishop's stomach turned as news rolled in about an attack striking sections of the power grid across the Southeast United States. The outages draped the region in darkness, like a light switch flipped without warning. So sudden was the blackout, not even chaos had a chance to think.

Elliot stood by a window in a lab that overlooked the MIT campus in Cambridge, Massachusetts. His arms crossed, he scanned the faces of the two people in the room with him. His friend, Jake, sat at the front of the room next to a large whiteboard, dragging a hand through his chaotic hair. Elliot could see bags under his eyes. Sleep had evaded them both since the signal infiltrated their lives. He felt a pang of guilt for putting his friend in danger.

His eyes moved to a woman who had shown up less than twenty-four hours ago. She called herself "Emma." Elliot didn't believe that was her real name, and he didn't know what else she might be hiding. Her eyes held thoughts her words avoided. She caught his look and shook her head as if apologizing. For what, he didn't know.

Elliot cycled through various news networks, CNN to FOX News to MSNBC. Normally poker-faced news anchors were perplexed, grasping at words as details came in. Breaking news banners in bright red scrolled across the bottom of each channel: *Power grid in Southeast shut down. Millions without power.* All were covering the outage live, different versions of the same map showing the steady march of blackouts across the Southeast like someone moving pieces on a Risk board. The high-priced news readers circled the same talking points. *Cyberattack* was thrown around like a buzz word, the word flashed across their chyrons seemingly without purpose or meaning. Their useless theorizing bounced off the cold concrete walls of the empty MIT lab.

The three of them sat in silence as the news droned on. Florida, Georgia, and parts of Alabama were hit within the first hour. The next hour, county by county, Mississippi, South Carolina, and the lower half of North Carolina were thrown into darkness. Concern shifted to reports of gas supply lines from Texas experiencing lockouts. The chaos spread steadily, systematically with no end in sight. And nowhere to point a finger.

The ominous maps and breaking news reports were periodically interrupted by interviews with locals and any official willing to talk—all of them a jumble of information and wild, unchecked theories about the cause of the blackouts.

"Jesus . . ." Jake said, his eyes glued to the television.

"You think this has anything to do with the signal?" Elliot asked as he paced the room, his hands buried in his hoodie pockets. No response. He continued, thinking out loud, "What if this hits us?"

He looked to Emma, who offered no response, her eyes still fixed on the screen, then continued to pace.

She murmured, "It's started."

Elliot stopped, exchanged a glance with Jake, and turned to Emma. "You expected this?"

She faced forward with a thousand-yard stare. "I'm expecting worse."

Chapter 2

Three weeks earlier

Elliot dove into the glass-like lake down the hill from his family's cabin in Lovell, Maine. He'd done this a million times as a kid, but back then it was much less graceful. He'd catch a running start and leap, arms open, while his father sat in an Adirondack chair trying to hit his young receiver with a Nerf football before he touched the water. He couldn't say his father never played catch with him, even if it was more like fetch.

Now, the cool water was a welcoming respite from the summer heat. A few seconds later he surfaced and climbed onto a floating dock anchored fifty feet from the shore. Other than a couple passing kayakers offering a friendly wave, the lake was quiet, peaceful. He could just barely see the White Mountains over the treetops in the distance.

He slicked back his short, dark hair to remove the excess water. His eyes squinted from the sun's glare off the surface of the lake. He lay flat on the dock, looking straight up into the sky at nothing in particular, then closed his eyes. The dock soaked up the dripping water and cooled the surface for a moment. It didn't take long for him to dry in the hot rays that had traveled 8.3 minutes to reach him from the sun. That was one of many science tidbits he'd picked up from his father as a kid.

An hour later Elliot made his way back up to the cabin and sat at a desk in his father's study. Windows extended across the outside facing wall, giving a full view of the lake, dock, and surrounding wooded area. Elliot understood why this was his father's favorite room—there was total privacy from the outside world.

The bookshelf along the back wall was jammed with dust-covered college textbooks his father had collected over the years as a professor, as well as some of his favorite sci-fi novels from Asimov, Heinlein, and Huxley. The study had one rule: no technology allowed. Only analog devices and books. Elliot had broken the only rule the moment he brought his laptop into the room. He sat in front of it now, staring at a blank document.

Distracted, he checked his email, deleting the few social media notifications he'd received without opening them. A distraction he could fix if he shut them off from the source. But what if something important came through? It was never important, he told himself. He opened an email from Trevor, his editor at *Science & Sky*, one of his consistent freelance gigs.

He enjoyed writing for *Science & Sky*. The publication had been around since the early 1950s, and their monthly magazine could still be found in doctors' waiting rooms, airport kiosks, and university science departments. Neatly organized rows of them lined some of the shelves in his father's study. Elliot mostly wrote short pieces for their online publication. These still got noticed, but not like articles in their monthly publication. His father had always been the first to read Elliot's articles. He was Elliot's harshest but best critic. His father had wanted Elliot to follow his footsteps into academia, a topic which had found its way into annual holiday conversations.

E—

I know you're away this weekend. But hoping I can get a first draft of your story by end of next week? In other news, check out this closure at the Green Bank Observatory in West Virginia—might be an interesting follow-up. Hope you're doing well. If you need anything, let me know.

—T

Elliot sat back and sighed heavily. He didn't respond to the email or look at any of the links or attached stories Trevor included. He could tell Trevor was treating him with kid gloves. He wasn't the type to be so lax. Even if they were friends, he still had deadlines. Elliot wasn't sure how to feel about it. Everyone in his life was treating him differently since his father passed. An instinct, he figured, the gentleness of others toward someone carrying the burden of fresh grief, but he wanted nothing more than for it to all be normal again.

He looked at his blank document again. First draft by Monday. He didn't bother with the additional link Trevor sent. He wanted to get this piece done and then start what he came up here to do—clean out his father's office. Fifteen minutes later, with one word typed, he stood up and walked away. Tomorrow's problem.

#

Elliot made his way to his father's workspace in the basement, which was on the ground level since the cabin sat against a hill. Sliding glass doors opened out to a path that led to the lake. There was a main room with a small wood-burning stove, and a living area with additional couches and a TV, which only saw use when his father watched Red Sox games. Elliot and his family lived in New Jersey when he was growing up, but his father was originally from Maine. His parents had met in Boston, where Elliot was born, but moved to New Jersey when his father was offered a teaching opportunity he couldn't pass up. For Elliot, New Jersey was home, but his family were New Englanders at heart. A connection this cabin offered.

Two additional rooms broke off from the main room. One was a bedroom with bunk beds, where Elliot's younger cousins would sleep during family gatherings. Over time, with fewer and fewer family reunions, it became a storage space littered with boxes containing the past. The second room was a larger space, lined with bookshelves and, now, more half-filled boxes left behind by his mother when she attempted a cleanup. She'd given up halfway through, not ready to clean out the last of her husband's life. His sudden death a few months earlier was still fresh in their minds; neither of them were quite ready to move on.

Books and magazines about astronomy and astrophysics lined the bookshelves. Once the collection back home in Jersey took over multiple rooms, his mother put an end to it. The cabin was the archive of last resort for his father.

Elliot scanned the room and took a deep breath, trying to find the best starting point. His father was organized, neat; there was order to everything he did, including his workspace. His father used to say, *A clean desk is a clean mind.* The mess Elliot found had him concerned, saddened, and feeling guilty for the distance between them before his father passed.

He ventured around the room, checking out the bookshelves, poking in the half-full boxes his mother had abandoned, getting a sense of what lay ahead. The space was disorganized, like debris floating in orbit around the desk. Notebooks, mapping tools, and books were scattered across the floor. It was like his father had stopped working mid-thought.

Against the back wall was a desk covered in papers and more books on astronomy, their pages bristling with sticky notes. Elliot hadn't been down here in a while and the sight of the room suddenly flooded him with emotion. He fought back tears, pulled in a shuddery breath, filling his lungs to capacity, then let it out slowly. He needed to take the edge off or else he'd abandon this journey like his mother did.

He moved the half-filled boxes to one side of the room and organized the loose papers into piles. He didn't want to throw everything in a box and toss it. He needed to parse through it all, throw out what was unnecessary, and keep a few things for himself. There was more than he expected. This would take a while. He couldn't wade through a life's worth of collections in a short time.

Once he stacked the loose books, magazines, and papers, he moved the various astronomy equipment his father had collected over the years. Some were for show, older telescopes that were collector's items, but others were still of use. Elliot figured he'd donate some of the equipment, knowing he couldn't fit it all in his one-bedroom apartment back in Boston.

The summer heat didn't help. Box fans pushed air through the main room. Sweat still crept down his forehead. Break time. He grabbed a drink then returned to the basement, sitting down in his father's chair. He leaned back and the chair gave a creak he remembered hearing as a kid. The sound conjured a memory of his father sitting and working in this very spot.

"Jesus, Dad, got enough shit down here?" he said to an empty room like it cared. He wiped his forehead and took a sip of his iced tea.

He shuffled through papers spread across the desk. Pages and pages of notes, coordinates, and scale drawings of various stars, or what seemed like random spots in space. It looked like his father was mapping something, but it wasn't clear what.

Elliot flipped through a few loose pages that had been torn from notebooks. All of them listed dates and timestamps running down the page in three columns. Each page had what seemed like random groups of times circled in red. But as he studied them further, he realized they were consistent and repeated at various hourly and weekly intervals. The scribbles continued on other pages. More times, more groupings over the years.

"What the . . ." He'd flipped through two notebooks of timestamps. He checked the front cover of the one he was holding, which was labeled JAN 2018–JULY 2018 in Sharpie in his father's handwriting. There were about ten similar notebooks on the desk, with more stacked on the floor in the corner of the room.

He gathered all the notebooks and the loose pages of timestamps, stacking them neatly on the desk. Next to the desk was a small amateur radio station. His father was big into ham and satellite radio, listening to the sounds of space and communicating with others. As a kid, he remembered hearing his father chatting with someone across the globe and thinking it was the coolest thing ever. It still was.

His father had everything from an old Hallicrafters SX-110, a shortwave radio receiver from the '60s Elliot remembered using as a kid, to a Kenwood TS-820 transceiver, a single-sideband model built a few years before Elliot was born. Although it seemed his father had upgraded and had mostly been using a packet radio modem that could transmit datagrams across radio frequencies. His setup was built to listen to chatter from amateur radio satellites in low orbit, launched by volunteers and students all over the world. A simple way to connect to anyone. Elliot had already packed away the photos of his father helping launch a few with his students.

Elliot tested some of the equipment to see what worked and what didn't. Other than a layer of dust, they were in working order—his father had kept it all in impeccable shape. As Elliot tested, he noticed a logbook tucked under some of the equipment. He pulled it out and flipped through pages and pages of logs, not of connections to people, but with more coordinates and timestamps with associated frequencies. The word *Sunspot* and the letters *GBO* appeared a few times, grouped together and circled in red, multiple times. At the top of one page was the word *satellite* written a few times along with the phrase *latest lie*. An anagram. A pattern of obsession leaving its mark on the future.

"An old man chasing conspiracies in the basement. Fantastic," Elliot said as he closed the logbook and tossed it on the desk. Another thing to pack.

Chapter 3

LiLo took a quick sip of coffee between her hurried typing. An unnoticed reflex, muscle memory, that was part of the process. Her latest sip revealed the cup was low—she needed a refill. She placed the cup on the edge of the table, a sign to the barista she needed more. She sat huddled over her laptop at an uninviting table, barely built for two, in the corner of a small coffee shop in East London. Her life, like the table, didn't have room for another.

The retro couches, reclaimed wood counters, and low lighting took the edge off the hip industrial space. The shop was always busy but never overwhelmingly so. Other than the occasional train passing behind the building, the noise was reasonable, and the shop was within walking distance of a flat she'd been renting. The intoxicating coffee aroma filled the warehouse's high ceiling, something LiLo needed after a long night.

She continued typing, with brief pauses as her eyes darted between her digital and physical worlds—a habit formed in her younger years by the paranoid people in her life. Her corner seat gave her a good view of the entire shop. She had no concern about standing out among the younger crowd, many of them displaying tattoos and piercings that would make an older generation blush. She fit in like she belonged, even if she didn't. She pushed up her long sleeves on both arms, another unnoticed reflex while working.

The soft clicks of her keyboard sounded like an orchestra at work. Her fingers moved with precision. She could feel each key's reaction with every stroke. It melded with the mix of Miles Davis coursing through her headphones. She'd tried listening to Coltrane, but his elaborate mixtures of time signatures and scales painfully pierced the brain, like his music wasn't built for humans to understand. With Miles, each keystroke was like a note of jazz—balanced, smooth, perfect. It brought memories of her father, who introduced her to jazz as a child. Whenever he'd return from his long trips, they'd sit in the living room and listen together.

This was LiLo's second visit this week, a usual cadence for her. Enough visits over the last five months to get acquainted with the staff and a few regulars. Not ideal. It'd be time to leave soon. The extent of *knowing* anyone was first name basis only, and listening to stories of terrible relationship statuses she could not care less about. To them, she was Emma, a single, and not interested, American in London on a temporary work visa. A flex of the truth. Still, she made all the right faces and replies one expects in social situations. Not that she didn't want to know more about any of them, she couldn't. Her aloofness was a habit, a process, built into her, like sipping her coffee.

To anyone who walked in—and even the few who knew Emma—she was just another person behind a laptop. Putting together reports, spreadsheets, or a presentation for a big project. No one knew she went by the anonymous online handle of LiLo, or that a photo of her, with shorter, blond hair, could be found on the FBI's most-wanted list of cybercriminals. She hated the photo for many reasons, its fallacy being one, but it excluded her from a normal life. That normal life had been taken from her as a teenager, leaving her in constant survival mode ever since. Plus, she hated her youthful facial piercings being documented in any shape or form.

It would be tough to look at that photo and recognize her at a glance today. With different clothes, the piercings gone, and her shoulder-length hair dyed in varying shades of under-the-radar brown, she was another person. She wasn't concerned about her local barista coming across the outdated photo of her, or any public photo of her. They didn't exist. No social media photos. No photos with a significant other, or a selfie with her lunch, or a group friend shot at a bar covered in smiles and spilled cocktails. To the world, she was a ghost—a nobody.

Mostly, no one bothered her outside of the occasional come-on from a guy seeing her sitting alone. She'd politely turn each of them away. No room at this table.

A barista stopped by LiLo's table and gave her a quick look, with raised eyebrows and a glance at her cup. LiLo smiled and nodded. The barista returned the pleasantries, topped her cup off, and disappeared. The orchestra of keystrokes continued over a Miles solo.

LiLo was in a zone. Her eyes bounced from window to window, skimming the freshly written code which lit up her dark screen with subtle color. Each statement, each command, building upon each other like cells of an organism. An organism that could penetrate and infect any machine—a nightmare for the recipient, but total control for the creator. Building such things wasn't a job she wanted but had become a necessity for survival.

Between her rhythmic typing in a terminal window and the messaging app, she took short sips from her refreshed cup. Cup number three—the trivial detail bounced through her mind and quickly left. A useless data point. Her eyes bounced up from her screen. There were fifteen people in the cafe. Twelve customers, three workers. Since she'd arrived, it had fluctuated plus or minus two. Conversations passed through her ears like a recorder. In her opinion, the flirtation between coworkers would come to nothing; the woman one table over should dump her distracted boyfriend; and the pair in the corner muttering about NFTs had no idea what they were getting themselves into. It wasn't a skill she cultivated, just muscle memory working for her without her needing to think about it—a task she could run in the background.

Her eyes bounced from the screen to surroundings. Seventeen people now. Were there always seventeen? *Ignore the mundane, focus on the problem.* More code appeared on her screen. Focus had been balancing on an edge all day. Was it the lack of sleep in the past seventy-two hours? Another interfering data point.

Her messaging window lit up with a subtle flash. A new message from her contact.

YELLOWJACKET: *Updates?*

She glanced at the message and let it sit for a few minutes. Letting them, whoever they were, stew. She wasn't sure what infuriated her more: the stupid handle, or how pushy they'd become. They had her at a disadvantage, which she didn't like. And not knowing who they were scratched at her like an obsessive thought. The handle was icing on the cake. She couldn't risk being in the dark about anything, but Yellow-Jacket didn't exist, and it bothered her. They came to her through a trusted source, the only source she'd ever trusted. She couldn't turn it away, even if she wanted to. Moments later, another message.

YELLOWJACKET: *??*
LILO: *testing.*

If annoyance could be heard through a message, her reply screamed it in its dry simplicity. The period at the end of a single-word response should make that clear.

She had assumptions about who YellowJacket was. A low-level contact for a hacker collective group, and given their resources, probably doing state-backed work for Russia or North Korea. Not something she was comfortable with, but she had little choice. Correction. They didn't give her much choice. It was the only way to fix her mistake and save a friend she shouldn't have made in the first place. She could tell by what they asked for, how much they offered, and what they had to leverage her with, even if they didn't realize it. She was still getting paid for a job she would've done for free, given the circumstances.

The code she had cranked out between cups of coffee looked like a digital poem within her text editor. A small portion of a script that, by itself, wouldn't do much, but at large scale could be a serious problem for anyone on the receiving end. This type of work was typical, offloading smaller tasks via a coordinator. Not having all the eggs in one basket meant if one piece was compromised, they could shift the work and recover.

A macro from a designated program could trigger the script she built via an email attachment. Once someone opened the attachment, the intended program would enable the macro, which would kick off the script. The script itself was the bread and butter. Once it started, it would reach out and grab an image file with data encoded in it—invisibly, which was the key. At its core, it acted as a simple phishing scam, but behind the scenes it was an elaborate key to a standard lock. A point of entry a recipient would have no idea existed. The entire process ran in the background while the end user carried out their typical workday, with no knowledge they were being taken advantage of. All it took was two clicks of a mouse. A simple but effective sweep and grab method of getting credentials and access. Companies don't get hacked, people do—because people are always the point of weakness in a system. One of the first lessons she ever learned from the people that trained her. The same people that had her on the run most of her life.

#

LiLo ran a few tests of her script. Found a few bugs and dove into fixing them. As she worked, her message app lit up again and flashed behind her text editor and terminal windows. She switched windows with a sigh. *If this is YellowJacket.* It wasn't. It was her source, her friend, her mistake.

GEMINI: *hey . . .*
LILO: *hey*
GEMINI: *how are you?*
LILO: *fine. just trying to finish this job and move on*
GEMINI: *right. sorry.*
LILO: *so you've said*
GEMINI: *where are you? Can I see you?*
LILO: *not a good idea*
GEMINI: *:(I understand . . .*
GEMINI: *Thank you . . . again*
LILO: *sure*

LiLo closed out the messaging app with a hard click.

There had been chatter across various forums and IRC channels about a large attack being planned. Collectives and individuals were being hired for quick work, but the scale was larger than usual. LiLo paid attention to it all. Listening invisibly in the background, just like her script. People dropped hints and details they wouldn't even realize. Chatter like this usually meant a high-profile target, but the scale proposed something big, like a national government.

It wasn't her problem once she was done. Or, at least she did her best to tell herself that. What she did know is that she didn't want to be near wherever this was let loose. She had ideas of end targets: the US, Israel, and Russia were at the top. It didn't matter. She didn't have vacation plans to those destinations anytime soon.

After a few final tests, she was happy with her script. She took extra steps to hide the data needed to unlock a recipient's machine using steganographic techniques—information hidden within an image. This would help evade any company-issued security tools, including network traffic scanners. An elaborate key.

Her cup of coffee was, again, almost empty. She wouldn't need a refill this time. She reopened her messaging app and pinged Yellow-Jacket.

LILO: *sending now*
YELLOWJACKET: *cool*
YELLOWJACKET: *have another task if interested*

LiLo paused. She wanted out of this connection. The risk to continue working with them was too high. Her gut told her to move on, but her head told her to find out who this asshole was.

LILO: *I am*
YELLOWJACKET: *will send details later along with crypto payment for this*
LILO: *and Gemini?*

YELLOWJACKET: *we're all good there*
LILO: *good*

This was the highest-paying and shortest gig LiLo had gotten yet. An absurd amount, which triggered red flags. She'd signed up to get a friend out of a dangerous situation, a situation that could see them both dead, and while she might have gotten them out of immediate danger, she felt she was being pulled into something even bigger with a gravity she couldn't fight. She needed to stay low, not ruffle feathers. Over the years, she'd dealt with people trying to track her down, but lately it'd been quiet. Had her former employers picked up a new trail? She'd been careful with every move she made, but comfort breeds mistakes and Gemini was comfortable. It was possible YellowJacket was attempting to flush her out using Gemini.

LiLo finished up the last few sips of her coffee. She shut down all her apps, closed out her laptop, and dropped it into her backpack along with her headphones. She looked around, took in the space one last time. This would be her last visit, which was too bad—the coffee was excellent.

Chapter 4

"Alright. We have just a few items to cover today, so let's get started," Agent Aaron Blackwell said to his team as he entered the small conference room in DC. The stale-smelling, purposefully generic space was part of an FBI field office that was home to various Cyber Action Teams within the Cyber Crime division. He didn't like that he was running late thanks to a previous department head meeting he couldn't escape, but even his tenure hadn't been able to get him out of it. "Evans, you're up first," he said between efficient strides to the front of the room.

Paul Evans, the team's tech lead, and youngest member, started as Blackwell took his seat and shuffled through his agenda.

"No updates on the recent DDoS attacks we saw in Atlanta," Evans said, then took a breath, his shaky eagerness on display. "Seems they were one-offs, no demands or any chatter about motive. Feels like some newbie hackers dipping their toes into deeper water. We're going to continue to monitor but take no action." Evans leaned back in his chair, pleased with his report and ready to move on.

Blackwell eyed Evans, jaw clenched. His CO in his military days would've had him doing push-ups till the sun came up if he ever used the word *newbie*. But he decided to let it slip. The kid was as sharp as his degrees from Brown University suggested, even if he was a little green with his updates.

Blackwell nodded and shifted his focus to Agent Rachel Klein, second in command of the team.

"We've seen an uptick in infrastructure attacks. Most seem to prod, nothing substantial yet. But there is consistency to them we should stay aware of. And their use of Microsoft OneDrive as command-and-control servers is a new and interesting tactic to hide malware delivery through legit domains. Nothing to the NotPetya effect, but still a potential concern," Klein said.

Blackwell remembered NotPetya's destructive wildfire-like path, which took the digital world by storm. No server, PC, or connected device was safe from the heavy-hitting ransomware, which extracted data and demanded high payments in return.

"Any key identifiers?" Blackwell asked, not looking up from his notes.

"Most are hitting electric grids, pipelines, nuclear plants along the Eastern Seaboard using phishing scams on employees and contractors," Klein replied, speaking with her hands like a leader would.

Agent Mark Hansen chimed in, "They could try to pull access passwords for a cleaner or more precise takedown versus an overload attack like a DDoS." His focus was international group monitoring and state-funded hacks. His gray stubble barely covered up a small scar on his right cheek, the result of an occupational hazard from his past.

"Seems amateur?" Evans asked. His tone was a little self-assured for Blackwell's taste, the question delivered as if he was the smartest person in the room.

Klein had noticed his tone too, her eyebrows raised slightly, but she gave a straightforward answer. "It does, but again, the prodding and reimplementation of the same scam, but with a slight tweak, makes it seem like they're testing, not actually deploying." She paused for a moment. "We're also seeing some steganographic manipulation involved."

"Steganographic, what now?" Hansen asked.

"It's a clever way to hide a script or a key within an image for an already downloaded script to play off," Klein said.

Hansen nodded with a half-smile as if impressed. "New day, new hack."

"Fun stuff," Evans said to no one in particular as he tapped his pen on his notepad.

"We have any ideas of backers?" Blackwell asked.

"No, but if it's infrastructure I'd guess state-backed—China, Russia, North Korea, Iran," Klein said.

"Evans, do some digging. See if there's any chatter about this. Hansen, see if Homeland Security or CISA have heard anything, although I doubt they'll give us much," Blackwell said.

Evans and Hansen both nodded.

"Okay. That it?" Blackwell asked the group. Each member nodded as he looked around the table.

"Great. That's a wrap then. Let's get to work."

#

Blackwell sat in his unpretentious office organizing the team's debriefing notes. His desk was clean, almost bare. Across from him were two chairs for visitors. A filing cabinet he hadn't ever opened was tucked in the corner, and a few low-maintenance plants decorated the space. The desk was next to a wide window that overlooked the street. Nothing spectacular. A waist-high bookshelf, filled with books on military tactics, annual FBI protocol reports, and a copy of the *Art of War*, lined the opposite wall. The only human touch in an office torn from a catalog was a photo of his military unit sitting atop the bookshelf. To Blackwell, it made little sense to clutter a room which wasn't occupied. He spent most of his time in the field or in briefings. He didn't have time to decorate.

His office door was ajar when a knock came. Blackwell didn't look up from his laptop. "Yes?"

Evans pushed open the door and entered with a slight hurry in his step but took the time to close the door behind him. He stood in front of the desk, waiting like a student in the principal's office.

"Evans, how can I help you?" Blackwell said, not looking up. The kid still radiated apprehension in one-on-one situations.

"I have something you should look at. Some interesting IP traffic from an observatory in West Virginia."

Blackwell paused, leaned back in his chair, and glared at Evans like this was an annoyance. *Why didn't he bring this up at the debriefing?* Evans handed a folder to Blackwell, which he flipped through. After a moment of reviewing what was in the folder, Blackwell said more to himself, "What could anyone want from a telescope?" Then to Evans, "Are these findings accurate? Have they been checked?"

"They have. And I did some extra digging. They match what we saw in Sunspot."

Blackwell glared up at Evans. "Sunspot was human error. A unique situation."

"Yes, sir, but these findings, as you'll see on page four, are too similar."

Blackwell paged through the rest of the data, taking a moment to think. "Let's pull the team together and review. Have we been in contact with"—he flipped to the front page to check the name—"anyone at the Green Bank Observatory yet?"

"No, sir. I can have the team together in an hour," Evans responded.

"Good. Let's keep this circle small for now."

#

The team regrouped shortly after Evans sent a message via their internal messaging system for a quick check-in.

"Green Bank. What do we know?" Blackwell asked the room. Although he'd already looked at the report, he wanted the group to brainstorm and show they knew what was going on.

Evans jumped in first. "Green Bank Observatory picked up a series of FRBs this past week—"

Hansen raised a hand like he was in science class. "An FRB?"

"An FRB is a Fast Radio Burst. They're highly intense radio wave bursts from space—nebulas or extragalactic activity that generate a ton of energy and shoot across the galaxy. They last a few milliseconds, which makes analyzing them difficult. Most researchers have chalked up FRBs as single anomalies," Evans said.

"They're not that common," Klein added. "Well, until recent years. A few hundred have been discovered, but places like Green Bank Observatory now have radio telescopes sensitive enough and large enough to capture such things."

Hansen nodded. "So, space history splashing its radio waves across the galaxy."

"Something like that," Evans said. "Repeating FRBs are becoming common but not at the scale that Green Bank just picked up."

"Why do we care?" Klein said, looking around the group.

"Because, although they're being marked as FRBs, their core signature is unique—more powerful, repeating, and bouncing between sources. Pair that with some interesting IP activity coming in and out of the observatory from places like China and Russia, and this looks like something else," Evans said.

"Bouncing between sources?" Hansen said.

"Initial reports from Green Bank's public data archive show this signal is pinging from some source and Earth."

The group went silent for a moment.

"What's the red flag? Can we reach out to Green Bank and discuss it with them?" Klein asked.

Evans gave a tight-lipped smile. "The red flag is data is missing."

"Why would data be missing?" Hansen asked.

Evans looked to Blackwell, knowing the response was above his pay grade.

Blackwell was silent for a moment, deep in thought but completely aware of the conversation, before answering, "It's because we've seen this before in Sunspot, New Mexico."

He brought his gaze back to the room; all eyes were on him.

"A high-powered signal was found. We suspected a surveillance test which wasn't ours." He looked down at the report Evans had given him. "But it wasn't as powerful as these are showing, nor as fast, hence why we could tail it back to a source. We then shut down the Sunspot observatory and found some issues and missing data. That was the end of it."

Blackwell left out the details that had kept him up at night during the investigation. The public report was generic enough, and the story died within weeks. What wasn't in the public report was the discovery of a faint signal picked up by the observatory. The FBI and Blackwell's team were brought in because of suspicious IP traffic coming out of the observatory. Then they discovered a signal was linked to the IP traffic. It caused issues with equipment routing and local network shutdowns. Chalked up as an anomaly, then put on the back burner. But to a dedicated conspiracy theorist, it made a convincing argument for little green men.

"Do we think these are connected?" Klein asked.

"Possibly. Maybe it's an improved version of the last. Won't know until we get the data," Evans added.

"What about the NSA? If we think this is surveillance related maybe they'll have something. Hell, they know what I had for breakfast," Hansen said.

"Even if they did, I don't imagine they'd be quick to share. Talk about a group that doesn't trust anyone," Klein said.

The group paused, mostly waiting for a response from Blackwell on what the next steps would be.

"Okay. Let's prep and get to Green Bank and collect all data on site. If we need to, we'll close the site but please stay away from the term *shutdown*. We need to move quickly and isolate the lab and data," Blackwell said.

"Why not call it a shutdown?" Evans asked.

"When you shut down an observatory, people immediately think aliens," Klein said with a smirk.

"Ahhh, got ya."

Blackwell stood and paced the front of the room, then focused on Agent Hansen. "Let's talk to local authorities, I assume it's a sheriff down there, get them authorization—have them clear out the facility except for all lab techs. Until we get there. Discreetly if possible." Hansen nodded. Blackwell then shifted eyes to Agent Klein. "Let's also get a press release ready on behalf of the observatory about why they're closing their doors. Lead with equipment failure and go soft on unusual IP activity."

"You got it," Klein said with a nod.

Blackwell paused, momentarily lost in thought as his team waited to be dismissed. His mind drifted back to Sunspot. If that wasn't just a test and this was the real thing, would they be ready? Would anyone?

Doubt creeped its way in. He snapped back to the moment, then continued, "Okay, let's get to it."

Chapter 5

By lunchtime the next day, Blackwell and the team had cleared red tape, prepped, and arrived on site. Blackwell's insistence on keeping the team small was paying off with its flexibility—they could mobilize and get things done at the snap of a finger. He always thought a team of three to five was perfect. Even from his military days as squad leader, he preferred working with a single fire team of five versus the typical two teams of four. In his mind, a strong-willed team of five, with a hard work ethic, could overcome any odds. Their ability to get in and out without notice was much greater.

In addition to his full team, they had four field agents for support and crowd control if necessary. These types of scenarios were nothing new to him. He'd coordinate with agencies like the DHS or CIA if anything landed on his desk that was beyond a domestic threat. Until then, this was his investigation and planned to keep this quiet unless absolutely necessary. He had nothing but time and planned to use it all.

They pulled up to the observatory in two black SUVs. Alone, they didn't stand out but seeing two of the same vehicle drive in a tight formation was hard to not notice and might raise eyebrows. Two local cop cars were already parked in the lot. Blackwell was happy to see the local sheriff and his team had done what was asked of them only a few hours earlier. It'd make this process much easier.

Blackwell led the team into the observatory Science Center like they owned the place, which, from this point forward, they did. He spotted two deputies in the lobby then eyed the sheriff. It took him less than a second to piece together that the deputies had done the job of clearing out the building, and the sheriff was there to make it seem like he was earning his paycheck. This was the most action they'd seen in a long time, if ever, so overacting was part of the role they played. Made them feel like they had control, which vanished the moment the FBI pulled up.

The sheriff—with thin, slicked-back hair, beer-ball belly, and hands on his hips like a cowboy—greeted Blackwell. Blackwell's team dispersed in an efficient manner, double-checking the work of local law enforcement—certain standards had to be met, of course.

"Agent Blackwell?" the sheriff asked in a drawl that made it seem as if his tongue was too big for his mouth. He extended a hand to shake; his other held his hat at his side. Blackwell was unsure if the hat removal was a respectful gesture, or if the sheriff had overheated and needed a breather. Blackwell assumed the latter. The sheriff didn't look like the respectful gesture sort. Blackwell wanted nothing to do with the sheriff but went through the motions of pleasantries all the same.

"Yes, sir." Blackwell returned the man's handshake. "Sheriff Ben Davis, is it? Thank you and your team for assisting here today."

"Our pleasure, but, ah, any chance we can understand what's going on here? Would make our jobs a lot easier," Sheriff Davis said, trailing off in a lower voice so only Blackwell could hear.

"Routine investigation. You know how it is. We're tracking some IP activity and are just taking precautions," Blackwell said, as precise as a canned message. "Now, where is Dr. Keating and his team?" Blackwell was already done with the sheriff. He'd done his part, they confirmed, now he wanted him gone.

The sheriff, dumbfounded, wanted to pry, but didn't push the subject. "Uh, they're, uh, in the main lab. Just follow the signs to the left. What do you mean by IP activity?"

But the question was directed at Blackwell's back, as he'd already walked away.

Blackwell and his team moved through the space with intention. Staff spoke in hushed voices and avoided eye contact.

He entered the main lab, an open space with a handful of researchers and scientists lingering like it was their first day of school. His eyes scanned the room left to right. Two people sat at a large round communal table in the middle. An older man with a cool-dad vibe and a younger woman with thin-rimmed glasses. Blackwell could see their eyes bounce like ping pong balls from person to person as his team entered. Tense much?

Blackwell spotted a ragged Seattle Mariners baseball cap on the table and approached.

"Dr. Keating?" Blackwell asked as he pointed at the seated man, putting him on the spot.

"That's correct," Keating said.

"That makes you Dr. Jennifer Liu, correct?"

Liu nodded.

"What's this all about?" Keating asked.

Blackwell, wearing his dark blue department-issued nylon windbreaker, which prominently displayed *FBI* in big yellow letters on the front and back, showed his badge and ID, as if his jacket didn't confirm who he and his team represented.

"I'm Agent Aaron Blackwell of the FBI. We're closing the observatory today and for the foreseeable future. Your cooperation is highly recommended."

He let that soak in as he watched Keating and Liu exchange a look.

"Great. Is there a space we can talk?" Blackwell asked.

Keating was silent for a moment before standing and pointing to a bank of closed doors. "Yes, of course, my office."

As they entered Keating's office, Blackwell nonchalantly put a piece of gum in his mouth as he checked out the various baseball related photos hanging on Keating's walls. Keating took a seat at his desk.

"So, what's this all about?" Keating asked.

Blackwell circled the room.

"Big Mariners fan, huh?"

Keating didn't respond.

"Been awhile since they were good, though." Blackwell glanced at Keating with a sympathetic expression.

"Yes, it's been a while. So, I know you didn't just shut down my observatory so we could chat about baseball. What's happening with my team right now?"

Blackwell could hear the irritation in his voice. A mask for nerves, he was sure. He didn't answer right away but continued to walk around the office, looking at awards, photos, and a collection of books.

"We'd like all your notes about FRB-200508. We'd also like to interview any researcher who was involved in discovering FRB-200508," Blackwell said as he perused a collection of plaques Keating had on his wall.

"FRB-200508? Why does the FBI care about some common space noise? It was probably radio feedback."

Blackwell whirled on his heel to face the scientist, his hands casually in his jacket pockets. "The reason why is classified. And considering this is one of the most remote and radio silent observatories in the country, your explanation that 'it's just radio feedback' is a little insulting, and I might add it's not well advised to minimize." He didn't want the science guy thinking he was a total stooge.

Keating smiled back at him as he broke eye contact. "We need to do more testing. More research. The signal is still a recent development."

Blackwell stood at the front of Keating's desk, his hands gripping the edge like he wanted to flip it. He didn't have time for this verbal volley of bullshit.

"More testing won't be necessary on your part. From this point forward, the observatory is closed until further notice, and we'll need all research notes and documents you have related to FRB-200508," Blackwell stated.

"This is ridiculous," Keating said as he shifted in his chair.

"If you say so, but this is what's happening. I'd like to work with you on this transition, so please, your cooperation is appreciated." Blackwell's tone was cold, forceful—he was done repeating himself.

"Transition? Sounds like there is more to this than just research notes."

"As part of the closing of the observatory, all researchers here are being transferred to other observatories. Any key personnel involved directly with FRB-200508's discovery will be moved to specific locations, as recommended by my team with your input of course."

"I see," Keating said, leaning back in his chair.

Blackwell could tell Keating was done fighting for control. "Now, given the sensitive nature of this discovery and conversation, I hope we're on the same page. We'll have paperwork—NDAs and so on and so forth—for you and your team to review and fill out."

"Of course," Keating said.

"Great." Blackwell handed him a folder.

"What's this?" Keating asked.

"It's your new gig, doc."

Keating opened the folder and skimmed through the documents. "Seattle?"

"Yes, we have you set up at a new location in Seattle. You'll be a research consultant at your old stomping grounds, AeroTech." Blackwell gave him a tight smile.

"This is—"

Blackwell raised his hand as if calming an enraged beast. "Ridiculous? It's not ridiculous, doc. Like I said, this is a classified situation. This is the best outcome for you and your team. If any details about why this observatory is being closed or the nature of FRB-200508 are shared outside of these walls, well, the circumstances will change. Are we on the same page?"

Keating nodded; Blackwell had handcuffed his tongue.

"In case we're not, we'll be watching you, but glad we're able to work together on this. Makes life easier for everyone. Now, all the information you need is in the folder. We'll brief your team and get everyone where they need to be," Blackwell said.

"How will this be explained outside of these walls?" Keating asked.

"We have a press release ready and will send it to various news outlets. Pretty standard."

"When does this all happen?"

"It's effective immediately. I'll have my team gather your things and escort you out."

"No need. I know where the door is," Keating snapped as he stood, grabbed his jacket and a red backpack, and headed for the door.

Blackwell moved behind Keating's desk, calling after the departing scientist, "Look on the bright side, doc—more Mariners games."

Chapter 6

Elliot's apartment was a six-hundred-fifty-square-foot box in a complex just outside Boston. The one bedroom was enough for one person but not enough for the boxes he returned with from Maine. He had more work to do at the cabin, making a second trip necessary at some point.

He unpacked the boxes, two filled with notebooks and other loose items from his father's desk, and two filled with the basic listening equipment his father had set up at the cabin. He stacked the notebooks by date next to his makeshift office desk, which took up half his bedroom. The warm summer air was thick. He had every window open in his small apartment, hoping to create some relief from the heat. Window fans blew hot air around, the sounds of the city passing through like white noise.

Elliot set up the equipment before diving back into the notebooks. He wasn't sure what his father was up to, but his curiosity got the best of him. His father's death was so sudden he'd never had a chance to say goodbye, and they hadn't talked for a month leading up to his passing. No particular reason, no argument—just life moving too quick. But there had been distance between them long before that. Elliot never understood why. Regret sat like a brick in his stomach. His father had never mentioned this side project, which he'd been working on for a while it seemed, and to an obsessive level. Maybe his father thought he'd ignore him, consider it another wild idea to chase.

It didn't take him long to get things in place. The tinkering was cathartic, a coping mechanism. The equipment was more than dusty transistors in metal boxes, it filled a space with memories. He remembered spending hours taking apart some new piece of equipment his father found at a tag sale or picked up at the local Radio Shack and putting it all back together just to learn how it worked. Or mapping stars with basic telescopes and analog tools, all before an app on his phone could easily show him anything he wanted. A memory attached to a tactile process.

Elliot cleaned everything and made his new toys look less like an eyesore—well, as best he could. A few connection issues, but nothing he couldn't handle or remember how to fix, like riding a bike. It all flooded back to him.

He started digging through the stuff that had been sprawled across the desk in Maine: a few notebooks with timestamps, and an old handmade star map with basic constellations and points with latitude and longitude markings his father added.

His father was hooked on something, but what exactly he wasn't sure. Even if it went nowhere, he felt a need to understand what his father was working on.

According to his father's notes, whatever he was tracking changed position constantly. Same bandwidth, same frequency, but the location was inconsistent. He could see as the notes progressed, they became increasingly messy. Frustration in written form. Could his father not figure this out? Why? He was a pretty smart guy, and this was his domain.

Elliot fired up the equipment and started tuning to different frequencies, not looking to chat with anyone, but getting a feel for it and just listening to see what he could pick up in the sky above. Elliot wanted to believe there was more out there than just human voices, even if his father took a more logical approach to the subject. If there was, we'd have already heard from them, was his thought. The only voice we'd ever hear would be human. It struck Elliot as odd for his father, who was always pushing his son to think big.

After a few attempts with the equipment, he glanced over his father's logbook and ran through a few timestamps, finding ones that matched the current time and day of week. His father had marked repeating signals at various intervals. Most were weekly or monthly. Elliot wasn't sure what to expect. He picked a set of frequencies and started listening. Nothing. Another set. Nothing. A few more, still nothing.

After a couple hours of reading through scribbled notes and tuning, he was about to give up when he pulled out the large hand-drawn map his father made.

He wasn't sure what he was seeing—to him they were random points in space. Whatever his father was tracking he could've easily figured out with some open-source software, but his father was old school and wanted to do everything by hand. To him, it showed you understood what you were doing. Elliot always had issues with that philosophy—he wanted to move quickly.

After staring at the map for a moment, he picked a random lat-long point and looked up the corresponding frequency and time stamp from one of the notebooks. He tuned his receiver to match the co-ordinates and frequency his father had noted. He listened. Nothing. A few seconds passed. He fine-tuned the frequency. A couple more seconds passed—then, a faint ping. A blip. Then, nothing. A few seconds later the same faint ping. It repeated, like a stretched beep, with no interference.

"What the . . ."

He sat up, smile stretched across his face. He flipped through the logbook, his fingers running down the page, checking dates and times, then flipped to another page. He jumped to the last page with listings. His finger hovered over the last entry. The day before his father died.

#

It'd been a few days since Elliot had heard the faint ping using his father's notes. He'd spent the days and nights since scrolling through pages and pages, tuning and listening. Double-checking his father's work, the ones grouped hourly and daily, and others to check after a week.

The timestamps, coordinates, and frequencies sometimes connected and made sense, but most times they didn't. Was his father drawing patterns for the sake of it, or was something buried here?

A sudden knock on his door broke his concentration. Time for a break anyway. He answered the door to find Jake, smiling.

"Heeeey," Jake said.

"Hey," Elliot returned as he walked back into his apartment.

"You didn't return any of my texts. Figured I'd stop by and make sure you didn't slip in the shower and, you know, die or something. Because that'd be a terrible way to go," Jake said as he closed the door behind him.

"You want anything?" Elliot asked from the kitchen, grabbing himself a water.

"I'm good. So, how's the cabin? The lake still watery and the cabin still, uh, made of wood?" Jake plopped himself on the couch.

Elliot smirked and moved to the living room. "Yeah, it's fine. But I did find some weird stuff my father was working on."

"Your old man was working on something weird? Please, go on."

"He had notebooks and notebooks full of timestamps, coordinates, and frequencies. Kinda freaked me out. Seemed like he was tracking something."

"Late-night ham radio chats?"

Elliot let out a chuckle. "No, jerk. But I started checking out some of the stuff he was listening to and actually heard something. Like a faint blip or ping."

"A faint blip? Well, you've piqued my interest."

Elliot showed Jake the setup and notebooks in his room.

"Wow. Look at this . . . junk. This stuff from when we were kids?" Jake leaned over the old equipment, inspecting it without touching it like he was in a museum.

"Some of it, but apparently he picked up some more sophisticated items along the way." Elliot handed Jake the most recent notebook.

Jake flipped through a few pages. "What the hell is this? When was the last time you chatted with your old man before he passed?"

"Maybe a month? And even then just a few quick chats on the phone or an email here and there."

"He seem . . . okay?"

Elliot shrugged. "Yeah, he seemed . . . fine." He pulled out the giant fold-out map. "Then there's this."

"Sweet Jesus. I give your old man one thing, he was always very old school, usually meticulous too. Which would be two things. But this is kinda messy, so I'm taking that last one back."

Elliot watched as Jake glanced over the map. "Strange, right? I'm not sure what to make of it."

"Satellites."

"What?"

"These points. They're satellites in LEO—low earth orbit. You not figure that out?"

"Well, no—"

"What do you write about every day?"

"Well, lately—"

"It's okay—you've been busy listening to late-night Rita on the ham radio. I understand. Here, let's open this up." Jake brought the map over to the kitchen table and spread it out. A few inches of the map hung over the edges of the table.

"Look." Jake pointed to numbers listed next to each random point on the map. "Mind you, this is a very, very educated guess, but since it's within range of the others he marked, those first numbers I'd say are distances in kilometers. The average being around fifteen hundred means it aligns with most sats that are in LEO. We could easily check this without going all Newton on it and scribbling it on paper."

"How'd I not put this together?" Elliot pointed at the numbers under the distance. "Ninety point something is its orbit time, then sixteen, the number of orbits per day."

"Yup, and look he even marked a few in MEO, which would mostly be navigation sats."

"So it explains the groupings of this ping at various intervals," Elliot finished.

"That tracks, but is it the same sound?"

"Yeah."

"Interesting," Jake said.

They were silent for a moment, studying the map, when Elliot's phone buzzed. He looked down at the screen then answered, "Trevor, hey, sorry I didn't get back to you. Just got back from Maine."

"It's okay. How you holding up?" Trevor asked.

"I'm good. Thanks."

"Good. Well, did you get a chance to look at that GBO stuff I sent?"

"No, not yet, but I will."

"Okay, good. I think it'd be a good bounce back story for you, and if you do pick it up I'll cover all expenses for this one."

"Really? That interesting?" Elliot asked.

"Yes, that interesting. Check out the links I sent. Not every day an observatory discovers an FRB and then gets shut down by the FBI. You believe that? Feels up your alley."

Elliot hung on Trevor's comment. "Wait, closed by the FBI?"

"Yeah, apparently they showed up, cleared the place out. Very hush-hush still. Just like Sunspot a couple years ago."

Elliot's eyes widened. "Trevor, hang on a sec," he said as he rushed into his room. He rummaged through a few of his father's notebooks, tossing some to the floor, searching for a particular one. He checked the cover—the dates ranged a few years back. He frantically flipped through pages like Johnny 5 reading a book, his phone pinned between his shoulder and ear. His eyes moved quickly on each page. Then he stopped at a scribble from his father that read *Sunspot*.

"Trevor, when can I leave?"

Chapter 7

LiLo sat in a chair at a small desk in her apartment, her right leg tucked under her left as she stared at her laptop. The computer was the only light source in the room and lit up her face in the London evening. Besides a small couch and a mattress on the floor, the loft-style space was bare. A speck of living space tucked away in a large building. The outside wasn't pleasant, but paying cash month-to-month didn't get you anything more. No lease and no questions was the priority for the last six months.

Her time in London had passed by like the snap of a finger. Not since she was a kid playing hide-and-seek in the backyard in West Virginia with her younger brother had she called a place home. She wouldn't let the word touch her tongue and quickly scrubbed it from her mind when it tried to take hold.

In her time in London, she'd gotten to the edge of comfort. She'd been sloppy, creating patterns, making acquaintances who could remember her, even if they knew nothing about her—creating a breadcrumb trail to her real identity. She'd broken her first and only rule for survival, zero trust. Like a network infrastructure, any device should not be trusted by default. In LiLo's case, it kept her alive. A plan of three months turned into more when she met someone. In her closed network, she couldn't even trust herself. She'd become the point of weakness and allowed intrusion.

Now she was cleaning up. She'd overstayed her welcome. She scrolled through train departures and short-term apartments across Europe. Decided her next move.

After she finished planning her journey, she opened a password-protected folder on her laptop and scrolled through photos and documents she'd collected over the years. Pieces of her past that didn't fit together and a photo of her most recent mistake—Gemini. The photo showed a tall, athletic woman in her early thirties. Her dark hair draped over her shoulders; bangs squared her face and highlighted her sharp facial features.

Before coming to London, she'd made a contact through various darknet forums who had listed small-time script jobs LiLo could do in half the time. At first, she needed a quick paycheck to cover the basics—food, a roof to sleep under, and transportation. In time, this contact and LiLo had built a rapport while LiLo bounced around Europe. After a few months, she decided to find her contact. She didn't enjoy talking to people for extended periods of time without knowing who they were. A one-sided introduction led to paranoia, and paranoia had brought her to London and put her in a situation she didn't like.

When she arrived in London six months earlier, it hadn't taken her long to track down her contact, known as Gemini, in East London. Gemini was good at covering tracks, but LiLo was better at finding them.

She monitored Gemini for two weeks before making contact: her browsing history, websites she visited, stores she visited, her favorite bookstore and coffee shop. Building a profile, following behavioral breadcrumbs until an opportunity presented itself. She knew it all, but her reasoning became blurred. It was another target, or was it her paranoia, or a slow-building infatuation? A longing to reach out to someone after years of silence.

She didn't think Gemini had a clue LiLo was watching her. They continued to chat over IRC the entire time LiLo was in London. LiLo searched for holes in who Gemini appeared to be. She couldn't find any, and it worried her.

An opportunity opened on a Wednesday afternoon at Gemini's favorite bookstore. LiLo was nervous on approach but managed a few words about a couple of books on the shelf—in particular, her favorite, Kurt Vonnegut's *Breakfast of Champions*. Gemini was so enthralled by LiLo's thoughts on a "planet dying fast" that they continued their conversation over a cup of coffee. LiLo introduced herself as Emma. The small lie she'd used a million times, but a lie about who she was. This time, it stabbed her in the chest.

Gemini had a soft English accent, only accentuated by key words that dragged it out of her. It made LiLo smile.

It didn't take long for them to get close. LiLo knew this was a problem. The relationship would have to end sooner rather than later, but she enjoyed the moment while it lasted. After two months, LiLo came clean about who she was, skipping the part about her being on the FBI most-wanted list and the rebellious eyebrow ring she had in her youth.

LiLo had never opened up to anyone, and she'd only known this person for two months, but it felt like a lifetime. Details about how her family had been killed when she was young weren't a total lie. LiLo skipped over what happened after the deaths, saying simply that she'd lived with a grandparent. The truth—that her mother and brother were murdered as a cover up for her father's military involvement—was a box she didn't want to open. Not even for herself.

With Gemini, LiLo settled into something that felt like a real life she hadn't had since she was a kid, listening to Miles Davis with her father or watching her younger brother meticulously assemble a Lego set while her mother assisted. It made her feel at ease, even if there was an itch behind her heart telling her this was wrong.

It wasn't until Gemini came to LiLo seeking help that her world returned to the way she knew. The way she'd lived it since her family was taken from her. Gemini was involved with a risky job above her skill set; she didn't know it until she got pulled in. Which was too late. YellowJacket had been Gemini's contact, and when she couldn't deliver on the job, they resorted to aggressive tactics and threats. Gemini came to LiLo for help. LiLo agreed, knowing it would change everything.

The job extended LiLo's stay in London. Gemini was wrapped up in something bigger than some script kiddie job, brute forcing email passwords. No, this was intricate and well-funded, a sign to LiLo this was bad news. They both needed to get away from this once it was done. And LiLo needed to move away from Gemini. It had to be abrupt, like pulling off a Band-Aid. The only way LiLo knew how to manage the situation.

LiLo deleted the photo of Gemini and closed her laptop. Dim light from the street sifted through her window as she gazed out into the London skyline. Another past she wanted to forget.

#

LiLo woke to sunlight skimming through the large windows of her apartment. She showered and packed her backpack with all the belongings that mattered. Anything else was thrown out. She'd spent her last night in London compartmentalizing Gemini, pushing the idea of closeness to the depths of her mind. A failed attempt at a clean cut on the surface.

Her focus now was on figuring out who YellowJacket was. Her gut told her it was her former employers getting too close. She needed to deal with it before it became more than she could handle. YellowJacket assured her Gemini was out of trouble, but in her zero-trust network, assurance from another meant nothing. As much as she wanted to move on from Gemini, something wasn't right.

LiLo planned to head back to the Continent. Travel between countries was easier, and she'd gotten a lead on YellowJacket that pointed her to Antwerp. They weren't easy to follow, but YellowJacket had left breadcrumbs in forums, requests for jobs in the depths of hacker communities.

She caught the National Express from Elephant & Castle in London to Dover—from there a ferry to Calais, France. The first leg of the trip to Dover was over three hours. The train reminded her of weekend trips with her father as a child. His work with the US government and military meant her family had moved around quite a bit. She curled up, her knees to her chest, as she thought about the train trips in the Pacific Northwest, her favorite, where they were stationed for a couple years.

The hours went by like they'd fallen off the face of a clock. LiLo snapped awake, mid-dream or nightmare, a recurring scene of being chased. A subconscious speaking loudly. She'd arrived in Dover, a small port town at the edge of the UK, like an outstretched hand to Europe. The ferry to Calais ran every hour. She made her way to the port, purchased a ticket. Since it crossed a country's border, she'd need to present a passport. The fake one she put together was good enough. She spoke enough French to pass as a local returning from business. Speaking four different languages had its benefits, as did being able to forge passports that could sell for the highest bid. Staying anonymous in the real world was just as important as it was online.

The ferry ride was about an hour and a half. By this time, London was well in the rearview mirror. LiLo decided she'd spend the night in Calais before heading to Antwerp. She'd found a small, cheap hotel near the train station. It had Wi-Fi, four walls, and a roof. She'd eaten some terrible Thai takeout in her hotel room, showered, and was enjoying a local lager she picked up at a Carrefour City grocery on her walk to the hotel.

She needed to reset and focus on finding YellowJacket. It had consumed her since leaving London. An obsession bubbling to the surface of reason. A distraction, but she couldn't shake it. She kept following the digital paper trail, every step a new breadcrumb leading to another stop. Many of those breadcrumbs were organizations YellowJacket had infiltrated. Various banks and corporations across Europe and the US.

She made progress as she sipped her lager, but something bothered her. The trail was too easy, too obvious. A trap? A honeypot pulling her in? If YellowJacket was working with TELOS, her former employers, trying to flush her out, get her to make a mistake—they were doing a sloppy job of it. She added a secondary layer of proxy servers to channel traffic through as a precaution. She found herself deep within the systems YellowJacket had touched. Searching for any other clues, all she could find was a consistent IP address within log files that bounced through the same stable servers in Antwerp. She knew YellowJacket wouldn't physically be in Antwerp; there was no doubt it was a command-and-control server, part of a hacking infrastructure, and YellowJacket could be anywhere in the world. But it kept her moving. Remaining stagnant wasn't an option.

As she wound down her search, she poked around another financial institute YellowJacket had visited. Argenta was the fourth-largest bank in Belgium, headquartered in Antwerp. She was digging through log files, bin folders, when she came across an oddly named file in the system folder, where level-one executables ran for minimal system requirements. The file contained a string of numbers. An important directory, but common. She copied the file locally, cleared log files, and disconnected from the servers.

She opened the file to see what was in it. Her eyes shifted through the complex code, line by line. A script, an executable, which looked like it could scrape data, among other tasks she wasn't sure of. Odd for something like this to be stored here. She noted it and returned to the other organizations YellowJacket had been, checking for this script. Each one had it, just sitting in their system directories. Hiding in plain sight.

Her mind raced. What was YellowJacket up to? Something was off.

Her late night carried over into the morning. She wasn't much of an early riser, so waking at 10:00 a.m. to catch the train to Antwerp was cutting into her sleep time. The trip would take the afternoon, giving her plenty of time to think about the script, YellowJacket, and her next move. The train provided a moment of peaceful pause from her paranoid life. She slept the first hour before hitting Lille-Flandres station. The sleep, more like a passed-out nap, partially remedied the fog that engulfed her head from drinking too much the night before. She caught the transfer to Antwerp.

After lunch, she was regaining her ability to interact with the rest of the world. Thankfully, the train had Wi-Fi. She connected with her usual precautions to cover her tracks and caught up on world news. A frequent stop was the FBI website, the hope being that maybe one day her photo and status would come down. It hadn't. Her photo, listed with other high-profile targets, sat front and center like an embarrassing birthmark. She checked out the latest postings and press releases, some of it signal tactics to offer a glimpse of their hand to enemies of the state. Hoping one would bite and slip up. A common tactic in espionage practice.

The last article headline caught her eye: *FBI Closes West Virginia Observatory to Investigate Potential Security Breach.*

Chapter 8

Elliot clicked between open tabs in his browser, his head propped up by his left-hand fist against the side of his face. The position of rabbit-hole research. He gently rocked back and forth as the train made its way over an old railway bridge in a small Connecticut shoreline town. The conductor announced the next stop. Elliot still had over two hours left of his trip to Newark. He'd decided to stop and visit his mother in New Jersey before heading to Green Bank in West Virginia. His hope was to find anything his father might have left behind to explain what he was investigating.

He'd set up work in the café car of the train as passengers gathered in line to get snacks. His phone vibrated with an alert that his rental car would be ready for pickup in Newark. He returned to his research, reviewing details Trevor had sent about the GBO closure, including a handful of links to various tech blogs and videos. One story, with the headline "Green Bank Observatory Closed by FBI for Suspicious IP Activity," included canned responses from an FBI spokesperson, an Agent Mark Hansen, saying the closure was for a security breach at the observatory. Not much else was provided. Conspiracy theories were quickly dismissed. The story was a few days old now, an eternity in the digital news cycle, and had already disappeared. As soon as it was established aliens weren't involved, no one cared.

Hours later Elliot arrived at his childhood home, his mother was ready to greet him with a hug. A touch of guilt gripped him. He hadn't been home since his father passed. He and his mother spoke regularly, but he'd pushed her away to deal with his own grief, which he didn't know how to handle. They each needed their own time to process, but it was good to be home.

"I got your text. Why the visit?" she asked. She'd worked a majority of her life as a nurse and being direct saved lives. It was a communication style she'd found hard to leave at the office, but her disposition and aura made the curtness seem trivial. They made their way inside to the kitchen where she was prepping dinner.

"I'm headed to West Virginia for a story," Elliot said as he took a seat at the kitchen island.

"A story? What about?"

"An observatory was shut down by the FBI."

His mother nodded enthusiastically, as if this was the most interesting thing she'd ever heard. A mother's way of making their child feel special at any moment.

"I was up at the cabin last weekend." Elliot paused, rotating the water glass she'd set in front of him. "I cleaned out Dad's stuff, his office. Well, most of it."

His mother turned and leaned against the sink, which was across from the island. "Thank you for doing that."

"Of course. Was Dad . . . Was he okay toward the end?"

"Was he okay?" she repeated like she trying to find the right words. "Well, the month before he passed he was having issues."

"What sort of issues?"

"He passed out a few times, was getting agitated frequently, and seemed preoccupied." She took a breath. "I pushed him to visit the doctor, which he did, but nothing irregular came back. High blood pressure, which he took pills for. Nothing out of the ordinary."

"Did he ever talk about what he was preoccupied with or working on?"

"You know your father—he'd get into these states of obsession and go tinker for days on something, then would surface. I was so busy at the hospital, we were like ships passing in the night."

"I found piles of notebooks in Maine. He seemed obsessed with something," Elliot said.

"Well, he was up there quite often the last few months. Almost every weekend."

"Have you cleaned out his office here?"

She shook her head. "I haven't been ready yet."

"Let's clean it out together," Elliot said.

His mother smiled.

#

The next day Elliot headed to his father's office, which was an addition that extended out from the kitchen and connected to the garage. His mother hadn't been in the room for weeks. It had a stuffy, dank smell. Elliot figured that was coming from the garage and lack of air. He opened the two windows that faced the front of the house, which filled the room with natural light from corner to corner, and a sliding glass door that opened to the backyard.

A large bookcase ran halfway up and along the longest wall. Lined with *Science & Sky* magazines and books on physics, astrophysics, and astronomy, it resembled a university library. A thin layer of dust lined the tops of the books and the shelves. His father's desk was bigger and older than the one in Maine. The bulky, L-shaped behemoth was tucked in the corner, with one half under a window. John Bishop had been a tidy man, self-contained and organized. What he'd left behind wasn't from the man they both knew. The desk was littered with another mess of loose papers, notebooks similar to those Elliot had found in Maine, and another large hand-drawn star map. His father had overlaid his own mappings and handwritten coordinates over a basic outline of known stars. Deep down, Elliot wanted to put all of it in a box and throw it in the trash. But closer to the surface, he found he was more curious than ever. What had consumed his father's mind?

Elliot cleaned out the desk. His mother was busy dusting, vacuuming, and packing boxes. He went through the notebooks, packing most of them away, putting a few aside for his own purposes. The papers on the desk were, like those he'd seen in Maine, covered in coordinates with blocks of them circled in red pen designed for correcting student papers. The same red markup Elliot would find on his papers when he was a kid; his father always insisted on editing them before he turned them in. Having a father as a professor was both a blessing and a curse.

He placed all the loose papers in the same box he had set aside for things he was going to take. The desk was starting to clear, which gave him a better look at the star map that had been at the bottom of the piles of papers. There were timestamps, repeated coordinates, and lines drawn from one spot in space to another.

Elliot stared at the map, parsing, as best he could, the data in front of him. *What were you looking at, Dad?*

When they'd looked at the map he'd brought back from Maine, he and Jake had thought his father was tracking a collection of satellites, but this map showed something else. Sets of coordinates were circled, with dotted lines traveling from each one.

Then it dawned on Elliot, like a light bulb flipped on. His father wasn't tracking multiple satellites. He was tracking one very specific satellite.

Chapter 9

Elliot arrived in Snowshoe, West Virginia the next day, a small resort town thirty minutes West of Green Bank. Because the use of radio frequencies in Green Bank was so limited that cell phones and even microwaves were restricted on observatory grounds, Snowshoe was the best option with steady internet and a place to stay.

Before heading to GBO, he checked an email from Trevor, who had reached out earlier to connect with someone at the observatory, a Jennifer Liu, the assistant director.

The drive through the mountains was pleasant; the area was lush, with rows of towering trees lining the road. Every so often, an open field would emerge, followed by more trees. From the highway, the fields rolled into the next valley, making it easy to see the next range of hills and mountains, like a naturally repeating wavelength. Elliot passed an occasional farmhouse, most of the residences far enough from one another that getting a cup of sugar would be a bit of an effort.

Green Bank was a special town, an oddity to outsiders, located directly within the only radio-free zone in the United States. A dead spot, as it was known. The town, with a population of maybe two hundred, was home not just to the engineers and astrophysicists who worked at the observatory, but also to those who had moved to the area to be off the grid, wanting the ultimate digital detox. Within a twenty-mile radius from the observatory, homes barely had Wi-Fi because of the interference it could cause with the telescope. It was an isolated world.

Elliot passed a few more farmhouses, the local church, a middle school, and a general store. The town was quiet. No people rushing around, staring at their phones as they hustled across streets. No noises from, well, anything. He'd entered a different world, with a strangeness that he couldn't pinpoint. If someone had told him he'd just entered the Twilight Zone he wouldn't be surprised.

The telescopes were set far back from the road, and the main observatory building sat right across the street from a few homes. It looked like the entrance to a middle school at first glance. Elliot checked his cell phone and, as expected, had no signal. He was dead center of a radio quiet zone.

The observatory property had three different areas: the Science Center, the radio astronomy observatory, and the telescopes. Elliot pulled in through the main entrance, which led to the Science Center, the main facility that housed spaces for tours, exhibits, and a cafeteria. With fifty thousand visitors passing through a year, the place should have been buzzing with activity during the summer vacation season. Today, the emptiness was its own presence.

Elliot parked and noticed a few cars in what looked like a staff parking area. Otherwise, it felt like a ghost town set against the science-fiction backdrop of massive telescopes poking up at various points from the trees beyond.

The front doors of the Science Center were open. Nothing seemed out of the ordinary, other than the lack of people. Inside, there was a main desk with a security guard behind it, staring at a computer screen. If boredom had a face, his was it. He'd seen busier days.

As Elliot approached, the security guard muted whatever he was watching and looked up with a weak smile. He had a nametag that read Karl.

"Hi, my name is Elliot Bishop. I'm here to meet with Assistant Director Jennifer Liu," Elliot said, as he eyed the center's high concrete ceiling.

"What's it regarding?" Karl wore the uniform of a security guard but didn't come across as someone who'd had any formal training. He was a big guy, that was it. Maybe a bouncer at a bar that needed extra shifts.

"I'm a journalist covering the closure."

Karl didn't seem too excited to be interrupted by this, as he slowly picked up the phone and dialed an extension.

As he waited, Elliot looked around the building, sizing it up. Behind the ticketing and security desk was an open area with high ceilings covered in windows that acted like a hub for the rest of the center. Out the windows you could see, in the distance, the largest telescope or, as locals called it, the "Great Big Thing."

"She'll be right down," Karl said as he hung up the phone.

Elliot turned back to him. "Thanks. You guys still doing tours?"

"No tours. Just the Science Center is open for now. Since the closure, things have been bare bones here."

"Were you here when it closed?"

"Yeah. First, a couple deputies showed up, asked people to leave, then like two hours later, a couple SUVs pulled up and FBI agents poured out. Came in like they owned the place. Then everyone was sent home. Anyway, feel free to walk around the center and exhibit."

"Thanks." Elliot walked over to a telescope fact plastered on the wall: *Did you know the surface of the Green Bank Telescope (GBT) is perfectly smooth to a noise level of 260 microns (5 human hairs)?* Elliot didn't.

A moment later, a woman with long black hair, neatly pulled back, and thin-framed glasses walked past the security desk. She glanced at the guard, giving him a nod of thanks.

"Hello, Elliot?" she said.

Elliot turned his attention to her. "Yes."

"I'm Jennifer Liu, assistant director here at Green Bank. Nice to meet you." She extended a hand, and they shook. "So you have some questions about the recent closure?"

"I do."

"Well, we can head to my office and walk through those. But before that, would you like a quick tour of the facility?"

Elliot smiled. "That'd be great. Maybe we can cover my questions during the tour. Two birds."

"Sounds good. Follow me."

They walked through the main hall of the Science Center. The exhibit area was like any other museum, highlighting discoveries made by the observatory over the years, mixed with astronomy 101. There was a lecture hall and auditorium for classes and large audiences. A gift shop with mini telescopes and T-shirts. With no visitors the place felt like a forgotten textbook. Audio from the exhibits continued to play for the phantom listeners.

"I'm surprised the center is open. I thought it was completely shut down," Elliot said.

"Everything was closed for a few days, but we recently reopened the Science Center and exhibits. The telescopes, radio observatory, and our research labs are still closed," Liu said.

"What staff is left?"

"A handful of security guards, myself for any inquiries, and a few maintenance staff, but even that has been limited. We're closed on Mondays and Tuesdays usually, and now have limited hours the rest of the week, so a smaller staff is fine."

She led the way into an exhibit hall labeled Catching the Wave, which touched on the history and fundamentals of radio astronomy.

"I'm surprised you wanted to do this in person," Liu said.

"I wanted to see the site for myself. I'll admit, as an amateur astronomer, I'm embarrassed to say I've never been to this facility."

She smiled. "There's a lot to see out there, so it's fair."

"So what exactly happened the day of the shutdown? I've read there was some security breach?" Elliot asked.

"Honestly, we weren't told much. The day of, we were contacted by the local sheriff, who told us to evacuate the facility. An hour later, two deputies showed up to evacuate the observatory, visitors and staff included. Then two hours later, the FBI showed up with reports of strange IP activity."

The response felt canned, like the FBI's in the article Trevor originally sent Elliot. Elliot sensed she was holding back. Why wouldn't she know more? After all, she was the assistant director of the observatory.

"What was the feeling like here when this all went down?" Elliot asked.

She let out an explosive breath, like bottled stress. "It was a little crazy, to be honest. We didn't know what was going on and once the FBI showed up, we were confused. It made it hard for us to understand and help."

"Did they take anything in particular or spend time in the control rooms or engineering labs?" Elliot asked.

She paused again, being cautious and selective of her words. Elliot was glad he'd done the interview in person, so he could get a better read of her. These nuances could be lost over a video or phone chat.

"They took nothing. They visited the labs for a bit, asked about what we were working on, but that was about it. Told us to shut down all activity until notified and that the observatory was closed until further notice."

By this time, they were back in the main hall of the Science Center.

"What happened to the rest of the research staff?" Elliot asked.

"They were all relocated to other facilities with an option to return when the labs re-open."

"Any sense of when that might be?"

She shrugged. "Unfortunately, we have no idea."

Elliot looked around the center again. "This facility is great, by the way. Reminds me of the tours I'd do as a kid with my family."

"Thank you—glad it brings up good memories," Liu said.

"Is there anyone else I could speak with about the closure? Is Dr. Keating available?" Elliot asked.

Liu fiddled with her glasses, then refocused. "I'm your best point of contact here. You could reach out to the local sheriff if you'd like. As for Dr. Keating, he's been relocated. So it might be hard to get in touch with him."

Elliot pushed. "Relocated? Where?"

"Seattle."

"Seattle?" Elliot repeated. Dr. Keating was well known in his field, especially his contributions to various SETI—Search for Extraterrestrial Intelligence—projects. Elliot had read that twenty percent of GBO's time was focused on SETI projects. He'd been here for years and seemed to always make himself available for interviews when it had to do with science and space. Keating had become closely identified with the facility, and it was surprising he'd be relocated so abruptly.

She nodded. "I believe he took on a temporary project with AeroTech while the station is closed."

"How did you and Dr. Keating end up working together here?"

"He was a mentor of mine when I was in grad school at Stanford. He helped me get through some tough times there, and he connected me with my first job and real project at NASA. Then an opportunity opened up here, and he asked if I wanted to join. Rest is history."

"NASA? What project?" Elliot asked.

"My background is in propulsion engineering. I worked on a few things, but mostly focused on any recent telescope or satellite launch projects."

"Like the James Webb Space Telescope?" Elliot asked.

Liu nodded with a modest but proud smile. "That was one of them."

Elliot nodded, impressed. "Do you have a contact at the FBI by chance?"

"I do. An Agent Blackwell gave me his card. He was leading the investigation here and spoke with Dr. Keating before he left."

They finished their walk around the Science Center and headed to her office. She provided Elliot with the sheriff's contact info and Agent Blackwell's card.

"Would you like to see the labs and telescope?" Liu asked.

"I'd love to," Elliot said, his face lighting up.

"We can take a cart out there," Liu said.

Their first stop was the labs, housed in a series of rooms with heavy measurement equipment and tools that Elliot didn't know the first thing about. The main lab was an open space, mostly filled with computers and monitors that crunched tons of data daily. It was quiet now, with everything shut down and no staff in place. The control lab was immense, able to reposition the immense main telescope, the Great Big Thing, like an antenna on a TV.

After checking out the engineering labs, they made their way to the field to see the main telescope itself. It was one thing to imagine something taller than the Statue of Liberty, with a dish the width of two football fields, but to see it in person overwhelmed Elliot. The sheer size gave him goosebumps.

As they made their way up to a platform that ran along the base of the telescope, Liu explained that this telescope only received signals, never sent them. Its focus was on finding signals from deep space, searching for extraterrestrial intelligence. Its size didn't deter from its extreme accuracy, which could narrow signals down to an accuracy of one arcsecond. Like seeing the width of a human hair thirty-four feet away.

"What's the wavelength range on this?" Elliot asked, trying to show he knew *something*.

"It can handle wavelengths from nine feet long down to one-eighth of an inch. So plenty of range."

"This is amazing. I could use one of these in my backyard—which looks nothing like this." Elliot gazed out at the view of the Allegheny Mountains and the Monongahela National Forest that stretched out behind the telescope.

"You can get a miniature at the gift shop. Might fit better," Liu said without missing a beat.

"I heard you discovered a new FRB? They're a minor research interest of mine."

Liu perked up a bit, seemingly excited to talk about the science. "Well, we think it is. It has all the makings of one, but since the closure we haven't had a chance to dig into the data, which takes time."

"When did you discover it?"

"Oh, a little over a week ago."

Elliot wondered if he'd be able to find something that corresponded to the FRB in his father's notebooks—maybe a repeating pattern that had left signatures in the past. "Do you remember the exact date and time?"

"I'm sorry, I don't," she said firmly and guided them back to the Science Center, her brisk pace signaling that the interview was over.

Elliot mulled her response, curious why she was avoiding details.

"Thank you again for the tour and for answering my questions. It was helpful," Elliot said when they finally stopped, back in the main building.

"My pleasure." Liu pulled out a business card and wrote something on the back. "If you have any further questions, just let me know." She handed Elliot the card and smiled.

Elliot looked at it and turned it over. On the back she had written a phone number. Since cell phones had to be shut off in the area, giving out numbers happened the old-fashioned way, via paper and pen. Elliot looked back up at her and smiled. "Thank you. I may have a few more as I organize my notes."

She walked Elliot back to the front security desk and said goodbye.

"Have a nice tour?" Karl asked, staring at Elliot with a lazy grin.

Elliot glanced again at the number Liu had written on the card. "I did, Karl, thanks," he said as he walked out the front door.

Chapter 10

Elliot returned to the connected world and the Mountain Lodge back in Snowshoe. He walked through the lobby, noting the large open space, with couches and heavy wooden coffee tables spread about. It was early summer, yet a fire was burning in the fireplace to lessen the evening chill. He got back to his room, which was more like a small condo with a kitchenette.

He slumped into the soft couch that was probably older than him. His conversation with Liu left him with less than he'd hoped. He hadn't pushed hard, but she seemed cagey when he brought up the FRB discovery. Which was odd. Was she hiding something? Why? He'd come this far on a hunch and scribbled notes from his father. He'd need more for Trevor to consider continuing this story.

He opened his laptop on the coffee table in front of him and pulled a few of his father's notebooks from his bag. He'd brought a select few and the hand-drawn map along with him. He started to transfer his father's notes to a spreadsheet, organizing them as best he could. Some of it made no sense, some of it was more of the same: coordinates, frequencies, and timestamps. He flipped through pages, searching for any mention of GBO, leaned back in the couch's embrace, and sighed. Dead end before it could start.

The conversation with Liu cycled through his brain over and over.

"They discovered the FRB about a week ago?" The thought escaped his lips.

Then it struck him.

He sat up, shuffled through the small stack of notebooks, and pulled out the one that led up to the months before his father passed. He flipped to the page where his father had noted Sunspot. Flipped a few pages forward. Checking the listing of timestamps, he spotted on the right side the letters GBO underlined, next to a few selected lines. The dates were months ago.

"What did you find, Dad?"

The conversation with Liu was still biting at his thoughts. He eyed the card she gave him at the observatory. He took a moment, then called her. It was short notice, but he played a hunch that she was anxious to share more information.

#

A few hours later, Elliot made his way to the lobby to meet Liu. There was a bit more life to the space tonight. People milling around, preparing to head out for dinner. Elliot sat by the never-ending fire, in a large green chair that was more comfortable than his bed, watching people come and go as he waited.

He was startled when a woman's voice spoke from behind him. "Comfy?"

Elliot turned, adjusted his demeanor, and looked up at Liu. "Oh hey, yeah, a little. You should try these chairs," Elliot said, his tone a bit more aloof than he intended.

Liu smiled. "Maybe another time. Grab a drink somewhere?"

Elliot nodded as he broke his cozy stay in the epic chair and stood up.

They walked to one of the few taverns in town, sat at the bar, and each ordered a beer.

Elliot could still feel some apprehension on her part as the conversation took a bit to get going. She had more on her mind about his questions earlier today. For a moment, they sat in silence until the bartender delivered their drinks and both took sips.

"So, why are you here?" Liu asked point blank, tapping the side of her glass with nervous fingers. She looked at him through her thin-framed glasses.

Elliot paused and took a breath, thinking. "I'm a journalist. I seek the truth," he said. "I think there is more to the closure."

She let out a subtle chuckle, turning her gaze back to the bar, like that was a naïve response. She wasn't wrong. Elliot wanted to believe what he was doing was important and attainable. He didn't want to get into the fact that he was here because of some red scribbles in a pile of notebooks he'd found in his father's office. Or that those same scribbles had been poking at his conscience for weeks now, keeping him from sleeping at night.

"The truth," she repeated. "What truth do you think you'll find with this story?"

"I'm not sure, to be honest. It all seems cagey and canned so far. Except, well . . . this right now," Elliot said. After a moment, he asked directly, "Is there more to the closure?"

She glanced at him; her eyes scrunched in concentration. She took another sip of her beer, like she was preparing to let it all out. Elliot did the same, mostly because he didn't have anything else to do.

"The fast radio bursts," she started.

Elliot looked at her, his ears perked. "FRBs?"

She nodded. "The day we discovered them, we saw a higher-than-normal number of them. Like never before seen. Multiple short bursts over a two-hour period." Liu turned to face him after a quick glance around the bar.

"We know where they're coming from. At least we have a theory," she continued in a lower voice. Her leg shook at a steady pace. "We pinpointed them."

Elliot could feel the concern and dread of what she was about to tell him. It seeped out of her pores.

She continued, "We think they were coming or came from a satellite—again, a theory."

He leaned back as the image of his father's map came into his mind. A pit formed in his stomach. The old man was tracking this.

"I may just be an amateur, but aren't FRBs signals from deep, deep space? Like from thousands upon thousands of light years away?" They both knew the science and what they were, but he wanted to see her confirm it.

She nodded and took another sip of her beer.

"So why does it involve the FBI?" Elliot asked.

"I don't know. I wasn't involved in those conversations. Only Keating was. When the FBI showed up, they quickly tightened the circle of knowledge to a select few."

Elliot's brain was still working through the logic and trying to connect dots. None of it made sense. There wasn't a clear connection he could see, yet. He took another sip of his beer like it might help, then another.

"You mentioned Keating was relocated to Seattle. I'm going to assume that was less volunteered and more of an order?" Elliot asked.

Liu nodded.

They both turned to face the bar as a collective *what the shit* moment washed over them—well, mostly over Elliot, but he could sense she was relieved to be telling someone about this. Her shoulders rolled down, the tension she'd emanated now easing.

"Look. You need to be careful where you tread here," Liu said, with genuine concern in her voice. "*They* were direct and compelling about what we could and couldn't talk about, but I have some theories and they scare the shit out of me."

Elliot turned to face her again, and she quickly backpedaled. "I shouldn't be talking with you. This conversation should probably stop now. I've said too much."

"What? No." Elliot took a deep breath. This was a break he needed for his story, and for himself. " If you have more, you can tell me. I can get the truth out there and break this open. They're clearly covering something up." He had to build trust with her, someone he'd met only hours ago.

They were both about finished with their drinks when Elliot looked at the bartender and signaled for another round.

"Look, I'm here on a hunch and what I thought was a wild goose chase. I have reason to believe my father was possibly tracking *this* satellite. But he never finished his work. It sounds like Keating is important to you, and he also didn't get a chance to finish his work. All I'm asking is to know what theories you did come up with." He'd rely on the scientist's impulse to share a theory.

She paused a moment, finishing her beer as a fresh glass was put in front of her. "If this signal is coming from a satellite in our orbit, that's pretty close to home. Too close. From what we could tell, based on the initial burst of data, the signal was repeating. My first guess would be that it's from a compromised system."

"Compromised? As in hacked?" Elliot asked.

She nodded. "Why else would the FBI be involved?"

He remembered the mentions of "illegal IP" and "security breaches" in the FBI statements. "What about the data? Isn't that archived for public use?" Elliot asked.

"We put a hold on the archive after the first burst that looked like an FRB. We wanted to do a full analysis before releasing. Keating was hesitant, always thinking there was something odd going on," Liu said.

"Where is the rest of that data?"

"I don't know." Liu took a sip of her beer.

Elliot wasn't convinced she was telling the truth. "If you're worried about Keating, I'll leave him out of anything I write."

She shook her head. "Keating is like a father to me . . ."

Elliot nodded and shifted the focus. "The FBI contact. Blackwell, right? What about him?" Elliot asked.

"He was the lead of the team that came into our lab. He knew his stuff and was quick to get things in control, under his control," she said. "It was crazy. They had everything—documents, release forms, confidentiality agreements, all this paperwork to review and sign, a plan for staff employees. They were prepared for this."

Elliot held on to that comment. Were they attempting to cover this up?

"He wanted you to contact him directly. To control the narrative . . ."

They were both silent for a moment. Their second round of drinks going quicker than the first.

Liu finished her last sip and stood. "Be careful of Blackwell but"—she scribbled something on a napkin and slid it to Elliot—"*if* you find yourself in Seattle, looking for an aeronautics consultant for AeroTech, tell him we talked and I said, 'Go A's.'"

Elliot smiled and looked at the napkin—an email address. "I will."

She reached for her wallet. Elliot waved his hand, declining. "No. I got these. You were more than helpful to someone you barely know. Thank you."

She smiled. "Good luck finding your truth," she said and walked away.

Chapter 11

Elliot returned to the lodge. The lobby was now empty, the only noise coming from the crackling fireplace no one enjoyed but was ready to look good when someone was around. Elliot made his way to his room. Throwing down his backpack, he pulled out his notebook and laptop. His chat with Liu didn't give him closure. It sprung more unanswered questions. He was wired. Sleep wasn't an option, even though he needed it. He knew his next step was getting in touch with Keating. Given how his conversation with Liu had gone, he expected it to be less fruitful. The fact Keating was in Seattle didn't make things any easier.

He couldn't shake the idea of the FRB discovery. The short bursts repeating within hours. Although FRBs were more commonly spotted these days with the technology available to seek them out, he'd heard of nothing like this. Liu's theory that an FRB could be coming from a satellite in low orbit was baffling. It didn't fit the definition of an FRB, but maybe the signal was designed to look like one? *But why?*

He opened his laptop and a chat client. The blue light from the laptop lit up his face in the dim room. He needed to talk to someone, someone he knew would be up at this late hour.

ELLIOT: *Hey man, you up?*

JAKE: . . .

JAKE: *yup what's up? Where are you btw?*

ELLIOT: *West Virginia*

JAKE: *wtf in all that is holy!*

ELLIOT: *Following that story Trevor has me on*

JAKE: *ahh right, your life story ;-)*

ELLIOT: *ha, yeah*

ELLIOT: *you know much about FRBs?*

JAKE: *the fast radio kind? Sure, as much as the next astrophysicist*

JAKE: *whatcha need?*

ELLIOT: *is it easy to find out if there have been spikes or recent reporting of them? And is it possible they could relay off a satellite?*

JAKE: *whoa so many questions at once. Not sure on spikes, but I can do some digging. Should be public data mostly. As for the satellite part, that's crazy talk. This have anything to do with your dad's mapping?*

ELLIOT: *Not sure. As for the crazy talk . . . I thought so. Thanks. If you find anything let me know*

JAKE: *will do*

Elliot paused in thought. A theory was forming.

ELLIOT: *think an FRB could bounce and seem like it's coming from a different source?*

JAKE: . . .

JAKE: *possible. Waves can bounce, higher output level, higher the bounce. Earth's magnetic field can also produce a bouncing effect.*

ELLIOT: *thanks*

JAKE: *np*

Elliot jotted some notes in his notebook, then dug up the email address Liu had given him. He drafted an email, trying to keep it simple, with an introduction of who he was and what he was working on. He threw Liu's name in, hoping it might help get a response and show this wasn't some cold call. The additional message of 'go A's' from Liu should be icing on the cake.

After a few rereads, he sent the email. Given the three-hour time difference he might get a reply. Being a bit desperate, he knew this was it. If Keating didn't respond, this would kill his story, his inherited obsession. He could still contact the FBI, but with no concrete evidence to work with, they'd give him a runaround response.

Still unable to sleep, he fell down a rabbit hole of research. His eyes glued to his laptop screen, he created an indent in the couch. His legs stretched out to the coffee table. One click to the next, to the next. His obsession bleeding through his eyes. He scanned every tech, science, military site he could think of for references to FRBs. Tracked FBI and military activity. *Maybe there was something or maybe I'm connecting dots for the sake of it,* he thought. He just needed to find some pattern, some conversation around the closure, around any other reported FRBs. The lack of information led him to serious conspiracy theory forums, which contained nonsense, nothing supported by any data that made sense. Amazing what the human brain comes up with when it doesn't have an answer—or one it doesn't like.

Hours passed like minutes before Elliot took a break. It was either very late at night or early morning—hard to tell without checking the time. He peeled himself away from the blue glare of his laptop screen and stood up. Blood flowed to his Jello-like legs, his eyes refocusing on the real world. He dragged himself over to the fridge to grab a seltzer, hoping it would snap him out of his internet daze.

As he opened the can, the initial burst of fizz and hiss echoed in the room. His phone buzzed from the table. Two quick vibrations signaled a new email. He put the can down and leaped over to his laptop, typed his password in faster than ever before, and opened his email. A response from Keating. A phone number with a simple message: *Call me tomorrow at 8 p.m. ET.*

#

Elliot finally slept. Not much, but enough to get him moving. The impending conversation with Keating ate at his consciousness. It was 6:00 p.m. Elliot paced his room, nibbling at his thumbnail, pulling his thoughts together into a coherent story. He needed to be precise with Keating to get the most out of him. If he stumbled, it would be a brief conversation. Keating was smart and wouldn't waste time. Elliot had a timeline, key players, and a theory, albeit a weak one, but he could work with it. Worse case, he could name-drop Liu to keep the conversation moving and maybe gain his trust. That could also backfire completely.

8:00 p.m. came faster than he expected. He picked up his phone and dialed the number Keating provided.

Within two rings, Keating answered. After a slight pause, he asked, "Who is this?" His voice was soft, hushed almost, like he was talking with someone else in the room.

"Elliot Bishop." He shook his head, trying to clear the nervousness from his voice.

"Hello, Elliot. I want to be clear and up-front. I will hang up in five minutes. I'm only doing this because you've clearly talked with Jenn. Only she knows how much I dislike the Oakland A's."

Elliot needed to make every moment count. There was no need for small talk. They both knew why Elliot was calling, so he got right to it. "I understand. What do FRBs have to do with the GBO closure?" Elliot asked.

There was a pause on the other end. Keating went on, doing his best to avoid answering. "Elliot, you need to understand this situation is delicate. My advice is to forget what you know and move on."

"I appreciate the advice, but don't people need to hear the truth? Don't you?" Elliot asked. Out loud, it sounded idealistic—because it was. But it put a nice gloss over his obsession. His father's obsession. Deep down, he wanted answers. *He* wanted the truth, but he didn't care who else got it.

Keating took a moment before answering. Elliot could almost hear his smile of disbelief. "Idealist. You clearly have dug into this and stumbled upon a detail that wasn't meant for mass consumption." Keating paused, then continued after letting out a slight sigh. "They're not FRBs. They only look like them. If you've spoken with Jenn Liu, then you know the source."

Like a scientist, he cut to the facts in front of him with precision. Elliot remained silent, as Keating still owned the conversation.

"Look, that's all I can say. I will repeat my advice—stay away from this, Elliot. Lives are at risk."

Before Elliot could respond, Keating hung up.

"Keating? Keating?! Shit," Elliot said out loud to an empty room. He dropped his phone on the desk and ran his hands through his hair in frustration. *Now what?* He needed more. Keating wanted to open up, but the hint of paranoia pulled him back. If he wouldn't talk over the phone, he certainly wasn't going to reveal anything over email. *Was he being monitored?* Elliot wouldn't put it past the FBI, who accounted for everything when they closed Green Bank. It certainly would explain the paranoia and brief conversation. *Lives are at risk.* Elliot repeated the comment to himself. This wasn't a normal security breach or equipment failure.

He opened his laptop and pinged Jake.

ELLIOT: *are there known signals that look like FRBs but short distance?*

JAKE: *Doubt it, we'd know what they were if they were short distance. The handful of FRBs recorded since 2007 are unaccounted for, because they're short bursts and from far distance. Hard to pinpoint exactly what they are and where they come from.*

Elliot opened his browser and reviewed articles he'd pulled earlier about fast radio bursts. Multiple FRBs had been picked up just about every year, with only one instance of a repeat. It didn't help but only opened the gates for what could cause them. Most had been categorized as extragalactic origin, coming from a dense stellar core, a neutron star near an extremely powerful magnetic field like a massive black hole or one embedded in a nebula. Green Bank Observatory discovered one in 2011 through archival data that suggested the burst was up to six billion light years away. Over the years, more and more had been picked up, but each lacked any pattern and were filed away as singular events, like supernovas. The first repeating FRB had been observed in 2012, but again wasn't attributed to anything as local as a satellite.

Elliot thought back to his conversation with Liu. She mentioned a compromised system. Maybe it wasn't the observatory, or any data they had, that was compromised. They had a theory it was a satellite. If this signal they discovered was coming from a satellite, then someone put it there. FBI involvement could mean it was someone we didn't trust or didn't want tinkering with satellites above the United States. That could be any global power with advanced enough technology to launch satellites or any hacker with a semi-decent laptop—even a domestic organization could be involved.

But why did the signals appear to be FRBs? To mask their true nature and where they came from? How was that possible? Satellite security had never been the highest concern of the engineers who built them.

Elliot texted Trevor, letting him know that the story was leading to Seattle and asking to chat. It wasn't so late he'd be intruding, but he knew needed to collect himself. His next request would require an explanation, which wouldn't come through over email. He wasn't sure how much he should divulge. He'd absorbed Keating's paranoia.

Trevor called within thirty minutes of Elliot's text, asking, "Seattle? What the hell is in Seattle?" before Elliot could say a word.

He wasn't angry, just playing tough editor. Elliot knew if he gave him the right information, he'd be open to it. He wanted to be careful about using the phrase *conspiracy theory*, but it might get Trevor's juices flowing.

"Yes, Seattle. I found something potentially big. But I need to verify with someone in Seattle," Elliot said, pacing around the room.

"Big, like how, big? Give me something. You know I'm happy to pull the trigger, but I just need to know why so I can sleep at night."

"I have a few theories, but I need to talk to the former director of Green Bank Observatory, who was moved to Seattle after the closure."

"What? You're kidding?" Trevor said. "Keating was director for years—why would he leave?"

Elliot felt Trevor knew the answers to these things, but he pushed people with obvious questions so they'd spill the beans. Make them feel smart by answering stupid questions.

"I'm still tracking this down, but I've spoken with the director's assistant and she said that Keating would know more, but I should be cautious. So, I reached out to Keating. We spoke over the phone, and I don't think I've ever heard anyone more paranoid."

"Paranoid? The FBI showed up to Green Bank, shut it down, disclosed nothing to anyone, and shipped the staff and director out of town? I'd be paranoid too."

Elliot nodded in agreement as if Trevor could see him.

"Okay, what the hell are they covering up?" Trevor asked.

"I have theories. The team here said they were seeing an increase in FRB traffic, but they pinpointed it to a satellite. That doesn't align with our understanding of FRBs. When I spoke to Keating, he said they weren't FRBs." Elliot stumbled over his words with nervous excitement.

"Meaning, if the FBI shut it down, they could know it's coming from another source?"

"Exactly. The assistant director, Dr. Liu, she's still here in Green Bank. I had an off-the-record conversation with her and she mentioned a compromised system. And I think Keating knows more."

There was a pause. Elliot waited for Trevor to convince himself to green-light the trip. Trevor was clearly thinking through the ramifications. It took less time than Elliot expected.

"Okay. Get to Seattle. Expenses approved and for any follow-up. Just keep me in the loop before moving."

Elliot smiled. "Will do. I'll be grabbing the next flight out."

"Elliot," Trevor said, pausing for a moment, "be careful. If this is anywhere close to what you or I are thinking it is, it could mean . . ."

Elliot finished the alarming thought in his head. He sounded genuinely concerned; Elliot never heard him like this.

"I know. I'll keep in touch."

Elliot dropped his phone on the table, opened his laptop, and booked the first flight out in the morning. This was moving quickly. After booking his flight, he took a moment to pack his things, gathering up the scattered papers covered with notes. He felt rushed, even though there was nowhere to rush to. He took a deep breath before his anxiety took over. He knew momentum was in his corner. He was starting to crack a shell of whatever this was. A truth was purposely being hidden for reasons he wasn't sure of.

Keating's comment echoed through his head. *Lives are at risk.*

Keating meant everyone.

Chapter 12

It had been years since LiLo was last in Antwerp. She made her way directly to the Airbnb, which she'd booked for a week's stay with a prefilled gift card via one of her crypto accounts. She wasn't sure how long she'd be in town but didn't expect or want it to be longer.

The studio apartment was simple, more like a college dormitory than a place you'd want to live for an extended period. Being a basement-level space, it provided quick access to the street. The tiled floors made it feel cold. All the furniture and cabinets were the same light brown in color. There was a small desk with a lamp next to the entry, a kitchenette barely big enough for one person, and a double bed in the middle of the room.

LiLo dropped her bag on the desk and pulled her laptop out. She stretched and took a shower to clean off the trip and reset her mind. The hot water was relaxing for a moment, but even as she closed her eyes, her mind pinged from thought to thought. Gemini. YellowJacket. Home. Her parents. Her brother. Recurring thoughts she couldn't escape. The time away from a normal life was seeping in, the loneliness bringing her to tears, which washed away with the hot water. Her mind operated like a computer, but underneath, she was still human.

She suspected YellowJacket was tied to her past. Another agent, maybe? Or a freelancer hired to track her down? It'd been a while since she needed to go on the offensive. Either way, they'd gotten close enough for her liking.

After her shower she lay on the bed, refocused on YellowJacket and the script she'd found that trailed their every move. Her mind jumped to the article she'd read on the train, about an observatory in West Virginia being shut down by the FBI for a security breach. The observatory didn't matter to her, but the reference to West Virginia summoned early childhood memories. She remembered playing in the backyard with her younger brother in their home in Charleston. Before the family bounced around the country for her father's work. Another life buried in memories, which surfaced more and more.

She sat up on the bed, stretched, and finished getting dressed. Time for the past was over.

She opened her laptop and started poking through everything she had on YellowJacket—the servers they'd been to, the script that trailed them, the log of IPs she'd pulled, strangely left behind like an amateur. To call it sloppy was being kind. The IPs she kept coming across traced back to a location in Antwerp. She could pull up a latitude and longitude for a general location, but more importantly, she pulled up an ISP name: Digital Grid Inc. The generic name wasn't convincing; she did a quick search for the company on the EU Business Register. Not much, no website, but a business listing and mailing address that led to a local mail service, Belgian Post Group or Bpost, PO box location. Nothing else. *A shell company?*

She figured the physical location of this fake company would be within a short distance of the Bpost listed. As much as they weren't advertising, they were still a registered business, which meant they would get official mail. Still facets of the world that lived in paper. She pulled up Google Maps and scanned the local area. *Where would I set up a fake ISP?* An industrial area sat about a mile from the Bpost location. A start, but still a needle in a haystack.

Hours passed as LiLo sifted through property records, business listings, and even reached out to commercial real estate groups for recent purchases in the area. She was pinpointing Digital Grid's location by proving where they weren't, through process of elimination. Working in reverse. She narrowed her list down to two likely locations.

She found local traffic footage she could grab online, then waited and watched. Who came in and out of the buildings over a forty-eight-hour period. One had too much foot traffic and no trips to the Bpost. Her list was down to one.

The address she pulled was a fifteen-minute walk from her Airbnb, on the edge of an industrial area that broke off from the city. She wasn't planning on heading right for the building. Instead, she headed to the Bpost where the PO box was set up. The surveillance she picked up from the traffic cams showed one person going from the Bpost to the building she'd identified. A middle-aged man, maybe in his early to mid-forties, tall, lanky, with scruffy brown hair. Like clockwork, he'd head to the Bpost and return.

She made her way to the Bpost, a short time before her timely target would arrive, and sat on a bench across the street. Traffic was light. The noises of the city waking up. As expected, the lanky man arrived, checked the PO box, then departed. LiLo noted details about him and the area. She returned to her Airbnb for the night.

The next day she returned, same spot, same time. Her target arrived as expected. He wore a leather jacket and black jeans. *YellowJacket?* He entered the post office and checked the PO box. She sat up straighter on the bench, full focus on him. She tracked him as he left, keeping her distance. He'd led her to what looked like a vacant residential building on the edge of an industrial area, a few floors high, about a mile away from the post office. The building she'd pinpointed. He entered. LiLo moved closer. Few people were in the area. She would have to be careful as she'd stand out doing anything out of the ordinary. *Next move?* She waited and watched.

A few minutes later, the same man exited the building and got into a car and drove off. LiLo made a move toward the building. The front door was locked, the windows closed, with bars running from top to bottom. She wanted to avoid breaking anything on the first floor. She wasn't sure if anyone else was inside. She made her way around to the back and found a small sliding basement window, one of a few she could fit through. *Locked.* She took off her jacket, wrapped it around a rock to mute the sound, and cracked the window. She unlatched the window and slid it open. Small chunks of glass crunched as she climbed into the basement.

Once inside, she noticed how organized and clean it was—not finished but prepped, with sealed gray floors. The small basement windows let in the only light, but it was enough to navigate. The temperature was colder than expected. She could hear the hum of computers, servers, and a cooling unit. She moved further in.

A staircase was on the other side of the room, the only way in besides a newly broken window. A portion of the basement was partitioned off with a false wall where the hum was coming from. She inched closer and looked behind it, seeing racks of servers lining the clean walls. Lights flashed. *A server farm. A relay point.* Was YellowJacket channeling traffic through this farm? High probability. A proxy that they likely rented out to other hackers who wanted to hide their digital tracks.

She made her way to the staircase and climbed to the first floor. She opened the door to a hallway. Directly in front of her was a living room, shades drawn, desks set up with desktop computers and laptops. *A hacking station?* She checked the other rooms on the first floor—a dining room with more laptops and a smaller station. No one was around. She didn't bother checking the second floor. She needed to know what was going on here.

She cracked into one of the laptops. It was easier than breaking a basement window. She opened the text editor, which pulled open the last file the user was working on. A script similar to what she made for Gemini. She checked the directory the file was in. It had a list of files, scripts, and a text file named README. She popped a USB drive she had into the laptop and copied all the files from the directory. Before she closed everything out, she decided to leave a little something behind, a backdoor. If YellowJacket was using this server farm, she could use it to find him and whatever else he's been up to. She loaded a program she had preloaded onto the USB drive. It would bury itself in the system files and take them too long to figure out it even existed. She closed everything out like it had never been touched, put the USB drive in her pocket, and started for the basement.

When she hit the hallway, the sound of a closing car door caught her attention. Time to move. She dashed to the basement door and fled downstairs. On the bottom landing she paused and listened as the front door opened and footsteps sounded across the floor above her. She prowled toward the broken basement window like a thief. The window sat higher than she could climb to. She dragged a small table over as quietly as she could, then climbed the table and out the window into the backyard. She brushed off some leftover glass and made her way around to the front. The back and sides were all fenced in. Jumping to another yard wasn't an option.

She poked her head around the corner of the building and spotted the tail end of the car she'd heard earlier. Her eyes darted up and down the street. Nothing else. She was in the clear. *Almost.*

But before she'd gotten a few steps out from behind the building, a startled voice yelled out from the other side of the car in Dutch, "Hey, who are you? Don't move!"

It wasn't the same person LiLo tracked from the post office—this was a bulky man. His head shaved down to gray stubble. He moved around the car toward LiLo. She looked at him and backed away, her hands out like this was no big deal, responding, "Mistake, wrong yard," in Dutch, hoping to disarm the situation.

He continued toward her, put his hand inside his jacket. *A gun?* LiLo didn't want to stick around to find out. She ducked, turned, and ran.

She had a good head start. His bulky frame slowed him. He might lose wind, but his anger might overcome it. She just needed to get back to a busy intersection she could get lost in. She held her distance. Cut through yards, dodging traffic. He still pursued.

She was getting closer to the city center; more foot traffic meant more obstacles. She cut through a park and headed toward an open mall area with a large crowd. He'd managed to close ground. The mall might not work if he was this close. She'd have to slow her pace.

She spotted a bus coming to a stop near the park and diverted her path toward it. People had finished loading and unloading. The doors were just about to close before she squeaked on.

She paid her fare and kept her head down. Winded, she made her way toward the back of the bus to gather herself. The man stopped when he got to the street, tucked away the gun, forgetting he had it out in public, and looked both ways, red-faced and angry. LiLo smiled and sat back in her seat.

Chapter 13

The next morning, Elliot hit the road early. He'd slept, but the bags under his eyes suggested otherwise. He wore the same shirt and jeans he'd started the trip with. His clean clothes were dwindling. Getting to Seattle was going to be a journey. He drove for a couple of hours to the Charleston, West Virginia airport. He had a couple hours before his flight and attempted to sleep, to no avail. After a layover in Chicago, he was finally on a flight to Seattle. His satellite theory was spiking at his sides; he'd done some digging the night before, looking for anything on recent foreign power moves in the satellite industry, commercial or military.

The FBI said the closure was because of a security breach. Was the satellite the security breach they were talking about? He wanted to know as much as possible before connecting with Keating—if he could even find him and convince him to talk. Keating was tight-lipped over the phone; a personal visit might set him off. Elliot thought if he came asking the right questions, Keating would open up. It was a long shot, but he had to try.

He'd chosen an aisle seat, preferring the freedom to get up whenever he wanted and not be part of a claustrophobia-inducing human sandwich. He jumped at the first passing of food, snagging a bag of chips and a Coke. It took him minutes to finish his poor man's lunch, which was fine. He was eager to work.

The couple sitting next to him were cuddled up, using each other as pillows, which gave Elliot a bit more elbow room. He opened his laptop, connected to the Wi-Fi, and started pulling up articles he'd bookmarked the night before.

He bounced from article to article, all of them discussing how satellites were the next frontier of military advancement. AeroTech, a leading commercial manufacturer of airliner and space aeronautics, kept popping up. The recent, and very large, deal they'd inked with the DoD would set them up as the leading defense satellite communications partner for decades to come. Other future-focused articles described satellites as being at the cusp of a technological and geopolitical revolution, with major global powers having a serious presence in Low Earth Orbit (LEO). Super-secure military communications networks to the US had accused the Russians of tailing one of their spy satellites. Even India was getting into the game by deploying "space weapons" and claiming to have successful tests of anti-satellite weapons.

Earth's orbit, once an uncolonized space, was now the scene of an unseen arms race. The new frontier of war was shifting over their heads. Treaties controlling Low Earth Orbit had been created in the late 1960s but hadn't been updated since and were now outpaced by new technologies. Anyone under the glare of the sun could send a satellite to the ocean of stars above.

As someone who worked and wrote about these topics, Elliot was confident he had a good pulse on what was happening, but the pace at which the world was advancing made it hard to keep up. The Air Force had a defense contract to build out a satellite system that would beam solar energy to Earth to deliver armed convoys full of fuel to power remote military outposts, and potentially for civilian use in remote areas. Hell, the military had even finished the deployment of an ultra-secure communications network.

When the flight attendant passed by Elliot, he asked for another Coke with ice. He needed something to do with his hands while he read. As he continued to click through and skim articles, a common theme pulled together. Surveillance. From commercial to military. Everyone was tracking everyone. Most countries were building weapons to destroy satellites, but there was little information on satellites being hacked. Military-grade satellites would have prepared for hacks, but existing communications arrays, probably less so.

Elliot thought about the damage that could be done if a spy satellite was hacked and redirected, or if a supposed secure communications network was compromised. If someone wanted to get in, they'd get in. Hacking for gain was about tapping into a system with mass impact. The larger the number of impacted users, the larger the return. Whatever that return was—whether financial, social or political disruption, or information. Data.

He rubbed his eyes. His body was telling him to shut down or it'd do it for him. Before he did, he captured a few more notes: *Data has all the value, greater than any currency. The one with the most actionable data wins or at least controls the board.*

He knew there were over four thousand satellites in orbit already, a number only growing as the commercial sector deployed at a constant rate. He'd read that, within a few years, the world would generate hundreds of exabytes of data daily. Which governments or individuals would control that data and harness its power?

Keating knew what this signal was doing—or at least he knew enough to put his life in danger. Elliot got the feeling Keating was right. He should stay away from this.

#

The sky was partly cloudy but with no sign of rain when Elliot arrived at Sea-Tac international airport. His flight landed on the late side. He was exhausted, and he had no idea where to find Keating beyond following the trail to AeroTech, which had offices throughout Washington state. So he booked a hotel in downtown Seattle, a central location.

AeroTech had been around since the early 1900s—a blue-chip company that survived every political and financial storm throughout the years. It helped they provided parts and planes for the military over the years, so business was good. However, Keating was in astrophysics. While AeroTech did have satellite and space defense programs, those were back in the Virginia area; most of the facilities in Washington were focused on aerospace and plane production. *Burying Keating in the Pacific Northwest is certainly a way to keep whatever he knows hidden,* Elliot thought.

The journey from the airport to his hotel was about twenty minutes, a quick ride, but it felt like hours after being inside a metal tube for half the day. The hotel wasn't over-the-top, but nicer than most and a close walk to the historic Pike Place Market. Elliot figured if this whole thing went to shit, he could at least check it out before heading home. He was prepared for this to fail and be on a plane back to Boston. Part of him preferred that outcome. He wasn't sure what he was getting into.

He checked into his room. It'd been a few days since he'd talked to his mother, so he called her to let her know where he was. He could tell she appreciated it. He texted Trevor to let him know he'd landed in Seattle.

Now here he was, in Seattle, unsure where to start. He thought about contacting Jenn Liu. He doubted she'd know where Keating was. Visiting various AeroTech offices made no sense, and Keating might not even be listed in a company directory. He decided to just email him. Keating might not respond at all and maybe that was how this whole thing ended. He could take a tour of the Space Needle, spend a day writing up what he had so far, and head home. While it wouldn't be the worst outcome, it'd certainly be the safest.

After crafting five or six versions of an email, he scrapped them all. Frustrated, he decided for short and sweet:

Keating,
I'm in Seattle. Can we meet?
Elliot

Lazy but direct. No room for walking around. *He's either in or he's—*

Before Elliot could finish the thought, his phone rang with a call from an unknown number. He accepted the call but said nothing.

After a moment's silence, Keating's voice. "My idealist. Couldn't stop, could you?"

"The truth interests me too much."

Keating chuckled. Elliot sensed Keating didn't believe him or thought he was naïve.

Keating continued, "Well, you made the trip. Tomorrow. 9:00 a.m. There's a set of water fountains next to the Seattle Aquarium. I'll be on a bench. Don't be late."

"Okay. How do I recognize you?" Elliot asked.

"Mariners hat and red backpack," Keating said, then hung up.

#

Elliot had never been to Seattle, or even the West Coast. The furthest west he'd been was to Chicago with his father to attend an aeronautical exhibition. He expected constant rain in Seattle, but the clear weather held. The summer morning was cool. The sun pierced through the high-rises and into the streets, but in the shadow of the buildings, the temperature was noticeably colder. Elliot was feeling the repercussions from his long travel day. But it didn't matter—his anxiety had gotten him up and ready early.

The walk from the hotel to the aquarium was short. Elliot's heart ticked along a nervous repetition. Each beat tapped his chest. He was at the whims of his body's reaction to the situation. What if he fumbled the meeting with Keating? He needed to make an impression and get as much information as possible. Showing up a mess of nerves might shorten the conversation if he couldn't think straight.

The aquarium was right on the pier that fed into the Puget Sound, surrounded by shops and a boardwalk, which extended in either direction. Elliot could see the attraction for tourists, but it wasn't a place he imagined locals visited often. The waterfalls Keating mentioned were right next to the aquarium. Up a set of stairs, there was an open area with concrete benches built into short walls topped with flower beds. The few benches along the back side facing the street were empty. On the opposite side there was an elderly couple taking a break while a couple of kids ran around, burning off energy. Elliot took a few deep breaths to calm himself. It worked enough so he could focus. He stood for a second in the middle of this concrete area and looked around for a man in a Mariners hat with a red backpack. Nothing.

He checked his watch for what felt like the hundredth time since leaving his hotel—a few minutes before 9:00 a.m. Elliot realized he looked awkward, and certainly suspicious, just standing there. *It's fine, I'm waiting for my date or a friend, or maybe no one gives a shit because they aren't paying attention to me.*

He took another deep breath and grabbed a seat on one of the benches. He pulled out a book he'd been reading, *Stephen Hawking's Brief Answers to the Big Questions*, to make it look like he was a normal person doing a normal thing, not someone about to meet a contact with information about a potential global conspiracy and security breach of the highest order.

He flipped to the section he'd been reading—about time travel, another of his favorite topics. The letters faded into a mess as he stared at them. He looked at his watch again instead—9:05 a.m.

A man in a Mariners hat carrying a red backpack sat down a few feet away from him. "Elliot?" the man asked in a low voice, careful not to look directly at Elliot.

The Mariners hat hid most of his silver hair and dark sunglasses covered his eyes entirely. He wore jeans, a casual button-down shirt, and white sneakers. You wouldn't know he was one of the leading experts in astrophysics, or that he found and analyzed signals coming from outer space. He looked like someone's uncle heading to a baseball game.

"How could you tell it was me?" Elliot asked.

"You look like a nervous tourist looking for a guy in a Mariners hat with a red backpack." Keating cracked a tight smile.

Elliot smiled back, thinking that his father and Keating would get along.

"Let's walk," Keating said as he casually stood up.

Elliot followed alongside him as they walked down the boardwalk. Keating's voice was different. Maybe it was the public setting, but there was less paranoia behind it. Less shortness. Keating's relative calm brought Elliot's nerves down a few notches, allowing him to focus again.

"Have you been to Seattle before?" Keating asked.

Elliot shook his head.

"Oh, it's a great city. Green, vibrant, and plenty to do. I started my career here. Spent many years here before moving to West Virginia."

"AeroTech. Explains the relocation," Elliot said.

Keating shook his head and grinned, subtly acknowledging that he hadn't been given a choice. "I started out in aerospace engineering. Moved to their space defense facility in Virginia but ultimately ended up searching the stars as I looked for something a little less paced, if you will. Guess that got me far."

They had walked far enough down the boardwalk that the tourist crowd had thinned. There was an open dock area where people could fish off the railing and benches to enjoy the view. They grabbed a seat that faced out to the Puget Sound. It was a beautiful view and clear enough you could see the islands across the way and mountains in the distance. A rare treat, it seemed.

"Elliot, I don't know what you hope to achieve with this. But coming here wasn't a good idea," Keating started.

"The truth. You said the signal looked like FRBs but wasn't?" Elliot glossed over Keating's warning.

Keating settled in, let out a sigh, and relaxed his shoulders. "At first, we thought they were just another random occurrence. The day after we discovered the big burst was when the observatory was shut down. But, in the bit of data I could review, I found a pattern. One aligned with other FRBs in the past."

Elliot waited, soaking in everything Keating presented. Keating had a presence about him, a gravitational pull. Every word seemed like part of a bigger lesson. Always something to learn. It reminded him of his father.

Keating looked out to the water and continued, "When I did a source analysis, I found this signal had bounced around different medium earth orbit locations over time. It's as if it grew stronger. That's when I found it originated from an older communications relay satellite. A nothing-special satellite owned by—"

"Let me guess, your current employers?" Elliot cut in.

Keating nodded but said no more. The two paused at the thought.

"You think the signal is from multiple satellites?" Elliot finally asked.

Keating took a moment and leaned back on the bench. He'd started fiddling with a baseball he'd pulled from his bag.

"Anything is possible. If that's the case, there may be log files associated with the satellites . . ."

Keating turned to face Elliot on the bench. "Elliot, this is dangerous ground we're treading. I'm not sure you entirely understand how dangerous. The FBI is involved, and I fear it's bigger than that. I feel like every move I make is monitored. If you're identified and seen talking with me, this gets complicated, for me and you. If I'm named in this story—"

Elliot held up a hand to stop him. "I can leave everyone anonymous. Just presenting the facts, that's all."

"They'll know, and I don't want Liu or any of the team pulled into this," Keating said, his voice firm.

"Then what do we do?"

Keating stood up, collected himself, then tossed the baseball to Elliot. "Nothing. Catch a ballgame. Then go home and write a fluff piece about an equipment failure at Green Bank. Mention the satellite if you'd like, let the conspiracy theorists simmer on it for a couple of weeks, and it'll go away. Nothing more."

They looked at each other, Keating searching for confirmation from Elliot, who gave a half-defeated nod like he understood. It didn't matter anyway. If Keating didn't want to talk anymore, this was where it ended.

Elliot offered the ball back to Keating.

"Keep it. I have more. Goodbye, Elliot," Keating said as he walked away, leaving Elliot with the view.

Chapter 14

It had to be important if the board of AeroTech called on Chris Burns for an impromptu meeting. For the average person, this might instill fear or concern, but for Chris it was just another day at the office. He was a lobbyist for one of the largest corporations in the world. Late-night summons and fire-drill meetings happened more often than not. It's why Chris got paid what he got paid and got reservations at whatever restaurant he wanted. In arenas from Congress to the press, he was their bulldog. He was more than just a lobbyist; he was their problem solver when shit hit the fan. For AeroTech, shit had hit the fan.

Even at 7:00 a.m., Chris dressed like he was taking on the world. He strode into the meeting room with confidence and his game face on. He had a knack for absorbing information and reciting it back word for word. It was what made him good at his job and made people on the other side worry.

The conference table was large enough for thirty. At this moment, it only needed space for four. Three members of the board were already seated when Chris entered the room. This group had been in so many meetings together. Even as important as they were, there was still an air of casualness between them. These were the only people Chris took direction from, and they respected his opinion and approach. They invited him to barbecues at their homes over the summer. To say he was family was an understatement.

The board members were mid-conversation when Chris entered and made his way to a seat.

"What do we expect in terms of losses if this gets exposed?" Arlen Moss, one of the members, asked the group. He was the eldest present, in his late sixties, his pure white hair cut short with a clean part like he'd worn it all his life. He shot a welcoming nod to Chris.

"Financially, short term, we'll take a tremendous hit over the next three years. Stock will drop significantly. Long term is where I'm concerned," David Cason said. He was a veteran CFO type, early fifties. He was known around the corporate world as *the shark*. Even if there was no blood in the water, he was aggressive.

The last member, Charles Brooks, tapped the end of his Montblanc ballpoint pen lightly against his lips, a thinking tic of his. He snapped out of thought as Chris sat down. "Chris, welcome."

Chris nodded to the group. "So, what's the situation?"

His no-nonsense, get-shit-done attitude was what the group liked. Even if he was the most junior of the group, he knew what his purpose was.

"We have an issue with a production run of our satellites. Many of which are already in orbit and in use," Arlen started, then nodded to David to fill in the details.

"Our engineering team has found a security hole," David said.

Chris looked around the room. "Satellite security might be a little out of my jurisdiction. Can't it be fixed with a patch?"

The board members glanced at each other, concern flashing across their faces.

"This is our problem. It can't. Some of these are high-profile satellites for commercial and even government contracts," David said.

"Has news gotten out?" Chris asked.

"Not yet, but there is some . . . noise, if you will, stirring up, which might pose an issue for us," Arlen said.

"We can't have another hit like last year's test failure," David said, not hiding his annoyance at the situation.

Charles was now leaning back in his chair, seemingly distant from the conversation.

"So what do we know?" Chris asked the group.

David continued, "We know at least one satellite has been compromised. We know a listening station in West Virginia is poking around and has data potentially connected to it, and we know a journalist from Boston is there asking questions."

"Do we know what this data is?" Chris asked.

"No. It may just be coincidence, but it's a little too close for comfort as the FBI has shut down the station." Arlen walked over to the conference room window, overlooking downtown Seattle.

Chris quickly understood the repercussions of the situation. "I'll connect with the journalist. See what he has and go from there. Do we know anything from the FBI?"

"No details yet, but we know the team involved and who's leading it up—an Agent Blackwell," David said.

"Anything else?" Chris asked.

The group looked at each other. David and Arlen shook their heads.

"We need to keep our name out of this as much as possible, whatever this ends up being," Charles said, finally.

Chris nodded. "Understood. I'll get back with an update once I hit the ground."

Chapter 15

Elliot remained on the bench after Keating walked away. He wasn't sure what to do next. Sitting seemed to be the best choice at the moment. The sun inched further into the sky behind him. He could feel the heat from the rays as they lit up the pier. Fishermen filled in spots along the edges of the pier, along with tourists who had ventured further down the boardwalk. Elliot was fading into the crowd as he sat, defeated by the conversation with Keating. He had come so far, but he needed more.

What else does Keating know? Elliot couldn't let it go.

He made his way back to his hotel. The lobby was busy as people prepared to make their way out to see the city. Elliot stopped at the complimentary breakfast area, picking up whatever was leftover—a blueberry muffin, a toasted bagel, and some OJ. With his hands full, he headed to his lifeless room. He sat, ate his breakfast, and thought about the conversation with Keating. It absorbed all other thoughts. He repeated the same questions in his head: *Why did Keating give me anything? Why take the chance?* He dragged on the thought while eating his dry blueberry muffin.

Unsure what to do next, he lay in the queen-size hotel bed. Mentally drained, he pondered every detail he had in front of him. He thought about the notes his father collected and the article he could write, which would be another conspiracy theory to spread on the deepest of internet forums. He wasn't even sure he was here for an article. He'd taken an obsession and turned it into something it shouldn't have become. His father had been his crutch and now that was gone. He'd need to figure this one out on his own.

A couple hours passed; room service lunch had come and gone. Elliot was halfway through a cold Coke as he sat at his laptop. He made the best of the situation by writing up his article. It was a hollow lie. It presented the tip of what he knew about FRBs and the observatory closure, while staying away from conspiracy theory territory. He didn't include any names that would cause trouble. It was a portion of the truth. It didn't satiate his obsession, his mind.

He took a break after his first draft, which didn't take long to write. First drafts never did for him. He wasn't happy with it, but it was the process.

The sun edged down the coastline; early evening settled in. The golden hour blasted through the city for the perfect photo op. He called it quits. His eyes were dry from staring at a screen for so long. When he looked away, his eyes blurred with tears as they tried to readjust.

He postponed his search for flights home. He wasn't in a rush to leave town just yet. He'd call Trevor in the morning, give him an update, spend another day in the city, and finish a second draft of his article. He snapped his laptop shut. Time to get out of this fancy cubicle and get dinner. He put on his gray hoodie and headed down to the hotel lobby. As he walked, he felt refreshed, like he'd just stepped out of a cave and saw the world for the first time. The sunken-gut feeling of losing from earlier dissipated. This was where his road ended.

The concierge suggested a restaurant close to the hotel. A short five-minute walk. It had an open layout, with a large bar, but managed to still feel intimate and inviting with its low lighting and rustic feel. He snagged a spot at the bar. Three bartenders stood between the bar and a wall of bottles that would make any cocktail enthusiast giddy. Two TVs were recessed above the wall of liquor. One showed the Mariners game, the other world news, both with closed captioning. An upscale place trying to please all customers.

He ordered a beer and a burger. He watched the Mariners game for a moment—they were losing—before his attention was drawn to a news story about an increase in corporate hacks over the last two weeks by state-backed groups. AeroTech was mentioned as a target. Elliot smirked as he sipped his beer. He decided people-watching and reviewing his article was a better waste of time. He relaxed into his spot, his mind at ease with where he was. He hadn't felt that in a long time. He'd come to terms with his decision to not press Keating any further. A dead end and time to move on, get back to his life in Boston.

The burger was delicious. Elliot reminded himself to tell the concierge when he got back to the hotel. After a couple beers and watching the Mariners lose another one, he closed out his tab and milked what remained of his half glass. The restaurant was buzzing at this point, with awkward first dates and tourists filling tables like it was their last meal. He was in a bubble, safe and unnoticed.

He took another sip of his beer, getting ready to finish up and leave, when his phone buzzed. An unknown number. He swiped it away like any spam call. A few moments passed, another sip, then again, his phone vibrated. Unknown number. He stared at his phone to see if it would just go away. But it didn't and the ringing felt like it lasted an eternity. *How many damn rings does it take to get to voicemail?* Finally, it stopped. He looked up and shook his head, took another sip of his beer, happy to be left alone. A minute passed. Again, his phone buzzed. Unknown number. *For Christ's sake.* He paused, let out an audible sigh, then answered.

"Who is this?" Elliot said, fast and with a touch of annoyance.

"Elliot. It's Keating." His voice was whispered and shaky, almost out of breath.

"Keating? Everything okay?" Elliot asked, his angry tone for a confused one.

"No. We need to meet. You still in Seattle?"

"Yeah, I'm still here. When?"

"Tomorrow. 11:00 a.m. Pike Place Market. The fish stand," Keating said, then hung up before Elliot could respond.

#

The morning sky was draped in large patches of gray clouds. Seattle's preferred blanket of comfort. Elliot could feel the air holding back drops of rain, like it could pour at any moment. There was a strange comfort to it. He left the hotel with nothing else but his gray hoodie and Red Sox cap. He ran his hand across his chin. He hadn't shaved in a few days.

He strolled toward Pike Place Market, thirty minutes ahead of when Keating said to meet. It wasn't a long walk from the hotel, maybe fifteen minutes. He wasn't sure what to expect. Keating had been all over the place in terms of behavior. From their first call to their brief meeting to his whispered call last night. It put Elliot back on edge. He had been so close to escaping this feeling of empty pursuit. Now he was flooded with it.

For a weekday, the market was busy. Elliot assumed the location and timing was intentional. A crowd in a safe place. Nothing could go wrong. The market itself captured the charm and vibe of the city perfectly. One of the country's oldest farmers' markets, the historic arcade had shops tucked away in winding alleys that made for a delightful maze. Multiple levels of multisensory overload of sight, sound, and aromas. One could spend hours traversing all it offered. Elliot wanted to get acquainted with his surroundings, so he did a quick walk through the main alley. Keating mentioned meeting by the fish stall, famous for fishmongers acrobatically tossing fish between each other. Tourists loved it; locals were over it, but still had a spot in their hearts for it.

Elliot stopped at the fish stand, feeling a little less awkward than he had yesterday at the aquarium. He watched the show as fish were thrown between yelling workers. Some less messy, wrapped orders were gently tossed to customers, putting them at the center of the fun as smiles stretched across their faces.

There was plenty to be distracted by as Elliot strolled around, staying close to the fish stand. He stopped at various open kiosks, less intrigued by trinkets than by people's faces. The crowd got larger by the fish-tossing show, which occurred every fifteen minutes, cleared, then rebuilt. Tourists and families, coming and going.

He hadn't slept well the night before. Even with the late meeting time, he was having trouble focusing on faces. The number of people made for a claustrophobic situation. The walls closed in on Elliot, but before he got lost, someone passed by and called out to him, "Elliot. Walk with me." The voice was hushed but clear.

Elliot recognized it immediately. *Keating.*

Elliot turned, and without missing a beat, walked along with Keating. Before they got far, Elliot asked, "So, what's going on?"

They walked into one of the alleyways. Keating slowed his pace to a stroll, like he was window-shopping. The alley was narrow and crowded. Keating did a quick pan behind, like he was looking for someone, then touched Elliot's shoulder, leading him toward a shop.

"Here. Pop in here. Make it look like we're buying something," Keating said, still checking either end of the alleyway.

Once in the shop, they moved around with the crowd, looking at the shelves covered in tourist swag. Seattle cookbooks, guides, mini Space Needles. All the crap people give to someone who would throw it out in a year. It didn't matter. Elliot couldn't focus on anything but Keating's paranoia; it seeped out of him for Elliot to absorb and equal in weight.

"What's going on? Someone following you?" Elliot asked in a hushed voice.

"Yes. Well, someone is always following me, but since you showed up, it's been a bit more noticeable," Keating said under his breath with a tinge of blame. "It's their version of a threat. To remind me."

Elliot peered around the store and through the shop windows. He couldn't see anything out of the ordinary.

"Who?" Elliot asked.

Keating ignored Elliot's question as they moved around the shop. Finally, they stopped in front of a display of various knickknacks: shot glasses, small Space Needle replicas, key chains.

"You wanted the truth—well, you're about to get as much of it as I know." Keating dropped a small plastic item inside a jewelry box replica of the Space Needle with a top that closed tight. He handed it to Elliot, his eyes still scanning.

"Here. Buy this for your mother." Keating then walked around Elliot to put some distance between them.

Baffled, Elliot eyed the souvenir. He thought about his mother, with an uncertain hope she was okay. He headed to the register and purchased the gift. The woman behind the counter asked if he wanted it wrapped. Elliot shook his head, and she placed it in a bag, giving him the receipt and a smile.

Elliot walked out of the store and back into the stream of people. He looked both ways for Keating and spotted him ambling down to the end of the alley. Blending in. Elliot made his way toward him. As the alley opened up, Keating slowed further, giving Elliot a chance to catch up. They continued, like any two people making their way through a crowded market.

Keating, without acknowledging or facing Elliot, said, "That has all the data from Green Bank, from the observatory archive. I never had time to fully analyze it. It has all of my notes." Their pace picked up slightly, Keating glancing over each shoulder as they went. He looked at Elliot with confident eyes. "You wanted the truth. There it is."

Elliot shook his head, signaling he could trust him, but also felt a weight land on his shoulders. Keating walked away. Elliot, not realizing he'd stopped walking, snapped out of his haze and panned around to see if someone was watching. No faces jumped out. No one looked like they didn't belong. It didn't shake the feeling someone was watching, paying attention.

Elliot hurried back toward his hotel. His mind raced, unclear what Keating had handed him. He was now the one carrying the paranoid baton. *Was he telling the truth? Was it just data from Green Bank?* Elliot had no idea what he had on him. But he understood if Keating was suspicious, it had to be from fear of what he knew.

Once back in his room, Elliot rushed to the table and put the shopping bag down. He removed the tissue paper and the small jewelry box from the bag. The souvenir, like Elliot, was completely unaware of what it carried.

Elliot placed the ceramic gift on the table and removed the replica Space Needle top. The base was a box for rings and earrings. Inside was a small, square plastic case. He pulled it out and looked at the front. An SD card.

#

Elliot sat at the desk and put the SD card into his laptop, then opened it in file explorer. He scanned the list of folders, all titled with dates, except for one named "Notes." Keating's personal notes on his research. Elliot hesitated before opening the folder. A double click brought him a next level closer. His heart raced, most likely from the encounter with Keating. The folder had text files, again, all named with dates. The dates, Elliot noticed, started about two weeks before the observatory closure and extended to about a week after. A digital journal sorted by date. Another folder contained more text files with dates further back, as far as last year. Mixed in with the text files were database files Elliot couldn't access on his laptop.

Elliot scrunched his face in confusion, paused in thought for a moment. Then he opened the last file Keating created before the closure. The file read like a journal, full of scattered thoughts and theories relating to data Elliot now had in his possession. Keating was connecting old fast radio burst data with the more recent bursts collected at Green Bank. The bursts happened just before the closure. Most discoveries happened years after the data had been collected, when researchers had time to analyze their vast archives. It could be like finding a needle in a haystack. But with this recent burst, Keating had something strong to work from.

Elliot continued through Keating's notes. The day before the closure there was the burst of data, and a repeating FRB within hours of each other. According to Keating's notes, what caught him and Liu off guard was the additional data that came with the FRB. A massive amount, and repeating, which meant they would have an easier time identifying a source. A source they thought was an old relay satellite.

Elliot looked up from his laptop. *It doesn't add up.* The data was inconsistent. Portions looked like actual FRBs; based on radio wave dispersion, these were distance pulses. Other segments Elliot couldn't interpret. It looked like garbled nonsense, a running theme he sensed.

He leaned back in his chair. The room's AC unit hummed in the background in a steady tone. Elliot wiped his face with his hands, dragging the day's events away.

"Keating didn't have time to finish his analysis." Elliot's thoughts leaked into words that filled the empty room. The question was, what did he find that would make him so nervous? Nervous enough he wouldn't hand this over to the FBI?

Elliot needed help. He couldn't access the database files and some of Keating's theories, and data analysis was over his head. He zipped and encrypted the files on the SD card with a password Jake would know without a hint, then copied it to a shared drive. He paused for a moment, thinking back to Keating's comment and the danger this could bring. Was he inviting problems to his friend's front door?

He opened his chat client and pinged Jake.

ELLIOT: *Hey, have some interesting data for you to look at.*
JAKE: *mmmmk*
ELLIOT: *But, it's sensitive stuff, I'm hesitating even sending it*
JAKE: *easy three days of the condor. Send it.*
ELLIOT: *In a shared drive. Link sent.*
JAKE: *Cool*

Keating mentioned the "signal" was similar to an FRB but wasn't one. *What else is in this data? What did Keating find?* Elliot cycled through these questions ad nauseam—like if he kept asking, he'd suddenly have the answer. He bit his fingernail with a nervousness he thought he'd left behind, in the hope Jake would find something quick. He tried not to think about the fact he'd just pulled his friend into a situation he didn't know the seriousness of. A pang of guilt ricocheted through his body. If Keating found something the government thought was worth covering up, this could spell a lot of trouble for everyone connected.

ELLIOT: *Hey, whatever you find, just keep to us*
JAKE: *Of course*

In the moments that followed, Elliot's world got smaller. His wandering mind took over. He thought back to Keating's first warning, and Keating was sure someone was monitoring and following him. Elliot paced the hotel room now, senses heightened. *If the FBI is interested, does that mean someone else is too?* Elliot's thoughts were building conspiracies for him. Jenn Liu mentioned a compromised satellite. *Does that mean it was hacked? Whoever did the hacking would want to cover it up.*

He started scribbling thoughts on a hotel notepad: *FRBs in Hawaii/Australia—do they know? What is the signal doing? Who else would want to know?* There was nothing connecting the data he had to those observatories, but he would not pass up his only lead. Keating noted the current influx of signal patterns matched ones found in old data. *I should have Jake look at old data too,* Elliot thought. An FRB could bounce off a more local celestial body or magnetic field, making it appear stronger. *Could they have miscalculated?* Keating and Jenn Liu said it came from a communications relay satellite. *Could the signal from some far-off nebula have been picked up by the relay, which would cause its signal to strengthen?* Not out of the realm of possibilities, but a stretch.

Panic had capsized. Elliot took a deep breath. So many loose ends. So many potential connections. He sat in a chair in the hotel room by the window. The curtains were open, so he could look out across the city. He rubbed the side of his temples, his eyes closed, trying to work the piercing headache in his head out.

His phone buzzed on the desk, amplifying throughout the room. Startled, he shot up out of the chair and answered before it could go a second round. Thankfully, it was Jake on the other end.

"Dude. What are you involved in?"

"Not sure. What'd you find?"

"First off, the files you sent contain only partial data, but it's segments of this FRB-like signal spotted over time." Jake paused as if he was looking at a screen while talking, then continued, "From what I can tell it goes back pretty far, but I'm still analyzing to confirm it has the same profile as the one spotted before the closure."

"Okay. What about source? Is it coming from low orbit, like from an old satellite?" Elliot asked, still rubbing his temple with his free hand. The headache wasn't subsiding.

"Yeah, the stronger signal pattern is definitely coming from a satellite. The one Green Bank picked up."

Elliot was happy to get confirmation, but it only opened more questions. "What do you think it is?"

"Shit. Not sure. I'm running some pattern recognition against the more recent signal. It has the most data, given the frequency, time frame, and strength. Then I'll look into the old data."

"Thanks. Anything you find, add notes to the folder I sent over. Drive should be secure enough." Elliot figured if they could analyze and fill in the blanks, he could share their findings with Keating.

"Sounds good. I'll crank on this, hopefully have something in a few hours, but realistically tomorrow."

"Appreciate it."

"You good out there?" Jake asked.

"Yeah . . . I am. I think so at least." Elliot said hesitantly, not even believing himself.

"Well, take it easy. Let me know if you need anything else."

"Thanks, I will, but you're doing more than enough as is."

"Talk soon," Jake said before hanging up.

Elliot stood then walked around the room before returning to his laptop. He checked his email, which was filled with typical social media notifications, a couple of spam emails that had gotten past the built-in filters, and an email with the subject line *Introduction* from someone named Chris Burns.

Elliot clicked open the message. The word AeroTech nearly jumped off the screen. When Elliot could focus on the message, he realized Burns wanted to meet him for lunch to discuss the story he was working on.

Elliot's only thought was *How did they know I was writing one?*

Chapter 16

The low western sun pressed against the hotel windows. The curtains were half drawn, which caused a beam of light to cut across the bed. Elliot moved to the window and drew the gauzy under-curtain closed. He didn't want it completely dark; he wanted some sense of time. He returned to his laptop to reread the message from Chris Burns. *Did Keating mention something? Did the FBI talk to AeroTech?*

But Keating was wound too tight to say anything. The fact Elliot got anything out of him was a miracle. AeroTech had just inked a long-term government contract to develop secure satellite communications. They knew their system was compromised and they wanted to keep it quiet, but they'd tipped their hand even by reaching out.

Elliot started to pull as much info about Chris and AeroTech as he could. It wasn't hard to paint a picture with the public records alone. AeroTech was a behemoth of a company, which made it hard for them to hide behind shiny product launches and half-hearted pledges to be better social and environment advocates.

Chris Burns was their big-time lobbyist—never the headline of the article but mentioned enough for Elliot to realize he was the wizard behind the curtain. He went to battle with lawmakers and governments, carrying bags full of cash to get legislation passed or halted. Elliot found a long list of recent bills, mostly tax-related, that AeroTech was involved in. He also discovered news items about recent testing issues and contract failures with a few of their aerospace projects, so it wasn't a surprise to see they had increased their lobbying spend over the last two quarters to calm the waters in DC.

Now here they were, sending in their white knight to visit Elliot in Seattle. Elliot replied to Chris, agreeing to meet. His experience with lobbyists of this nature was limited; he felt like a rabbit heading into a cage match with a pit bull.

Lunch the next day was at a posh restaurant in Seattle's financial district, not too far from Elliot's hotel. The warmer than expected day caught Elliot off guard. He was expecting clouds and rain, but also didn't mind the sun for his short walk. The restaurant was large with an open-space layout and floor-to-ceiling windows that filled the room with natural light. Despite its size, the room still had an intimate feeling. The large windows looked out onto a busy commercial street, offering a view of life as it passed by. A two-way fish bowl.

A host, a suited gentleman who looked eager to serve, greeted Elliot as he entered and took his name.

He gestured for Elliot to follow him. "Your party is already waiting—this way, please."

Elliot instantly felt out of place. There was only a handful of patrons, mostly small groups of men in suits, having their power lunches. Not Elliot's crowd in the least.

Elliot approached the table. Chris, already seated, was sipping from a glass of water with lemon. He had wire-framed glasses and dark hair speckled with gray. Distinguished, but with a slight air of trying too hard. He wore a perfectly tailored, slim-cut gray suit. Elliot guessed it cost double his rent back home. He looked comfortable in it, like it was a uniform he was proud to wear, one that separated him from others.

About halfway to the table, Chris looked up with a subtle grin, like he sized Elliot up in the half-second preview. Elliot's jeans, sneakers, roughly ironed button-down, and week-old stubble made him stand out. Elliot hadn't planned to have a power lunch, so dressing for the part wasn't an option. Nor did Elliot care at this point.

As Elliot got to the table, Chris stood and extended a hand with a pleasant smile. They shook.

"Elliot," he said, like they were old friends, "it's a pleasure."

Elliot grabbed the seat across from him and nodded. "Likewise."

A waiter was at the table before Elliot could even sit down and handed him a menu. Elliot thanked him and asked for a Coke.

"Hope you're enjoying Seattle." Chris resettled in his seat, his body turned enough so he could cross his legs out from under the table. He leaned forward with one elbow on the table, his left hand gently holding his chin between his index finger and thumb. It was such a delicate move for a person as big as Chris and made it hard not to be enthralled by whatever he said.

"I am, mostly," Elliot said, waiting for Chris to talk about the weather next.

"Good." Chris looked back up from his menu and smiled. "So, I hear you're working on a story?"

"I am," Elliot said, tight-lipped. He had no intention of giving more information than necessary, at least until he heard what Chris and AeroTech wanted.

Chris placed his menu on the table and put his hands out like he was welcoming Elliot to the stage. "Have you spoken with a Doctor Keating recently?"

"I have," Elliot started, breaking eye contact and choosing his words carefully. "I'm covering the Green Bank closure and wanted to chat with him to understand what happened."

Chris leaned back in his chair like he owned the place. It wouldn't surprise Elliot if he did. "I thought that was a straightforward closure, no? Some equipment failures and a small security breach. A lost password, probably."

"Yup. That was pretty much it." Elliot gripped the arm of the chair under the table to work out his nerves.

"Then what are you doing here in Seattle talking with Keating?" It was a disingenuous question—even if he already knew the answer, he wanted to hear Elliot say it.

"I like to talk to folks in person, that's all. And he had some details around the equipment failures. You know, science stuff—it's what our readers want," Elliot said with a layer of sarcasm that could coat walls.

The arrival of the waiter broke the silent tension that had been winding tighter between them.

Chris shifted his attention from Elliot to the waiter. "I'll have the salmon with a kale side salad."

"And you, sir?" the waiter asked Elliot.

Elliot scanned the menu again. An appetizer cost more than his outfit. "The chicken sandwich. Thanks."

"Anything else at the moment, gentlemen?"

Chris politely waved and shook his head no. As the waiter walked away, Chris turned his full attention back to Elliot. "Have you spoken with anyone from the FBI yet?"

Elliot shook his head.

"I have a contact there you should catch up with. Agent Blackwell." Chris pulled out a business card with a casualness that felt rehearsed and slid it across the table.

Elliot examined it—the same one Sheriff Davis and Jenn Liu had given him back in West Virginia. "I'll be sure to reach out to him."

"He'll provide all the details you need. But in the meantime, if there is anything you need while putting this story together, don't hesitate to contact me." He pulled another business card and placed it on the table between them. "In fact, if you want to chat with Keating again, it might be good to reach out to me as well. I can coordinate meetings between us to be more efficient."

Elliot doubted it would be more efficient, but it would certainly allow Chris to control the narrative. "Why was Keating relocated here?"

Chris took a moment to sip his lemon water before answering. "Well, as I'm sure you know, he started here. He was a leading expert in our space and aeronautics department. Mostly with satellite development. He founded the department. Without him, we wouldn't be where we are today."

The answer felt soft to Elliot. He decided now was the right time to take a jab. "Where you are today, as in having multiple failed satellite launches, causing defense contracts to suddenly get questioned?"

The jab landed, a smirk pulling against Chris's face. "The company has had a few missteps, but that's exactly why Keating is here. To help us get back on track."

The conversation paused as the waiter dropped off their plates. Chris took a bite of his salmon, clearly savoring it. "Now, that is perfect," he said, dabbing at his lips. "Did Keating give you anything, by chance?"

Elliot shook his head slowly. "Nothing in particular." The conversation felt like a game of chess, each player waiting for the other to make a mistake. Chris did this day in and day out, leaving Elliot at a great disadvantage. His only defense was what he already knew and what he might learn from the data Jake was crunching—that and keeping his answers short.

"I just want to be clear. If you have any information, it'd be good to share, so we can work together on this. I want us to be cautious of what's put out there, that's all. And if Keating has any data or theories, we could work together on it. AeroTech has plenty of resources."

Elliot held back from looking up at Chris. *They know about the data? How is that possible?* Chris used the word 'us' like they were suddenly a team. A tactic to bring comfort to the opposition, but now he was getting a bit more direct with what he expected. "Of course. If I come across anything, I'll be in touch," Elliot said.

After they finished their lunch, Chris walked Elliot out. As they stood outside, Chris added, "Like I said, keep in touch with any details and if you should need anything from Keating going forward. We're happy to help."

Elliot nodded and gave a tight smile.

Chris, AeroTech, didn't want to help. They wanted to contain something. Like a lost, compromised satellite that had national security issues written all over it. They also knew about the data from Green Bank. *What would they want with it?*

Elliot started back to his hotel. The conversation sat heavier than the lunch. This wasn't a friendly gesture but a veiled threat. For Elliot, it confirmed his path. He had something to give Jake to look at. If one of their satellites was compromised, there could be others.

#

With Elliot's extended stay in Seattle, his hotel room had become lived in. The desk covered in notes, the bed unmade, the second twin bed covered in clothes and the rest of his belongings. His current life spread across the room in an unkempt mess. He didn't like housekeeping coming in and cleaning. He told himself he wanted it to feel like home. In reality he was concerned with privacy ever since his last conversation with Keating.

He needed to get in touch with Jake. His conversation with Chris Burns might have pointed in a direction—he had a feeling AeroTech's compromised satellite situation ran deeper. And he wanted to see if Jake had made any progress on the data analysis. Elliot knew Jake could get lost in data and forget about the world around him.

He called Jake, who answered like he was waiting for the call.

"Elliot. I got something," he said, quick draw, without any salutations.

Jake was the type of person, who, once involved, didn't let up. He'd tear something apart and put it back together just to learn how it worked. Then tear it apart again and rebuild it better in less time. Elliot appreciated this aspect of his friend; he was also the only person he could trust.

"Me too. You first," Elliot said.

"So, my first-pass analysis of the data set showed the signal pattern from the Green Bank spike matched all the entries Keating was looking at over the last two to three years. He'd only gotten a year or so back, but he was onto something. I also confirmed his theory—the recent spike came from a specific satellite."

"Let me guess—an AeroTech relay satellite?"

"Yeah. How'd you know?"

"I'll tell you in a second—go on."

Jake paused to regain his thoughts. Elliot could picture him adjusting his glasses. "So, the crazy part is, the other older signals have come from other medium or low orbit points. It's not just a single source."

Elliot took a moment to think. He scratched at the back of his head. His hair was an untethered mess. "Maybe the signal is bouncing in various points back at these satellites?"

"No, I think the signal is coming *from* different satellites. Obviously their placement has changed over time, so I can see the burst and will have to map the satellite placement to a point in time."

There was a moment of silence between them. Elliot realized his theory of multiple AeroTech satellites being compromised might have weight to it. He also remembered his father's mapping. "Focus on any AeroTech hardware first. I'll send over something else which may help."

"Sure. That will help narrow the field a bit. Worse case we can eliminate them from the list. Seems like you just shared what you had?"

"Let's just say I had an unusual lunch today with an AeroTech rep. They have an interest in my story it seems."

"What the . . .? Really? How do they even know you're writing a story that *might* involve them?" Jake asked.

"No clue, but I have a few hunches."

"Well, I have something more for you. You may want to sit for this one."

Elliot took his advice and could hear a rapid burst of typing from Jake before he continued. "So, after my first pass of the recent Green Bank data, I thought I'd look a bit more into the signal itself, the actual radio waves captured. I broke my research down into categories—over-time occurrence, source, and purpose." He stumbled over his words in his excitement.

"Go on . . ." Elliot said.

"Most of these fast radio burst type signals, as you know, are just noise from space. Nebulas or some large-scale electromagnetic burst from an entity way the hell out there, from a time before time. When it finally gets to us, the signal is short-lived and weak." Jake paused for a moment. "Well, this signal—the signal picked up at Green Bank—it's *doing* something, Elliot."

Elliot sat in silence.

Jake went on, "This is still theoretical and I'm still investigating, but I think it's acting like a transmitter."

"A transmitter of what?" Elliot knew the question was stupid and obvious, but asking it out loud let both their minds open to ideas.

"That's the sixty-four-million-dollar question, friendo. From what I can tell, it uses less power than, say, a flash memory drive—like an SSD hard drive, but at a very, very large scale."

"Holy shit," Elliot said. *If that is even remotely true, what do we have?* Keating's paranoia wasn't unfounded. Understanding this technology and its implications opened up why anyone would want the data.

"Yeah, holy shit is one way to describe it," Jake said. "I'm gonna keep pushing on this and see what I can find. But I thought you might enjoy that little nugget."

"You tell anyone about this?"

"Hell no. This is deep-state shit, Elliot."

"Yeah, you're telling me. Let's keep it that way, at least for now." Elliot stood and began pacing the room. "Keep anything you find off your local and MIT storage and just on our secured drive."

"I'm a step ahead of you." Jake paused then asked, "You okay?"

"I don't know."

"What's your next step?" Jake asked.

He didn't have a plan. This was new territory, dangerous territory. He could contact Keating, but feared AeroTech's reach and whoever else was on Keating's tail. By now they were probably on his too. He realized he only had one more good move.

"I'm going to have a chat with the FBI."

Chapter 17

After her run-in with the not-so-friendly types at the server farm, LiLo took a short bus tour around the city followed by a scenic walking route back to her Airbnb to make sure she wasn't being followed.

Her legs were sore. Her body was exhausted. She collapsed on the bed. Even though she'd been running most of her life, she hadn't run like that since grade school track meets. She reached into her jacket pocket and pulled out the USB drive, stared at it, and smiled. Another dot, another connection to YellowJacket—and possibly her past. If they were routing traffic through that farm, there might be communication crumbs from those higher up than YellowJacket. Details she could use—that maybe would mean she could stop running.

Recovered, she dropped the USB drive into her laptop and sat on her bed with her legs crossed. *Time to see what's in here.* She opened the directory and scanned through the file list. She opened a few as she went. Scripts, similar to the one she wrote for Gemini. All doing different things—malware, spyware, phishing scams, control scripts for taking over remote machines. A full package and more advanced than some script kiddies doxing servers. This was professional work.

She opened the README text file; it had some weak password protection on it. It contained instructions on how to use each script and when. A list of to-do items, and a timeline. Dates tied to when each script was to be run. They were scattered over a few weeks, with a couple of key ones set for a specific day. Then the timeline ended. Each script was connected to the IP address of a different machine. She dug into where they were located; they matched servers YellowJacket had been in.

The end date was tied to infrastructure sites on the East Coast of the United States. This was a well-organized attack, and she had every step outlined in front of her. She knew her script was in here. It made her gut turn.

She switched over to the mysterious scripts she'd found when tracking YellowJacket. She'd captured log files from each server and analyzed the IP addresses left when the file was created. They all came from a satellite internet service provider. A company called AeroTech, based in the US. They were headquartered in Seattle but had offices and manufacturing sites all over.

What do AeroTech and YellowJacket have in common? She pulled a few more addresses that came from AeroTech satellites, and each was tied to various institutions across the globe— banks, military sites, universities—a wide variety. One in particular was an observatory in West Virginia. She shook her head and pulled up the article about the FBI closing an observatory in West Virginia, Green Bank Observatory. A three-hour drive from where she was born. She reread the article, which named the agent in charge of the closure, an Agent Aaron Blackwell.

She paused, let out a sigh, and stared at her screen. It only took her a second to process and decide on her next step. She opened a text editor and started to code. She was in another world as the blank screen filled with characters that could execute any action she wanted. Logical statements and checks that could break through any wall of defense. If it couldn't, it'd destroy itself. Line after line, she coded a back door—a back door she planned to drop on the FBI.

Before she could do anything, she needed to know what the FBI knew. They tapped enough people. She decided to return the favor. It only took a few hours for her to get into Blackwell's team communications. She now had eyes and ears on Blackwell's team.

There was always a way in, if you looked hard enough.

Chapter 18

Elliot stared at Agent Blackwell's card, which sat on top of a few loose pages from a notebook. After he hung up with Jake, he paced the room in thought. *Why didn't Keating give this to the FBI to start with? They were tailing him, right?* His thoughts passed through his lips in soft but audible sound bites to himself. He ruffled his hair, let out a groan. *Who can I trust?* With each pass by the desk he glanced at the card. *The FBI is already on to me, right? How do I start the conversation?* He stopped in front of the card and took a couple deep breaths. Picked up his phone and dialed Blackwell's number. It didn't get through a second ring before someone answered.

"Agent Blackwell." The tone was tighter than a drum. It ordered, *Don't waste my time.*

A pause.

"Agent Blackwell, this is Elliot Bishop." He paused so Blackwell had a moment to recognize the name, then continued, "I received your card from Sheriff Davis in Green Bank." Elliot didn't want to mention Dr. Liu—for the time being, the fewer people connected the better. "I'm writing a story on the Green Bank Observatory closure, and I—"

"Mr. Bishop. Good to finally hear from you." Blackwell's voice was clear, concise, in control, but with a casualness that didn't sit well with Elliot.

"You've been expecting me?" Elliot asked.

"At some point, sure. I heard through the grapevine you were working on a story. How can I help?" Blackwell asked the question like they were buddies and Elliot was calling for a favor.

Elliot paused for a moment. *What grapevine?* "I just had a few questions about the FBI's involvement with the Green Bank closure."

"Sure. We were working closely with Doctor Keating, who I think you've met"— he was no longer being subtle with what he knew—"about some equipment issues, mostly data breaches. It's fairly standard procedure for us to get involved in those situations."

Elliot settled into a steady pace in front of the twin beds, back and forth. "Can you elaborate on the breaches themselves? What sensitive data is at the observatory?"

"I can't get into too many details. But as a federally funded institution, if it is compromised in any way, we like to know." A canned response Blackwell had clearly said a million times. Information was on a need-to-know basis and Elliot didn't need to know.

Elliot paused, thought back to a story his father liked to tell about him when he was young. During a trip to an aerospace museum, the guide didn't have the answer Elliot was looking for, so he just kept asking *why* over and over until his father had to pull him back. Elliot felt the urge to push Blackwell the same way.

"How was the data compromised?" Elliot asked.

"Well, technically, the data wasn't compromised but their equipment was. Meaning, the data *could've* been compromised but we shut everything down before that risk could inflate. Right now, we're just trying to recover some missing data." Blackwell wasn't being coy—he'd just shown his hand to Elliot.

The move stalled Elliot—he wasn't sure where to go next.

Before he could figure it out, Blackwell spoke again. "So what did you and Keating discuss? Out of curiosity . . ."

Blackwell wanted Elliot to know he was being monitored, even if he didn't say so out loud. He was in a corner, but he had to answer. "Fast radio bursts. The mechanics of the Green Bank Observatory, more science-focused questions."

"Interesting." Blackwell paused. "Seems like something you could've just gotten over the phone?"

"I like to be face-to-face for interviews."

Blackwell took in a breath and released it like a sigh of relief.

"Well, that's good to hear. I'll be in Seattle in a few days." He paused for a moment. "We should connect—you know, face-to-face."

"I'll be here." Elliot said.

"Good." Blackwell's voice softened just a fraction. "Listen, Elliot, if you come across any information, it'd be good if we were on the same page. We could help each other maybe."

Elliot couldn't decide if this was a good or bad thing. Could he trust Blackwell? Keating's paranoia reminded him nothing seemed safe. "If I come across anything I'll be sure to let you know."

"Good. This situation is a bit sensitive. I just want to make sure whatever we put out there is accurate."

"Couldn't agree more."

"Good. I'll reach out once I'm in Seattle."

"Looking forward to it." Elliot hung up and dropped the phone on the table, paused from his pacing.

Thoughts raced through his mind. The FBI had something—they knew more, but didn't have the data Jake and Elliot had. He wondered, if this threatened national security, should he hand it over? Keating went through some lengths to keep it away from people, and even tagged it as life-threatening. *What else is in that data? Why would Keating keep it from them?*

Blackwell hadn't been subtle about what he knew of Elliot's contact with Keating. Elliot stood still, looked around his room. At his phone, his laptop.

Anxiety flooded him like a broken dam. The "grapevine" was Elliot.

Chapter 19

The air in the hotel room was stale. The last time Elliot had left the room was for lunch with AeroTech's all-star, Chris Burns, two days before. He'd barred himself in his hotel room, a physical cage that didn't keep his mind from wandering. To what extent had Blackwell, the FBI, been keeping tabs on him? Were they monitoring his email? His phone? Was his room bugged?

The curtains were drawn; the lack of light made it difficult to know the time of day. He'd unplugged the clock in case it was bugged. He stared at the ceiling, following the semi-circle swirls in the paint. Hands across his chest, fingers entwined. He waited to hear from Jake, a familiar voice.

He sat up and stared at the space in front of him. Contacting Keating was dangerous. But he had to talk to him. Share what he'd found, understand what was buried in the data Keating was so protective of. Elliot couldn't call him or create an email thread through normal channels. Whoever was listening had those avenues covered. He needed something more secure, to at least stall a track. Elliot opened his laptop. He grabbed a link for a secure messaging app and emailed it to Keating. No subject. No context. He trusted Keating would figure it out and use the number Elliot already had.

Elliot sat at the desk and glanced around his room. The chaotic mess of notes and papers had found their way to the floor. Lost thoughts, theories, ideas—scattered like stars in the sky. He'd seen this before; he had cleaned up this mess twice already for his father. *What am I becoming?*

The thought snapped him out of his seat. He picked up all the loose pages on the floor, stuffed them into organized folders. He moved his written notes to the secure drive with the missing Green Bank data. He cleared off the beds and made them. He organized his clothes, packed his bag with everything he didn't need immediately. His mind refocused, he showered. All he could do was wait.

He got out of the shower, dried, and wrapped the towel around his waist. He stood in front of the bathroom mirror, his stubble now a short, patchy beard. He didn't mind the unkempt look. He brushed his teeth, then started to get dressed. As he pulled his shirt on, his phone started to buzz. He stared at it for a moment, then leaped across the room. An unknown number. He hoped Keating would use the messaging app, not call him directly. He held the buzzing phone. Waited, then answered.

An upbeat voice chimed in, "Elliot? Chris Burns here. How are you?"

Elliot was thrown back in surprise. He didn't expect Chris Burns. He needed Keating or Jake. His mouth stumbled to a response. "Uh, Chris. Hi. I'm good."

"Great. I was hoping we could chat again?" His question sounded more like a statement.

"Uhh, sure," Elliot said, in the most unsure way possible.

"Great. How about today?"

Elliot stalled—time had eluded him. He opened the curtains; sunlight poked through in fragments behind the city skyline. "Today? Today isn't great for me."

"Oh, too bad. I'm walking past your hotel now."

Might be time to find a new place to stay, Elliot thought. "I guess, if you're right here, I can make it work." He wasn't good at lying on the fly. But he had an idea about how Chris could be useful, so he played along.

"Great. Meet in the lobby? Whenever you're ready."

"That works. I'll be down in five minutes."

"Perfect. See you shortly."

Elliot finished getting dressed. He looked around his room, not for anything in particular, but to make sure everything was accounted for. He wanted to make sure he could leave in a rush if needed. He packed away his laptop and final notebook and left his bag in a corner near the door. On his way out, he checked that the *do not disturb* sign was in place. He made his way to the lobby. *What tactic is AeroTech playing at?* They had an angle, they always did, but what was it?

The hotel lobby was busy, an afternoon rush before the weekend. Chris sat in a chair with a high back; he was tall enough his head rested a good half foot above the back. It looked like a dollhouse chair for this large person, when for most it'd feel like a throne. Elliot could see Chris's tight smile as soon as he walked out of the elevator. He was wearing a gray suit with a blue tie. Subtle compared to their first encounter. Elliot imagined Chris's closet was full of suits, like Elliot's drawers were filled with T-shirts. He respected the daily uniform—one less decision to make in the day.

As Elliot walked over, Chris stood and extended a hand that made Elliot's seem small. They shook.

"You like coffee?" Chris asked.

"I do."

"Well, you're in a great city for it. There's a place around the corner from here."

"Sounds good."

Their short walk was filled with pleasantries. Chris asked Elliot what he thought about Seattle and if he'd managed to see the Space Needle. Elliot hadn't—his appetite for tourist activities had diminished with each passing day.

The shop was small, intimate, a family-owned vibe with bright earthy coffee aromas attacking the senses. They each grabbed a cup and took a seat by the window. The morning rush was over, foot traffic was low. All that remained were a handful of college students hunched over their laptops surrounded by empty cups.

"So, any new insights for your story?" Chris asked as they settled in.

"No, nothing new." Elliot took a sip of coffee, then decided to lead the conversation. "You know, there is one thing."

"Oh yeah?" Chris said, looking intrigued.

"Yeah . . . I was digging through some data and noticed a few anomalies coming from AeroTech satellites. Older models still in orbit." It was a shot in the dark, but he felt confident, based on details from Keating, Liu, and Jake, that the signal had to involve an AeroTech satellite somehow.

Chris shifted in his seat and took a sip of coffee before answering. "That's interesting. You have data to back this up?"

"I do." Elliot knew how to drive this and what he needed. Chris could be valuable, but he'd need to play his game and offer him something. "The data I have points to an FRB-like signal—which, if you're unaware, is a fast radio burst, a signal which comes from deep space. But this signal is coming from an AeroTech satellite."

Elliot let Chris chew on that. He wanted to see what he might give up. Elliot had suspicions AeroTech knew about their compromised satellite and this was connected.

Chris presented his charming smile, the one that could probably get a date by itself. "Interesting. Well, it'd be great to get a look at that data."

"Sure. You know I have a theory . . ."

Chris peered over to Elliot without saying anything. Elliot had him on his back foot and he knew it.

"I think your satellite malfunctioned. I think your satellite is at risk and I don't think it's the only one. I also think you're here to make sure I don't piece this together and share it with the world."

"Interesting theory. And you're right. That is why I'm here. I need to protect something, whatever that cost is."

"I bet that cost is pretty high given your recent track record," Elliot said.

That patented smirk rolled across Chris's face. "And what's your price?"

"A favor—a connection in DC when I call."

Chris glanced up at Elliot. "Oh, when you call?" His tone was gently mocking.

Elliot nodded, playing hardball now. Preparing for the worst was his plan. If this got bigger, he wanted protection for himself and his friends.

"How do I know you'll keep my client out of this article?" Chris asked.

"You have my word."

Chris looked away and chuckled. "Your word?"

"I won't print any false information, but I can leave names out," Elliot said, his face locked and serious.

Chris took a moment, shaking his head in disbelief. He knew what was happening and he probably didn't like losing. "Anything else?"

Elliot paused. "What else does AeroTech want from this?"

Chris stared at Elliot, then gestured to the street outside the window. "You see these people?"

Elliot looked out the window as people marched by.

"You may not believe it, but we want to protect them."

Elliot turned to face Chris, chuckling like he'd just heard the stupidest joke. "You mean protect your stock price?"

Chris took another sip of coffee, then looked at Elliot. "So, who in DC do you want to talk to?"

"How far up does your Rolodex go?"

Chapter 20

As soon as he'd walked away from the meeting with Chris Burns, Elliot had focused on finding a new place to stay. Given the situation, it was time to change locations. The new apartment was in a small five-story brick complex, less than a ten-minute walk from the hotel. The space was clean, organized, as blank and impersonal as an Ikea showroom. Generic photos of landscapes adorned the living room walls; the dining room looked like no one had ever eaten in it. There was a single bedroom, plus a small den that had been turned into a library and workspace.

He'd checked in as early as he could. Got settled and took a shower. He needed a routine. The hot water from the shower cleansed his thoughts but couldn't wash away his tangled reality —an FBI cover-up, corporate alliances, and whatever game Keating was playing. His line of trust with Keating was wavering. *Is he playing a role? Does Keating have some other plan or is he working for someone?* He pushed the questions to the furthest reaches of his mind, where it would fester. He had to believe Keating wanted to help him.

It had been over twenty-four hours since Elliot had heard from Jake, the only person he could trust. The only person to keep him tethered to a situation spinning out of control. He'd played a heavy card with Chris Burns and AeroTech; it had worked, but it wouldn't last. This relationship only added to his growing sense of fear. He wasn't sure who frightened him more, a corporate monster with immense power or the FBI. Given AeroTech's reach, they didn't seem to be on the same playing field, which was a terrifying thought.

He dressed and took out his laptop. Even at his new location his current life belongings were contained within his backpack. Ready to go at a moment's notice. He put his bag back in a corner near the door, sat at the desk, and opened his laptop. His new home screen and program list was scarce. After the realization *he* was the FBI grapevine, he'd moved any important docs to an encrypted USB drive, backed up to a shared drive with Jake. Then he clean-installed his OS to a privacy-focused distribution of Linux Kodachi. Out of the box it provided more protection than he'd had before. He'd also moved to a secure chat client so he and Jake could talk.

He wasn't a security or privacy expert. He understood the basics and did enough research to make at least these basic changes as his trust in the technology around him evaporated. Ultimately, however, he knew if someone wanted in, they could get in.

He opened the chat client. It was the middle of the night in Boston—the time of the day when night bleeds into morning, when nothing good happens. But Elliot knew Jake often worked through the night. He would become obsessed until he knew every in and out of a problem or system.

Sure enough, as soon as the chat client loaded, he had a message.

JAKE: *we need to talk*
ELLIOT: *What's up?*
JAKE: *so, this is some serious shit*
ELLIOT: *tell me something I don't know*
JAKE: *you were right about AeroTech sats*

JAKE: *they're the source of the signal and have been for years*

JAKE: . . .

JAKE: *same for GBO burst. Your buddy Keating was onto this as was your father*

Elliot sat back for a second. Stared at the messages. Now he had the data to support his theory that AeroTech knew about the signal and were trying to keep it—or something—quiet.

JAKE: *there's more*

ELLIOT: ?

JAKE: *last time I mentioned the signal was doing something . . .*

ELLIOT: *yeah, like it mimicked flash memory*

JAKE: *exactly – well, it looks like it's pulling data and at massive scales*

ELLIOT: *what?*

JAKE: *yeah*

ELLIOT: *what data?*

JAKE: *any data it wants, like a giant fishing net*

JAKE: *came across this late yesterday . . . early today. Whenever. still trying to figure it out*

JAKE: *Elliot, this was put here by someone*

Elliot took his hands off the keyboard. Whatever this signal was, it was powerful. He hesitated before sending the next message, almost afraid of the answer he'd get.

ELLIOT: *if it can pull data, could it push data?*

JAKE: *already looking into it, but yeah, in theory*

JAKE: *this is pretty complex shit, and I feel like I just peeled back the first layer*

A swirl of thoughts ran through Elliot's mind. Was this tool capable of rewriting any data it managed to reach? Financial records, government databases, military intel, anything? Each step forward created more questions, but he was starting to see a path through the chaos. He feared what lay at the end.

JAKE: *in other news, how's your friendly neighborhood FBI doing?*
ELLIOT: *I don't have a good feeling about it*
JAKE: *you shouldn't – we just stepped in over our heads*
JAKE: *maybe we just hand this to them?*
JAKE: *this could be some surveillance prototype we stumbled on or something*
JAKE: *and I think I'm being followed*
ELLIOT: *what? By who?*
JAKE: *No idea. He's not being sneaky about it. Like he wants me to know he's there.*

Jesus, Elliot thought. He'd pulled his friend into this, and it would be on him if he got in trouble. Then he thought about others that might be in danger. *My mother?*

ELLIOT: *Okay, keep an eye on them. I'll be in SEA for a few more days – I need to talk to Keating. No phone calls.*
JAKE: *k*
JAKE: *another thing, I started digging into the signal exposure over time*
ELLIOT: *yeah?*

JAKE: *this signal may have been around even longer than we thought. I have data for the last year or so, but I think it may have been longer*

ELLIOT: *longer than a couple?*

JAKE: *definitely. I see faint occurrences that date back a decade. Could be anomalies, but it's all in the data Keating had.*

JAKE: *he and your father were onto something*

ELLIOT: *keep on it. Hit me up if you find anything. I'll be back in BOS soon.*

ELLIOT: *and . . . stay safe, man*

JAKE: *you too*

He had to talk to Keating before he did anything else. He hadn't heard anything from him since his last email. Blackwell was coming to Seattle, and Elliot wanted to be ready. What Jake found was a start, but still little more than a conspiracy theory. They were stuck. He needed Keating to open up—he was the key.

His phone suddenly buzzed. He checked the lock screen preview. A message via the messaging app. He unlocked the app.

KEATING: *Let's meet.*

#

Keating had picked the meeting spot. Midday at Discovery Park, which lay northwest of downtown Seattle and reached into Puget Sound on its far west side. Elliot found a bus route to the park that would get him there in under an hour. He brought only a small notepad that could fit in his back pocket. The gray clouds hung over the city like a shell. Just another day to the locals. Elliot wore a gray hoodie; he didn't have much else to protect himself against the cool temperature.

Elliot couldn't get past the compromised satellite angle. If someone had put the signal there, did they put it on older satellites too? Even if they were running COBAL or some archaic OS no longer used, how did outdated operating systems on inactive satellites connect to the latest signal coming from a newer relay satellite? Elliot hoped Keating could provide an answer or at least a direction.

Elliot arrived and headed for the visitor center. He was a minnow in a sea of tourist groups from various parts of the world. A senior tour group of at least twenty poured out of a private bus shuttle, immediately looking for where to head next. Chaperones corralled summer camp kids with loud voices and flailing limbs into groups. Locals passed by, heading directly for the walking trails which sprawled throughout the park or toward the lighthouse at the tip of western side. Elliot picked up a map and headed in.

The park was over a mile wide and just under a mile long. Keating had said to follow the Discovery Park loop trail toward the lighthouse, and he'd be about a half mile in by an open area with benches.

The overcast blanket of cloud cover had broken into less menacing patches. Sunshine sliced through where it could. Tall, thin trees lined the pathways. Through them, Elliot caught brief glimpses of the Olympic mountains, looking like resting giants. So distant, but so large they looked like they were painted in as an afterthought.

Locals jogged by with their dogs, cutting through small groups of people stopped here and there on the paths. It was busy for a weekday but not overcrowded.

It took Elliot about ten minutes to reach the open area Keating had described. A handful of benches were positioned against the tree line, all of them empty except one. From this distance, Elliot could see Keating's dark blue Mariners cap and the bright red backpack sitting next to him on the last bench.

He approached slowly, glancing around every few steps. A couple of joggers passed by, chatting about work problems. A man stopped to let his dog pee then moved on. A field trip of kids screamed down the path, but Keating didn't look up at the noise.

A sudden uneasy chill coated Elliot. Something wasn't right. Keating's head hung down and he was slightly hunched over, staring at the phone in his right hand, which rested on his lap. His left hand was positioned oddly on his leg. Elliot moved closer, the uneasy chill boring into his bloodstream. A small pool of thick, dark liquid—like an oil spill—reached out from under the bench where Keating sat.

"Keating?" Elliot called as he approached. No response.

Elliot looked around, then back at Keating. His hand and phone rested in a pool of red liquid, like he'd spilled a drink on himself. The red liquid dripped down through the bench like rain drops. An uncontrollable shiver spread throughout Elliot's body. The quiver turned into an upper body shake. A shake he had no control over.

He looked at Keating's phone, which was lit up. A connected 9-1-1 call, three minutes in. *Keating's last move? Or poor timing on Elliot's part?* He snapped his head up and scanned in all directions. The few people on the trail were fifty feet away and didn't notice a dead man sitting on a bench, or Elliot standing over him.

Elliot turned and backtracked toward the trail he came in on. His hands were trembling, so he shoved them in the pockets of his hoodie. A couple strolled by with their dog. The senior tour group he'd seen earlier meandered by, softly conversing. The sun burst through more clouds and lit up portions of the trail, but the spots of warmth didn't shake the chill from his spine. He pulled his hoodie up to cover his head.

He split down another trail; he remembered from the posted map that it looped back to the visitor center—a side trail but more direct.

He maintained his pace, attempting to focus on what to do next, but nothing made sense. Adrenaline pumped through him and reduced his choices to fight or flight. He was in flight.

His breathing increased with each step until he started to hyper-ventilate as his brain processed what he'd seen. Halfway down the quiet trail he leaned into the woods and puked. A dry heave with no substance. He'd never seen a dead body before. He wiped his mouth as a woman on rollerblades skated past, paying him no mind. He had to keep moving and get out of the park.

The visitor center was more crowded than when he'd arrived. An ambulance sat in the emergency lane in front of the visitor center, lights still circling. If he was being followed, he had some distance now. A safe spot in a sea of strangers. The world spinning, Elliot closed his eyes and the noises around him seemed to amplify. His body sank into an empty void. He'd been through this emotional state once before. His mind flooded with thoughts of his father. His support system was collapsing again. A voice echoed inside him: *Keating is dead.*

Elliot found himself in the last stall of the visitor center bathroom, a concrete block with a few stalls and a line of urinals, his body still reacting physically. He puked. This time his stomach emptied its contents. Tears trickled from his puffy red eyes. He took a few deep breaths to slow his racing heart, avoiding a complete breakdown. He needed to get out of there and back to the city. He splashed his face with water from the bathroom sink. The shake in his hands started to subside. He patted his face with a harsh brown paper towel and collected himself the best he could.

When he stepped out of the restroom, the sky had broken open entirely, the full warmth of the sun exposed. His eyes adjusted to the brightness. It didn't pierce the sudden haziness of the world around him. More people gathered at the park entrance, some whispering about a dead body, others oblivious to their surroundings.

Elliot suspected whoever killed Keating was still in the park. He sensed he was being watched—by who he didn't know. *AeroTech? FBI? If they'd killed Keating, why not kill me too?* Elliot chewed on the thought as he made his way toward the bus stop in front of the visitor center. *Maybe they think that, without Keating, the data is worthless? Is it?*

A bus headed back to Seattle pulled up. Elliot blended into a line of passengers waiting to board. He wasn't sure if he was being tailed; if he was, he couldn't see them. He thought of calling the police. But what good would that do? He'd explain he was meeting a friend in the park, he'd found him dead and now thought he was being tailed, by a corporate behemoth or the FBI. He could see their eyes roll as they filled out useless paperwork and he'd still be exposed.

He didn't have much of a plan other than to get back to his place, get his bag, and get out of town. He was alone with no options. He sat in the middle of the bus in an aisle seat near the rear door. The bus was at medium capacity, maybe twenty to twenty-five people. A mix of tourists, locals heading home, and drifters. The bus provided public cover. If a tail was on here with him, he might have a chance to spot them. His eyes were hazy; his body was still regaining control.

He tracked, as best he could, everyone coming on and off the bus. He tried to remember each face that got on at the park stop and separate them from the faces that were already on. Young professionals in suits, an elderly couple, a college couple, a man with sunglasses and a crisp new Mariners hat, this one in teal green rather than Keating's old-school blue. The image of Keating hunched over, dead, on the bench jumped to the front of his mind. He closed his eyes for a moment and took a deep breath, forcing his body to hold back any physical reaction.

There was one transfer on his trip back, and the next bus to downtown was much busier. He again took an aisle seat near the rear door in the middle of the bus. People had shifted and moved around. He lost track of who had been on the first bus. No one eyed him. No one stood out as an agent of death. *Of course, they wouldn't.* Whoever they were, they knew what they were doing. If they wanted him dead, there wasn't much he could do about it.

More people poured on at each stop, and Elliot gave up tracking everyone. He offered his seat to a pregnant woman and stood with his back against the rear door, peering up and down the length of the bus, seeing nothing. Just faces of people staring out the windows, at their phones, or talking to their neighbor. The pain behind his right eye subsided. The haze cast across his vision was lifting. His heart no longer pounded at his chest like it wanted to escape. *What now?*

He arrived back in the downtown area, closer to Pike Place Market. He was a fifteen-minute walk from his new place and figured it'd be better to get off earlier and walk through the market. If he was being followed, maybe he could lose them in the market crowd. Not the best plan, but his only plan. At this point he was improvising.

The bus emptied of passengers. Elliot hopped off at the rear door, looking at faces as they exited. Nothing stood out to him. He remained on guard, pulled his hoodie up over his head. A bank of clouds had returned to take over the city sky. The temperature dropped further. He put his hands in his hoodie pockets and started down the market alleys.

The market was swarming with people, even more so than his first visit. He blended into the moving crowds, stopping every so often to look at a storefront, check his surroundings, and move on. As he ducked into one of the many alleys, he scanned the crowd behind him. His eyes darted from face to face—a young woman, a young couple, a group of high school kids, an old man with his wife, a middle-aged man with sunglasses and green Mariners cap. He paused. His heart sank into his gut. *He was from the bus. He got on at the park.* Elliot dropped his head but kept his eyes on the man, studying his face. Light five o'clock shadow, Ray-Ban sunglasses, a crisp new Seattle Mariners cap a visitor would buy to fit in.

A spike of adrenaline rushed through Elliot. He turned, with his head still lowered, and moved into the alley. A few steps in, he peered over his shoulder eyeing his new friend. The man was ten or twelve people behind him. His heart rate jumped, but Elliot was in more control than he had been in the park. The noises of the market were a constant hum of people talking and moving about. Smells of baked bread and fresh seafood filled the alley, enticing noses to follow. Elliot moved with the crowd like a salmon heading upstream. It took him along. Halfway down the alley, Elliot stopped into a small bookstore. It fit maybe fifteen people in total. He wanted a better look at his mystery tail. Not a good idea, but he was already committed to it.

He stood close to the window that looked out to the alley. He picked up a book, skimming as if interested, while peering out to spot the man. A moment later the man walked by and glanced into the shop. Elliot was tucked behind a wall at an angle so he could easily see out while not being seen. At the last second the man turned his head to look back and caught a glimpse of Elliot. For a brief moment, they made eye contact. Elliot glared at him, noticing a small scar on the right side of his face. The man, realizing he'd been spotted, cut into the shop.

Elliot didn't take his eyes off him as they circled around the shop, the counter in the middle acting like a divider. The man got caught between a few people who acted like walls. Elliot dropped the book and made a quick move for the exit and back into the alley. Once out he looked both ways—no others perked their heads or seemed to be following him.

The maneuver gave Elliot a little breathing room, as he cut across the alley into another corridor of shops that went down to a second level. He tried to not look back, as it might stand out among the crowd. The second level was a more open space, but just as crowded. Elliot circled around, then up the stairs back to the first level. As he hit the stairs, he checked behind again—no sign of his tail. His heart was moving at a steady, quick pace. His breaths were short.

Back on the street level, Elliot made his way out of the market area and headed to the hotel where he'd stayed when he'd first arrived in town. Still, no one behind him. He moved with purpose, but he paced himself so his movements wouldn't stand out.

He hit the hotel in under ten minutes. Sticking to his plan, he walked through the main entrance, cut through the lobby, and headed for the restaurant. As he passed the host stand, the host asked if he wanted a table. Elliot said no and continued toward the exit, which would put him on the adjacent street on the opposite side of the hotel. Once at the doorway he peered out to the street. *So far so good.* He shook his head at the thought. *What am I doing playing spy games?*

He pushed the thought aside as he walked out to the street and headed toward his new location, just a few blocks away. *Was it far enough? Too late now.* He pulled his hoodie up further and kept his hands in his pockets. He avoided eye contact with those he passed. *Does that make me stand out more?* It didn't matter, he'd arrived.

The apartment complex had a gate that used a basic numeric keypad for entry, an added sense of security. Tenants could change their code as needed for guests or rentals. Before entering the code, Elliot paused and scanned both ends of the quiet street. Nothing stood out. A few people coming and going from their daily routines. He punched the code in and darted inside, making sure the gate closed behind him. He made his way to the apartment.

He entered the apartment, shut the door behind him, and immediately dropped to the floor. His body took over entirely, forcing him into a ball with every emotion possible expelling itself. He was having a panic attack. He couldn't do anything but ride it out as his body processed everything that had happened.

He kept repeating to himself, *I'm safe.* Even if it was a lie.

Chapter 21

Less than twenty-four hours had passed since Elliot found Keating's body in the park. He hadn't left the apartment since. Hadn't used his phone, checked his email, or even opened his laptop. The first few hours he'd huddled himself in a corner of the bedroom in a daze. After a while he made it to bed, curled in a fetal position, and slept. As the hours passed the sun dropped, shrouding the apartment in darkness. It was silent, other than his quiet breathing. He was alone, stranded, like in the park, not sure what to do. He needed to get out of Seattle, head back to Boston. That was his only plan.

He made his way to the living room and sank into the large brown leather couch. The lights remained off. Streetlights glared through the window shades, providing enough light to move around but not so much as to reveal someone was home. He opened his laptop and found a flight back to Boston. Wait, maybe a train to Portland, then a flight? Or head north to Vancouver first? *Would they know? Could I lose them?* His mind frantic, and illogical, he wanted to be as far removed from Seattle as possible. He needed to get home and forget about any of this. He'd tell Jake to delete any and all of the data, he'd write a short article about the closure, and that would be it. He could rest his mind.

The thought spun and conflicted with every fiber of his being. It wouldn't be fair to Keating. And what if this signal was dangerous? Who had control of it?

His face was lit up in a light blue hue from the laptop screen. He stared not at the screen but out the window. Flashes of Keating's body jolted across his eyes. The blood dripping from the bench, the lifelessness of a man he'd just met. The weight of the situation landed on his shoulders like a stone. He closed his eyes and took a deep breath as his head sank backward into the couch.

His phone buzzed on the coffee table, breaking the silence and startling Elliot out of his trance. He looked at the phone—an unknown number continued to buzz. He hesitated, then answered.

A direct, precise voice was on the other end. "Elliot. This is Agent Blackwell of the FBI."

Elliot, with a sudden burst of energy, sat up on the couch. He put his laptop on the coffee table. His mind raced.

"Hello," he said.

"I think it's time we meet," Blackwell said.

Elliot paused, neither agreeing or disagreeing.

Blackwell continued, "I just arrived in Seattle, will be here for a couple days. How's tomorrow? 10:00 a.m.?"

Elliot took a second before replying. He wasn't sure how involved Blackwell was—his trust was shattered. "I can do that. Space Needle Park." It was a statement, not a question. He wanted a public space, neutral ground. Not that it had mattered much for Keating.

"That'll work. See you then," Blackwell said, then hung up.

#

Elliot arrived at Space Needle Park right at 10:00 a.m. The area was busy, with plenty of foot traffic and people. Cameras in key spots around the park calmed Elliot's nerves. The park had a collection of tourist activities all tied together by a monorail. The Space Needle was front and center near the park entrance, surrounded by a large garden.

He waited outside the Space Needle welcome center, seated on a bench in front of the main entrance. Elliot had done some research on Blackwell the night before, finding pictures of him from various articles, impressed by his military career and his move into the Cyber Criminal department at the FBI. He sat firm, his right leg tapping like an active drummer. His hands were in his hoodie pockets, his head on a swivel, checking faces as they passed. If there was someone who looked nervous Elliot was it.

The wait wasn't long. A man—casually dressed in jeans, a light black jacket, and sunglasses—walked toward Elliot. He had a soft smile on his face and precisely cut hair with a perfect part on the left side.

"Elliot?" the man asked, stretching out a hand.

Elliot stood and shook his hand. "Yes." Elliot squinted in the morning light. Blackwell looked younger than he'd expected.

"Agent Blackwell." He pulled out ID and flashed it to Elliot, who nodded. "Nice to meet you. Let's walk."

They passed down a walkway that opened to the back side of the Space Needle and led to a larger park surrounded by various art institutions and museums.

"You're in quite a spot right now," Blackwell said matter-of-factly. "We know what happened to Keating."

Elliot glanced at him, then looked away, lost in a flash of Keating and his blood-soaked shirt.

"We know you were going to meet him yesterday."

A tingling sensation poked at Elliot's insides; a shot of prickly nerves touched the surface of his skin.

Blackwell continued. "Don't worry—we know you weren't in-volved."

The hairs on Elliot's arms relaxed, but tension still pulled his body taut. "You have any leads?" he asked.

"Not yet."

They continued into the park, making their way to the garden.

"Elliot, I need you to be up-front with me. There's missing data from Green Bank. We believe Keating stored this data on a drive of some sort. It's important we have that data. Did he ever mention this to you?"

"No. What sort of data?" Elliot lied.

Blackwell paused, looked out into the garden. "Data we believe to have national security implications." His words were gentle, but his tone was forceful.

Blackwell paused and gave a discreet scan of the surroundings. "We have reason to believe a satellite or satellites transmitting a signal were hacked. We think it's a surveillance tool from a foreign entity." He turned to look at Elliot. "We think Keating knew more, or had col-lected data that would help us pinpoint the source. Data that would possibly incriminate him."

Elliot chuckled in disbelief. "I can't imagine Keating withholding something like that. Why hide it?"

"We think he was involved in or providing intelligence to foreign agencies. We think he knew about whatever was discovered at Green Bank and decided to hide the data to cover his tracks."

Blackwell was providing more details than Elliot expected. *But why?* He knew Keating had given Elliot something—more information about the signal, without which he couldn't do anything. But what about the conclusions Blackwell had drawn? A foreign entity wasn't out of the realm of possibilities, but it didn't make sense. Claiming Keating shared intelligence or was a spy didn't add up either.

"What happens if this data isn't retrieved?" Elliot asked.

"We've already started to work on countermeasures, and opening investigations against foreign powers and potential threats," Blackwell said.

Was Blackwell painting this picture to push him into giving up the data and what he knew? "Why are you telling me this information?" Elliot asked. "And what prevents me from writing a story and including all of this?"

"Including what? You don't have much more than what would add up to a conspiracy theory with nothing to back it."

Elliot suspected Blackwell was trying to goad him into saying more, into admitting he had the SD card. If Elliot did he might end up on a bench like Keating. That last thought connected dots Elliot didn't want to accept.

"If Keating gave you anything, you need to tell me. I can't help you if you don't," Blackwell said.

Elliot thought, *Help me from what?* "I'll keep it in mind," he said.

They started to circle back to the Space Needle entrance where they'd met.

"How much longer are you planning to be in Seattle?" Blackwell asked.

"Not much longer."

Blackwell nodded. "That might not be a bad idea."

The circular driveway in front of the welcome center entrance curved into a side parking lot. Cars lined up to drop off and pick up. Off to the side in a nearby parking spot was a typical government-issued black suburban SUV with darkened windows. *Not subtle,* Elliot thought.

Blackwell paused in front of the welcome center and turned to Elliot. "I hope if you have any other information, you'll let me know." Blackwell started to walk away then turned back. "It took me too long to figure this out, but life is precious, not to be wasted."

"Like Keating's?" Elliot said.

Blackwell nodded, admitting the truth of the statement, then said, "We'll talk soon."

Elliot watched Blackwell walk back to the black SUV and get in on the passenger side. Another man stood outside on the driver's side, his back to the car. Once Blackwell closed the passenger door, the other man turned, flicked a cigarette to the ground, and opened the driver's side door.

Terror flooded Elliot's body as his eyes focused on a small scar on the man's right cheek.

Chapter 22

A couple days had passed since LiLo's run-in with her bulky bearded friend at the server farm. She hadn't left the Airbnb since. The door was locked with a chair shoved against it. The curtains were drawn and the lights off except for the desk lamp. For her, Antwerp had overstayed its welcome. But in order to leave, she had to figure out where she was headed.

She continued to monitor Agent Blackwell's team communications. There was no mention of the IP addresses YellowJacket had bounced between when hitting the observatory in West Virginia. Were they not aware of the attack? It seemed like an obvious detail to miss. What was YellowJacket looking for and why hit an observatory?

Emails and message chats were enough to keep tabs on them. Most of the communications were about tracking a Russian APT group called HoneySuckle. They were tied to various corporate espionage hacks in the States. She didn't think YellowJacket was aligned with any particular group or country, though she was still suspicious he was from the agency that trained her.

As she listened she painted a mental profile of Blackwell and everyone on his team—Agents Hansen, Klein, and Evans. She pulled up FBI recruitment data on each.

Blackwell was a government lifer with a military background, a computer science degree, and one mark on his sheet—an accident during a tour of duty that left someone on his team dead. According to the reports, she could see it wasn't Blackwell's fault. Orders that put them in a terrible situation, a situation that Blackwell had saved. She could relate to taking orders and thinking they were given for the right reason. You trusted that they were. After a few tours he'd returned and joined the FBI. Took up a position within the Cyber Crime division. Then spun up his own team, which acted as a conduit between agencies. A more autonomous and agile approach, also new for the red-tape-laden FBI. Based on his records, he was by the book. His personal life was simple—and lonely. No significant other, no girlfriends who lasted longer than six months. *Love life not important,* LiLo thought. His work consumed him. He didn't have much of a social footprint. Clean as a whistle. Never a late payment. Clocked in and out of work consistently. An overachiever. A Boy Scout.

Agent Rachel Klein, a career agent, bounced around departments before landing in cyber activity tracking with Blackwell. They were friends and had known each other since their FBI training days. She'd joined right out of college as an analyst. Like most government-issued photos, her profile photo was unflattering, but she did her best with a genuine smile. Her shoulder-length auburn hair made her light-colored eyes stand out. The photo told LiLo more than her FBI bio. Agent Klein had the all-American family: husband, two kids, white picket fence, and a golden retriever. Social media accounts revealed details about vacations, backyard barbecues, family portraits. Klein appeared happy with the perfect life she had, but LiLo didn't understand the appeal—just looking through the photos made her feel trapped.

Evans was fresh out of school—Brown University. He was smart, probably the smartest person in the room, but lacked experience. The definition of a computer nerd, he'd gone straight from college to the FBI and the cybersecurity team. LiLo was only slightly impressed by his credentials. He was good and knew his stuff but made eager mistakes. She felt bad for him. He was their cybersecurity lead, and she was about to infiltrate his life as easily as opening an unlocked door and walking in.

Hansen had only joined the team within the past year. Military training. He'd been in financial records from the start of his career at the FBI, had a background in computer science, and elected to move to the Cyber Crime division for international tracking. Wife, no kids.

LiLo was deep into each of these agents—she knew everything about them, even their spending habits. It put her on edge to be this close; she couldn't slip up. She'd spent her life running from them, and now she was in their digital backyard watching as they played.

She checked their recent travel. Blackwell and Hansen had been in Seattle. Parsing through chats and emails, she learned they went to find a Dr. Geoff Keating and an Elliot Bishop. LiLo pulled their names—Keating was a former employee of AeroTech and had been director of the Green Bank Observatory in West Virginia, before the closure and moving back to Seattle. *FBI shuts down your place of work, and you end up back in Seattle. A planned relocation.* He was also dead. Killed around the same time Blackwell and Hansen were in Seattle.

Elliot Bishop was a journalist from Boston writing for science and astronomy magazines and online publications. His social media was sparse—no girlfriend, or at least not anymore. *What does the FBI want with him?* The FBI already had a tail on Elliot and someone else named Jakob Fischer at MIT. She couldn't see the connection. The FBI had an entire file on Elliot and Jakob. She skimmed it, then set up a monitor on their messages too. Their email communications had stopped and switched entirely to a secure chat platform. The FBI already had a middle-man sniffer in place, but it wasn't working. She made it work for herself, but the FBI would never know.

Night had fallen. LiLo sat cross-legged in the dark on the bed, her face bathed in light from her laptop screen. She'd spent the entire day scanning through Elliot's messages to his friend Jake. She kept seeing mentions of some *signal* and that it came from AeroTech communications satellites. The FBI had mentioned surveillance tools. Was this *signal* connected? It was widely known AeroTech had large defense contracts with the military and US government, with a new satellite communications project on the way.

But the signal Elliot and Jake mentioned sounded different. She thought it strange the IPs she'd tracked earlier were coming from AeroTech satellites; the same IPs had dropped the mysterious scripts on servers tied to various institutions. Did they make a mistake? And why was YellowJacket following these script drops? She processed the pieces she'd started to pull together. Lines were thinning and merging.

She pulled up one of the mystery scripts she'd discovered and dug through the code. There was more to it than she first suspected. Self-replicating and self-updating? Was that possible? It was sophisticated and not something she'd seen used in the open market. The cost of developing something like this was too high for the return. One section of the code was a simple data scraper. Another looked like it could pull and push data to any connected databases on the servers where the script lived, but it could also ping out to other machines at set intervals. Then it could make a callback to a host IP, though it could adjust what it did based on where it lived. She tracked the host IP back to an AeroTech satellite, then mapped where else the satellite had pinged—Green Bank Observatory.

LiLo leaned back and looked out the small window in the room to the outside world. The soft city light filled the frame. She'd stumbled into something big. Her first thought was to delete everything, do a clean install, and leave town. She fought with herself. YellowJacket was connected to this. She needed to find him and this was the best lead she had. As her fingers poised to open her chat client, the app lit up before she'd issued the command.

YELLOWJACKET: *enjoying Antwerp?*

LiLo froze. Scanned the room, the windows, and listened. *Did I make a mistake? No way.* She was positive, she retraced her steps in her mind.

YELLOWJACKET: *talk to me*

She hesitated, stared at the screen.

LILO: *who are u?*
YELLOWJACKET: *a friend*
YELLOWJACKET: *in need, indeed*
LILO: *what do you want?*
YELLOWJACKET: *you do great work. could use another script*
LILO: *not for hire right now*
YELLOWJACKET: *yeah, I think you are tho*
YELLOWJACKET: so does Gemini

LiLo's heartbeat dropped to the depths of her gut. She grabbed her bag and packed what little she had laying around and put on her jacket. The chat client flashed, waiting for a response. She checked for flights that night out of Antwerp and booked one a few hours out. Time to leave.

LILO: *ok. Send me details*

LiLo closed out her laptop, grabbed her bag, and left. She hailed a cab to the airport. Cash made the transaction simple. LiLo stared intently through the backseat window. Light rain pooled and streaked across the glass, turning the passing city lights into a mosaic of color that reflected off her focused gaze. Intent. Always intent.

She arrived at the airport with not much time to spare; her insides shook with nerves as she approached security. Travelling by air wasn't her preferred method considering the paperwork and no-fly lists. She passed through security without issue, and given the time, the lines moved quickly. She arrived at her gate and watched as the last burst of people shuffled through while a woman at the airline counter made an announcement over the loudspeaker. "This is the final boarding call for Flight 1321 to Boston, Massachusetts."

Chapter 23

Elliot returned to Boston the day after his meeting with Blackwell. A welcoming sense of security ran through him, like the comforts of visiting the cabin in Maine as a boy. He opened the door to his apartment and scooped up a pile of scattered mail, then dropped his bag on his way to the couch. He threw the chaotic pile of credit card offers, food menus, and the rest of the mail on the coffee table. He kicked off his shoes and sank into the cushions with a sigh of relief. A quick text to Trevor to let him know he'd returned safely, and they should chat soon was all he could muster in the moment. Trying to push away the recent events for just a minute, he closed his eyes and took a breath, but his distracted mind kept him from getting the break he wanted. He sat up and sorted the mail, forming distinct piles for the useless physical spam.

As he shuffled through the last few pieces, he came across a small envelope addressed to him but with no return address. Intrigued, he opened the envelope and pulled out a folded piece of paper, maybe torn from a small notepad. Elliot unfolded the piece of paper and read the short handwritten note:

The signal has been around longer than we thought. Look to the past to solve the future. Think beyond what's possible. —Keating

Elliot dropped the note on the table like it was on fire, then stood and circled the room, creating distance between himself and the note from a dead man that lay on his coffee table. Jolted, he grabbed his bag to look for his laptop but instead he came across the baseball Keating had given him. A memory of Keating's body on the bench flashed through his mind. Everything had moved so fast he hadn't had time to process his death.

Elliot sat back down on the couch and stared at the note. Keating's mention of the signal being around longer than they'd thought didn't shock Elliot; they knew it had been around for a few years. *Did Keating mean even further back? Was that why he included historical data on the SD card? How far back could this thing exist?* If it was a hack, it could only be a few years old.

Elliot read the cryptic note again. *Look to the past to solve the future. Think beyond what's possible.* What did any of it mean? The handwriting looked hurried, scratched out on a pad, a passing thought Keating had as he pondered the data, or the scribbles of a man pushed to the brink of paranoia. First his father, and then Keating.

Elliot's trip to Seattle had raised more questions than answers. Any leads he had were being threatened by Blackwell, not to mention that the FBI was keeping tabs on him. Who was that agent with Blackwell? The man who'd tailed him from the meeting that never happened with Keating? And Blackwell had hinted that Keating was a spy. Why? It didn't make sense. Was Blackwell using Keating as a cover up?

#

A light afternoon breeze came off the Charles River as Elliot biked to Jake's lab at MIT. The lab was located in an older building on campus, part of the general science department behind the admissions center. A giant concrete block, the building looked like stacked gray Lego bricks alternating with windows.

Elliot locked up his bike outside and walked in through the building's main entrance, which was unlocked. The individual labs were locked down to students and faculty only, requiring key cards to access them. The place was almost deserted on this summer Saturday.

The inside felt as cold as it looked, perfect for labs and experiments. The institutional smell and overall feeling of the building reminded Elliot of his Catholic grade school in New Jersey, stuffy and concrete.

Jake's lab was on the first floor, at the end of the hall that led from the main entrance. Elliot could see him through the narrow glass window of the door, hunched over a laptop, glasses on, deep in thought.

Elliot knocked.

Jake looked up, focused for a second, and smiled as he got up to open the door. Dressed in jeans, New Balance sneakers that looked like he'd owned them since high school, and a Dinosaur Jr. tour T-shirt, he looked like just another hipster roaming the streets.

"Good to see you . . . alive," Jake said, with a big smile and open arms as he let Elliot in.

"You're telling me." Elliot chuckled with a true sense of relief.

"I'm digging the half beard, my friend." Jake checked the empty halls and closed the door before scurrying back to his laptop.

Elliot dropped his backpack at a table then walked around the lab, his stress-relieving baseball in hand. It brought memories of Keating with it but also comforted him in a weird way—as if it allowed him to channel Keating as he navigated the complex situation he found himself in. Rows of bench tables sat along one side of the lab. The rest of the room was filled with various scientific equipment and study stations Elliot didn't know the purpose of. All he knew was his friend spent more time here, at all hours of the day, working on his PhD than any other place.

After poking around like he was in a museum, Elliot strolled back to Jake, tossing the ball up and down to himself like a metronome. He grabbed a seat on a stool across from Jake. "So, you find any new info that might get us killed further?"

Jake let out a short burst of nervous laughter. "Uh, yeah, I found something, Sherlock."

Elliot smiled, at ease in the company of his friend. He needed this more than he recognized.

"That signal of yours is something." Jake peered over his glasses like an old professor—a sign of things to come.

"Stop teasing me already and get on with it."

"So we know it has the ability to pull data and seems it can push data. At least that's what everything is telling me. Of course, I still need to figure out exactly what it's pushing and pulling. But, great, right?"

Elliot rolled the baseball between his hands and nodded.

Jake continued, "The interesting part is it can do a lot of pushing and pulling. Like terabytes in milliseconds a lot."

"That's quite a . . . bit," Elliot said, pun intended.

Jake rolled his eyes. "Yeah, it is." Jake removed his glasses, now in full professor mode. "So I took a step back and started looking at how the signal was placed on *this* satellite and how it was picked up across other stations."

Elliot nodded. "Go on."

"The signal you have isn't the only one. I mean, it's the same one but it's coming from different satellites, from what I can tell."

Elliot paused and stopped fiddling with the baseball for a moment. "Like, it's been installed on other satellites?" Elliot thought about his father and what he was tracking. He had been onto something, but had no idea what.

"Kinda." Jake walked over to a giant wall-sized whiteboard in the front of the room and started to draw shapes. "I looked at the host satellite, we'll call it. The one that had the strongest and most recent output, the one picked up at Green Bank. Then I looked at activity across other AeroTech satellites when this signal fired. There's a weird correlation of when it had the strongest output to when the others basically came online. The source signal fired, then satellites of the same kind started the same signal all at the same time." He'd drawn a rough diagram of a central satellite with others connected by dotted lines.

Elliot stared at the crude drawing, his mind connecting dots like the diagram suggested.

Jake tapped the whiteboard marker against his hand.

"The others weren't hacked individually," Elliot concluded, his eyes wide and mouth open like he wanted to say more but couldn't find the words.

Jake nodded with a smirk. "How that's working, I have no clue. It'll take me time to figure out."

"It's a virus," Elliot said, his gaze shifted from the floor to Jake.

Jake's marker tapping stopped.

"It spread from one satellite to the next that matched specifications, which was any AeroTech satellite of the same make and model or ID or whatever."

"F me. That's some next-level shit," Jake said.

"Yeah. And it's some dangerous shit."

Silence fell between them. They could hear the concrete walls shift.

"If it can spread that fast what's to say it wouldn't connect to other satellites?" Elliot asked, gripping the baseball tightly.

"It already has," Jake said.

"What?"

Jake shifted back to the whiteboard and pointed at the host satellite in the center with the marker. "I crunched more of the data, and the signal isn't just coming from AeroTech satellites. It's almost as if this host satellite was a test, then it had a larger burst to identify others to jump to. Short-range bursts at the strength of the host satellite that act as a diagnostic check of any in the surrounding area. Then it jumps. Like a virus from computer to computer."

"Jesus," Elliot said. His mouth went dry, and his grip tightened further on the ball.

"Elliot. It makes sense that the FBI is involved then." Jake stood in front of the whiteboard, his arms spread out, an unconscious reflection of the enormity of the situation. "If this is tech run by a hacker group, another country, or whoever, this has some serious surveillance implications. Frankly, it's giving me the heebie-jeebies."

Elliot stood and paced the room, staring at the floor like it had answers. "We need to figure out what it's pushing and pulling specifically."

"I'm working on it, but this thing is complex. I'm still trying to wrap my head around the data alone. Honestly, from what I'm looking at, it's doing something impossible . . ."

A thought popped to the front of his mind like it was dropped there. "I got a note from Keating."

"Okay?" Jake said, his face scrunched in confusion.

"He's dead. And I got a note from him when I got back to Boston."

Jake's shoulders settled as his hands dropped to his sides.

"Jesus . . ."

"Yeah, I found him in a park in Seattle. There was so much blood." Elliot's face flushed.

"Elliot, what the hell. You gotta call someone about this. What about your FBI contact? We should share this data with them." Jake's hands were atop of his head, holding back his hair.

"I think they killed him. They're putting on he might have been a spy or something, but it all seems off," Elliot said.

"Shit. If they find out we have this—"

"I know. I know." Elliot paused. "They already suspect we have it, hence the tails."

Before either of them could say another word, the door to the lab opened.

Elliot's head snapped around to see who was intruding. A woman pushed the door open slowly and walked in. *A lost student?* Her light-brown hair was pulled back in a short ponytail. She wore black jeans, a solid color T-shirt, and a gray bomber jacket. She had a backpack slung over a shoulder. Her broken-in navy blue Onitsuka Tiger sneakers barely made a sound as she moved a few feet into the room. She glanced around as she closed the door behind her. Her demeanor sent a nervous jolt through Elliot.

Jake glanced at Elliot, then to the new guest. "Hi, and who are you?" The words were like a blunt machete swinging through the air.

Her eyes moved around the room, not making contact with Jake or Elliot. "I'm Emma."

#

LiLo was too busy eyeing the room from windows to corners to notice the shock on the faces that looked back at her. It was simple threat assessment—she knew the surprise would keep them frozen, which gave her the seconds she needed to understand her surroundings.

Their silence and body language said more than words. The one who must be Elliot was clearly processing whether or not she was here to kill him. That made the other one Jake.

She moved around the room like a tourist, her hands in her jacket pockets. She glanced at Jake as he placed a marker on the whiteboard tray and eased back to the table where a motionless Elliot sat. She could feel his concerned eyes fixated on her.

"Emma," Jake said to break the silence as he got to the table and closed his laptop.

LiLo nodded. She didn't look at either of them as she continued to study the room.

"Can we help you?" Jake said.

"Maybe," LiLo said, now in the middle of the room. She paused then finally looked at both of them.

"You lost?" Jake asked.

"Don't think so. You're Jake and you're Elliot, right?" she asked, pointing her chin at each of them.

Elliot nodded, his eyebrows arched.

"How'd you get in here?" Jake asked.

LiLo pulled her right hand out of her pocket, flashed a keycard, then dropped it on a table. She resumed walking around the room at a snail's pace, checking out each station and acting impressed at the expensive equipment.

Jake walked to the table and picked up the card. He checked both sides—there was no MIT labeling, just a blank card with a magnetic strip.

"I'm sorry. Who are you?" he asked.

"Someone with info on your signal."

Elliot and Jake exchanged looks.

"What signal?" Elliot asked.

LiLo glared at him, disappointed at his poor attempt at lying. "You're being watched by the FBI."

The two men traded surprised looks again.

"So, it's Emma, right? You don't work for the FBI. But you have info about some *signal*?" Jake said.

Elliot jumped in, his hands up like he was stopping traffic. "Hold on, who do you work for?"

LiLo stopped at the whiteboard and studied the crude diagrams they'd drawn. She pushed up her sleeves, and gently itched the inside of her right forearm. Her eyes dropped to the source of the discomfort. A small patch of dry skin had formed around the intricate, layered, colorful floral-patterned tattoo that adorned her forearm. It was hard to miss against her pale skin. Lost in thought, she stared at the small geometric bee design at the center of overlapping triangles. A covered-up detail of her history, who she was, a past she would soon face. Here she was, back in the United States; what was once home was now the most dangerous place for her to be. The thought collapsed and she returned to the whiteboard.

"No one." She picked up one of the dry erase markers and started to draw connections from Jake's makeshift satellite drawings to a giant circle in the middle. "And I know what your signal is doing down here." She pointed at the large circle they labeled Earth.

Elliot stood and paced from one side of the room to the other. Jake glanced at Elliot, then sat on a stool and faced LiLo at the whiteboard. "You can probably understand our shock right now. But, why should we trust what you *might* know?"

LiLo turned to face Jake. "You can't. You shouldn't. But we can help each other."

Jake rolled his eyes and shifted uneasily on his stool.

"Just an exchange of information, that's all," she said. She watched Elliot rub a baseball he'd picked up off the table in front of him like he was preparing for a pitch in the bottom of the ninth. She could tell the stress relief wasn't working.

"Look, I know your friend Keating is dead. I know you two have stumbled into some shit and found this signal and have no idea where it came from. I know shady stuff is going on with this FBI guy Blackwell and his team. I also know this signal can drop scraper scripts on any server it pleases. Complex scripts that can do a lot of damage. And I need to find someone who, I think, is connected and now I'm here . . ."

LiLo leaned with both hands on the table in front of her, letting the silence hang in the air. She turned to stare out the window and shook her head. *Why am I here?*

"So you've been listening to us?" Elliot said with an accusatory whisper.

"Technically, I've been listening to the FBI, who, in turn, are listening to you."

"Wait, you some kinda hacker?" Jake stood up.

LiLo shook her head again and crossed her arms, all body language closed off to this waste of time. "Something like that. Your names came up when I sniffed the comms of this Blackwell guy and his team. So I tagged your chat," she said as her eyes bounced between them.

Elliot looked up at the ceiling and let out a string of whispered vulgarities.

"If it makes you feel any better, everyone is listening to everyone and they don't know it."

Jake looked at her, displeased. She gave him a shrug. *Get over it.*

"Sooo, this is a lot to process," Jake said, breaking the silence.

She watched as they looked at each other, then back at her.

Elliot sighed. "Okay. Fine. Let's start with you showing us how these scripts work."

Chapter 24

Blackwell marched into the FBI field office in Washington, DC with efficient strides. His trip to Seattle wasn't as fruitful as he'd hoped. He knew Elliot had more of the data from Keating, he just couldn't prove it yet. Pressing Elliot any further wouldn't get him the outcome he wanted. He had bigger issues to deal with at the moment.

He passed through security and headed down a long hallway that led to a set of elevators. His team's office was a few floors up. Each floor could pass for the next. The same concrete decor and lifeless lighting that could suck energy from the sun. A simple maze of hallways, offices, and conference rooms. Blackwell came to a conference room that was locked behind a keycard. He tapped his card, red to green, and entered the room.

The room sat against an outside wall, with a stretch of windows overlooking the city and letting in natural light—a relief. The team was already together. Agent Hansen, recovering from Seattle jet lag, poured himself coffee at the small refreshment area and nodded to Blackwell as he entered. Agents Klein and Evans sat at the conference table reviewing their notes. The small group made the table appear bigger than it was. Blackwell headed for the front of the room.

"Any updates?" Blackwell asked.

Agent Evans started. "I've been tracking a few intrusion hacks linked to Russia and North Korea. A strain of malware-as-a-service written in Rust, which is a fun one. Nothing solid yet, but these seem to be happening at an increased clip lately. Still poking at infrastructure but nothing complex or preventable."

Blackwell stood at the front of the room, arms crossed, focused. "Okay, keep on it. Let's get in touch with a few security firms, find out if they're seeing anything. And connect with CISA to see if anything overlaps, otherwise keep a lid on details."

Evans nodded and typed notes on his laptop. Blackwell shifted his focus to Agent Klein.

Klein spoke on cue. "The Green Bank signal we narrowed down to an AeroTech satellite in LEO, based on the data we have. But that's about as far as we've gotten."

"Source?" Blackwell said.

"We have reason to believe it's a Chinese state-backed attempt."

"Corporate espionage?" Hansen asked from the side of the room, as he blew across the top of his coffee and took a sip.

"Possibly. AeroTech is the centerpiece for next-gen satellite infrastructure. They have deals with the DoD that stretch into the next decade, and just inked a deal with a handful of social networks."

"That doesn't sound bad at all," Evans said.

"Yup. They're providing hardware for satellite internet service," Klein said.

"Great, blanketing the world in shit posts," Evans said under his breath as he typed away on his laptop, not looking up.

Blackwell paced the front of the room in thought. "Any other agencies chattering about this?"

"Not yet," Klein said.

"Okay, let's keep it that way for now, but get this on General Conrad's radar."

"Air Force?"

"If the Chinese are hacking satellites—well, that's their area. Unless you want to suit up?" Blackwell asked with a quick smirk as he walked to the windows.

"And the White House? Heads might roll if they find out later," Klein said.

"Let's chat with Conrad first. I'm sure DHS will run to them once they find out. I want clean-cut intel before this goes any further up the ladder," Blackwell said.

Klein nodded and turned in her chair to face Blackwell. "How was Seattle?"

"Other than a dead scientist—uneventful," Blackwell said as he looked out over the city. "Any news from the field office out there?"

"Nothing yet," Klein said.

Blackwell nodded.

Hansen asked, "Should we continue to keep tabs on that Elliot kid?"

Blackwell glanced at Hansen. "No. He's got nothing. He'll write a story and it'll go nowhere."

Chapter 25

Elliot watched Emma scrutinizing the diagram she'd drawn for them. The entire wall-length whiteboard was covered with scribbles of code, equations, and ideas tagged with question marks. It had been over five hours of laying out what they each knew, taking turns adding new details. Elliot, lost in thought, repeatedly tossed Keating's baseball into the air and let it drop into his hand. Jake paced a steady route from the black-topped lab table in front of Emma to the midpoint of the room, his hair becoming more chaotic with each passing minute. While the tension in the room had decreased since Emma's self-invitation, Elliot still didn't trust her.

"Okay, so an AeroTech satellite gets hacked with a virus," Jake started, "then it bounces to another, creating like a mesh network or another point of access?"

"Right. Then it's dropping these scraper scripts wherever it wants," Emma said.

"And you came across these how?"

Emma hesitated. "I was tracking someone and spotted them. The first one was in a system directory, hiding in plain sight. But then I noticed more on other servers for different institutions, like banks and random corporations."

Elliot caught the baseball, paused, and looked at Emma. "Who were you tracking?"

Emma turned back to the whiteboard. "It doesn't matter."

"Uhhh, you sure about that *Acid Burn* hacker lady?" Jake stopped in front of the lab table. Shaking his head, he looked back at Elliot for support. Elliot shrugged.

Jake continued, "Maybe whoever you were tracking is dropping these scripts for you. Maybe they have nothing to do with our problem, and maybe you're just here as a mole or something. Maybe they're using you to find us."

Emma dropped her head back and let out a sigh like she was dealing with a stubborn child. "*Acid Burn*? I'll take that as a compliment. And don't flatter yourself." Emma stared at the board again. "It's not them. But they're poking around and know about these scripts."

"Why isn't it them?" Elliot asked.

"The person I'm searching for wouldn't do this. These scripts are almost polymorphic. Or they are like an advanced version of that concept. They tweak themselves based on the system they're on. Very complicated."

"So?" Elliot said.

"So, that's a lot of work. Expensive. And no pattern. And I've never seen it before."

"No pattern?"

"They're all over the place. It doesn't make sense. Legit hacks come down to money. Others are just script kiddies screwing around. Then there's data pulls, espionage. But these are on weather centers, astronomy archives—"

"Like Green Bank," Elliot said as he and Emma shared a glance.

"Okay, okay, so we know it can pull data and, based on the scripts, it could push data," Jake said.

Elliot returned to tossing Keating's baseball in the air. Emma leaned on the table, focused on Jake.

Jake continued, "And we know it can do this in massive chunks and fast."

"You going somewhere with this?" Elliot said, exasperated at the rehash.

"Maybe it's a data dump. Analysis." Jake went to his laptop.

Elliot stopped his mindless baseball toss and sat up. He looked at Emma. "Where did you say you were from?"

Emma turned and glanced at Elliot. "I didn't," she replied, then went back to staring at the board.

Elliot glared at her back. He wasn't ready to trust her, but he believed what she said about the scripts. She was passionate, curious about what she had found. Her tone had changed since she first arrived—mostly she didn't take shit from Jake. *But who is she?*

"I just think you know something—well, a lot—about us, but—"

"But what? Knowing where I'm from won't help you." Emma turned to stare at Elliot for a moment.

The direct comment hit him across the face so hard he broke eye contact. She'd shut him down—but she was right, it didn't matter.

"If we're to work together we need a little trust," Elliot said but knew she wasn't going to give in. He turned back to Jake, frustrated. "So there's this signal and these scripts on weather stations, financial institutions, and so on, that can send and pull data as it wants. What does that mean?"

Jake leaned back and let out a heavy sigh.

"It means it can easily manipulate systems," Emma said.

"It can go wherever it wants," Elliot quickly added.

"It can possibly change what's on those systems," Jake said.

The group was pulling together pieces to a scary scenario. Elliot walked the room, fidgeting with Keating's baseball. "So say this script is on the server of a major financial institution and could scrape data, what does that do?" Elliot knew he was asking rhetorical questions, but the step back was needed to really understand what they had found.

"Dig up any individual's banking information or corporate statements," Jake said.

"Find trails of where money is coming and going, maybe where it shouldn't be," Emma added.

"And if it can push data?" Elliot asked, continuing the brainstorm.

"I could take that permanent vacation I've always wanted," Jake said.

"Suddenly, any country, corporation, or individual could have more than they're supposed to," LiLo said.

"This feels like the tip of the iceberg," Elliot said as he zoned out in thought.

"We're the *Titanic*, aren't we? Please don't say we're the *Titanic*," Jake said.

"Well, it's starting to make sense why someone would kill for this," Emma said as the group exchanged looks.

"We should bring this to the FBI," Jake said.

Emma let out a sarcastic chuckle. "What's your plan? Just drop it off at their doorstep and say, 'Hey, we found this thing...'"

"Elliot, this is crazy," Jake said. "Keating is dead. This iceberg is much bigger than us. Let's hand it over to Blackwell and get out of this."

Elliot gazed from Jake to Emma, who was now leaning back in her chair waiting for his response.

"Not yet."

"What?" Jake said with a rattle of disbelief.

"I have someone who can help us. Maybe connect any missing dots."

Jake's eyes went wide as he shook his head in anticipation.

"A friend from Green Bank," Elliot said.

Chapter 26

Elliot wasn't sure what he was thinking when he offered Emma a place to stay. He had no clue who this person was, and she was clearly mixed up in plenty else beyond the signal. Elliot sensed she had her own problems to deal with, and he didn't want to get involved. But she'd also helped him and Jake with details about the signal, its function. Without her they would be staring at a whiteboard working through theories until the sun rose. As mysterious as she was, and as dangerous as this all seemed, his gut said he could trust her—at least he wanted to give her the opportunity to earn their trust. He also realized they might need her to figure this whole thing out.

What surprised him even more than his invitation was that she'd accepted. Hopefully it didn't get him killed in the middle of the night.

He came out from the bedroom with a blanket and a pillow. Disjointed and clumsy, he was nervous to have a stranger in his apartment. He wasn't sure of how late it might be, but the three of them had been in Jake's lab past midnight. The exhaustion of the last week was resting on Elliot's face; the bags under his eyes could've been checked on his last flight. He dropped the blanket and pillow on the couch where Emma sat.

"Hope this works. All I have," he said. It had been a long time since anyone had stayed at his place.

"It's perfect. Thanks."

"If you need water, cups are in the kitchen."

Emma smiled, laying the blanket out on the couch and arranging the pillow at one end. "Interesting place to store cups."

Elliot's face scrunched, realizing how stupid it sounded. They had been in a room together for most of the day, yet there was still a gulf between them. He supposed that was to be expected when you were thrust into a high-stakes situation with a stranger. Maybe just as well, given who had come and gone in his life over the last week. He turned and started toward his bedroom.

"Charleston, West Virginia," Emma said out of the blue.

Elliot turned to face her.

"Where I'm from. Originally." She glanced up to make eye contact with him for a moment then immediately lay down, pulled the blanket over her, and closed her eyes.

Elliot smiled and shut off the lights. "Night." Not a complete stranger now.

#

The next morning Elliot woke up to the smell of coffee filling his apartment. He was also alive—both good starts toward trusting Emma. He went to the living room, half expecting her to be gone. She wasn't. Her blanket was folded, pillow placed on top. It looked like no one was ever there. She sat at the small dining table, her face scrunched at her laptop. Elliot couldn't tell if it was concern or focus.

"Morning," Elliot said as he headed for the kitchen. "What's up?"

"Just chatter in forums."

For a moment she looked like she was going to say more but stopped herself. "Any connections to what we found?" he asked.

"Not sure."

Elliot caught something in her voice, a soft hesitation, a deep shake within the words. *Trust?* She was smart, and he believed she knew more than she let on. His guard was coming back up.

"What's the deal with your friend in Green Bank?" Emma asked.

Elliot poured himself a cup of coffee and sat down across from her at the small round table. "She was assistant director at Green Bank with Keating. She had a theory the signal was coming from a compromised satellite. I think she knows more, but she warned me to be careful," Elliot said.

"So much for listening."

Elliot let out a chuckle. "Yeah, true."

"What's the plan?" Emma asked.

"I need to get in touch with her, but before that we'll head to Jake's lab."

"Shut off your phone," Emma said.

"What?"

"Shut off your phone. We're going to make a pit stop before we get to Jake. You have any cash on you?"

An hour later Elliot found himself in a small convenience store with eighty bucks in cash in his wallet.

"Don't go to a major outlet or carrier, they'll want a ton of personal information even for a dumb phone," Emma said as she shuffled through a rack of prepaid phones.

"You could use a burner app on your phone in a pinch, but this all counts for nothing if you keep your phone on while you're moving. It's a beacon that pings cell towers as you move. Even the dumb phone. So off when not in use. Got it?"

"Seems . . . simple," Elliot said.

"Simple is what you need. Plus these are good in emergencies for battery life. I'll add a GPS app that I can connect to. Keep using a secure chat app but make sure it isn't one owned by a social network or any massive company that wants to sell you a phone too."

"Okay, I'm not a total idiot," Elliot said.

"It's not about being an idiot, it's about being aware," she said as she handed him a phone. "And always pay in cash. Every step, every action you take is a breadcrumb."

Elliot caught her eye. "Is this how you live?"

She paused, then nodded. "You get used to it."

Chapter 27

Jake was already at the lab when they arrived, huddled over his laptop. Elliot noticed the bags under his eyes, the Dinosaur Jr. shirt no cleaner than the day before, the makeshift blanket and pillow setup adorning one of the more comfortable-looking chairs. Elliot figured he got maybe an hour or two of sleep.

Elliot dropped his bag on a table. "Hey, what's up?"

Jake didn't respond, just picked up a TV remote and turned on the TV tucked in the corner of the room.

A news anchor was mid-update. "The situation is still unfolding and we'll bring you details as we get them, but what know right now is that a power grid outage in the Southeast has left millions without power . . ."

#

Elliot muted the television and turned to face Emma. He wanted to trust her, but she wasn't making it easy. "You're expecting worse? Does that mean you knew this was going to happen?"

Emma turned to look at him, a sad look washing across her face. "I helped do this."

"You what?" Jake said, anger shaking his voice. He stopped what he was working on and glared at Emma for an answer.

Emma hesitated, then stood and walked to the front of the room. A moment ago, she'd held herself like she owned the place; now she looked defeated.

"I helped a friend build a script. They were in trouble," she said.

"Trouble?" Elliot asked, his elbows leaning on the armrests of the chair. "Is this connected to the person you're looking for?"

Emma nodded. "I made a mistake," she said softly.

"A mistake?" Jake said as he stood up, his anger boiling over. "Are you kidding me? People are in trouble because of your mistake."

Elliot turned to Jake with his hands up to calm him.

"What? You believe this shit?" Jake said. "She shows up out of nowhere, spies on us, our conversations, and now this?"

Emma retreated within herself, her arms crossed.

Jake continued to rail on, with Elliot trying to calm him. Emma snapped out of her trance, walked to her laptop, closed it up and tossed it in her bag as she rushed out of the lab. Elliot stood to try and stop her then stopped himself—it didn't matter.

Jake was finally silent, and Elliot turned to him. "You happy?"

"What? You were thinking it too. Do you realize what we have here? The severity of this?"

Elliot paused and took a breath. "Yes, but without her we wouldn't have any sense of how bad this is, or what it could do."

Jake sat back down, his head in his hands. After a moment he broke the silence. "We need to get this to someone who isn't us. Preferably someone in a suit with a badge."

Elliot didn't answer but took out his prepaid phone and stared at it. *How many more people should be involved in this?* He pulled Jenn Liu's number from his other phone, then shut it off. He sent her a message from the prepaid and waited. It didn't take long before the phone buzzed in his hand.

"Hello?" he said.

"Elliot?"

"Yes, thanks for getting back to me."

"Am I going to regret this?"

"Maybe. But it's the signal. We found something."

"Like I said, am I going to regret this?"

"The attack today in the Southeast—I think the signal is connected."

"What?"

"It's dropping connection points onto servers and systems all over the globe."

"How is that possible?" she asked.

"Well, that's why I'm calling. Did Keating mention anything about the data he analyzed? Anything stand out to you?"

Elliot paused, he could sense Liu pulling back. Was it too soon? The last few days had moved so fast that Keating's death seemed like a forgotten blip. He was so caught up in the spiral he didn't stop to think about how Liu felt. Here he was, pressing her for answers.

"I'm sorry . . . about Keating. I know he was important to you."

"Thank you. He was more than a mentor. He was practically family. I can't believe he's gone," Liu said, clearly doing her best to hold back a flood of emotion.

They shared a moment of silence before Liu continued, "He was convinced the signal had been around longer than we thought. And it was a matter of our technology advancing enough to catch it," she said.

Elliot said, "We know it's a few years old or at least matches similar FRBs and radio noise seen."

"No, Keating was convinced it was even older."

"How old?" Elliot asked.

"Not sure. He was obsessed with the frequency that the signal landed on. He found a few matches that went back five or so years, but it never panned out."

Elliot repeated, "The frequency . . ." Jake perked up and looked at him, his face lighting up. He put his glasses on and jumped back to his laptop like a lightbulb had suddenly turned on over his head.

"He thought there was a connection, but nothing came of it," she said.

Elliot walked over to the window, looking out at the people passing by. The words from Keating's note moved through his mind: *Think beyond what's possible.*

"Did Keating leave anything behind, any notes?"

"No, the FBI cleared practically everything out, including the backups. Keating's office is empty besides the photos on the walls."

"Thank you, if anything does come up—"

"I'll reach out, don't worry," Liu said. "Stay safe, Elliot."

"Thank you," Elliot said and hung up.

Suddenly, the lab door clicked open. Elliot and Jake both turned to look. Emma had returned.

#

LiLo moved through the tension-filled room as if Elliot and Jake didn't exist. This trust-building thing wasn't her strong suit. You don't need someone to catch you if you don't fall in the first place.

She headed for the table in front of the large whiteboard, placed her bag down, and pulled out her laptop. Even without looking up, she could sense their eyes on her—they hadn't moved since she returned.

LiLo tapped away at her keyboard for a brief moment, then turned it around to face Elliot and Jake and pushed it forward for them to see. She stood with her arms crossed, waiting for them to look.

Elliot moved closer to see what she had pulled up, and Jake followed. They leaned in and stared at the screen for a few seconds. Elliot made the connection first, the surprise washed over his face, then looked up at LiLo, his mouth open and eyes wide.

"Oh shit," Jake said, taking a step back. "We have an FBI most-wanted hacker in our midst."

"This really you?" Elliot asked.

LiLo nodded, the most vulnerable she had been in a long time. She was a mystery, a ghost to most people. Only three people knew who she was, a mistake in London, and the two who stood in front of her. She couldn't let this be another mistake.

"I've been running for a long time." She fidgeted with a ring on her left hand, the only remaining physical memory of her mother. "Coming here was a huge risk for me."

"Why now?" Elliot asked.

"I've been tracking someone who goes by the name YellowJacket."

"Jesus, that's a dumb name," Jake muttered under his breath. LiLo rolled her eyes in agreement.

"You have any idea who this person is?" Elliot asked.

She shook her head.

"Sorry to ask the obvious elephant-in-the-room question that just shoved its way in, but how did you end up on the FBI most-wanted list?" Jake asked.

"My former employers didn't like how I quit."

"Who the hell did you work for?" Jake pressed.

"Pretty powerful people," she said, doing her best to dodge further inquiry. She could tell Jake was getting the hint, but she wouldn't be able to keep this hidden forever.

"Is Emma your real name?" Elliot asked.

She shook her head. "I go by LiLo," she continued. "I don't have many—any—friends. I made a mistake by attempting to have one and this YellowJacket asshole took advantage of it."

She watched Elliot put two and two together.

"So you built a script—"

LiLo nodded. "And then the hack happened."

"Do you know who they are connected to?" Elliot asked.

"I *think* they might be tied to my former employers," she said.

"Great." Jake's sarcasm leaked out of the back of the room as he paced around. "Now we have even more 'pretty powerful people' after us."

"I tracked his movements to a server farm in Antwerp before I came here. Shady hacker house."

"Says the shady FBI most-wanted hacker lady," Jake said to the room, his face pale with exhaustion.

"That's not me," she said softly as she glanced down at the laptop.

"So now what?" Elliot asked.

LiLo looked at him. "Let's talk to Blackwell."

Elliot's face lit up in surprise. Jake stopped pacing and stared, then walked toward Elliot and LiLo. "Well, I'm guessing you shouldn't do the talking considering, uh, *this*." He pointed at the laptop, the harshness in his voice barely masked by the humor of it.

LiLo glared at him.

"I'm not sure that's a good idea," Elliot said, still looking at LiLo. "They were in Seattle when Keating was killed. One of his guys followed me."

"I don't think Blackwell killed Keating," LiLo said. Her voice didn't shake. She was confident in the statement.

Elliot's eyes widened. "What?"

"Couldn't he have ordered someone to kill him? The FBI doesn't *actually* get their hands dirty, right?" Jake said.

"I cracked his phone's account and tracked where he went when he was in Seattle. He didn't kill Keating," LiLo said.

"You sure about that?" Elliot said as he leaned in. "Like *sure* sure?"

"Positive."

She paused for a moment as that sunk in, then said, "I also think he has a sleeper agent of some kind, a mole, in his team."

#

Elliot moved to take a seat and tried to process what he'd just heard. Jake stood in the back of the room, looking perplexed. His lack of sleep had taken its toll and then some. Elliot wasn't sure how much longer he'd last.

"A mole?" Elliot said among the silent trio. If the FBI's task force was compromised, could they even go to them?

"Do you know who it is?" Jake asked.

"No. But when I was tracking YellowJacket, I dropped a backdoor onto his command-and-control in Antwerp so I could monitor them. They're trading encrypted messages," LiLo said.

"How do you know it's an FBI agent?" Jake said.

"The language they use. The details he gave about the signal."

"Wait, the agent is sharing details about the signal with this Yellow-Jacket?" Elliot asked as he perked up in his seat.

"Yeah, but they don't have what we have."

"There was an agent in Seattle with Blackwell," Elliot said as he fiddled with his baseball. "He had a small scar on his right cheek. He followed me after I found Keating."

"I can do some digging," LiLo said as she sat at the table and pulled up her laptop. "He's got a small team of four that I know pretty well at this point. It won't be hard to figure out who was with him in Seattle."

Elliot paused a moment, feeling his way toward a decision. "I'll reach out to Blackwell. If we think he isn't compromised, and they're missing this data, they might be linking this to the wrong group."

"Sure, but maybe they want to link this to another group." Jake said.

Elliot hesitated, then took out his burner phone and entered Blackwell's number. He put the phone on speaker and placed it on the table. Jake moved to be within earshot. The phone rang a couple times, then Blackwell answered.

"Blackwell," Elliot started then paused, "this is Elliot Bishop."

"Elliot. How are you?"

"I'm fine. I have some details about the signal I wanted to share."

"That's great. Where did you get these details from?"

Elliot leaned over the phone. "That's not important yet, but it's what you're missing."

"Elliot what's going on?" Blackwell asked.

Elliot paused, then asked. "Can you protect me if I give you what I have?"

"Protect you from what?"

"Whoever killed Keating. This data is clearly important."

"What do you have?" Blackwell insisted.

"Can you protect me?" Elliot asked again.

"If you come in. If you come to DC I can," Blackwell said.

"I don't know if that's a good idea."

"Elliot, what are you not telling me?"

"How can I trust you?"

Blackwell paused, then said, "You have to take my word, but I need to know what you have."

"I can't give it all to you now, but just know the signal has been around a lot longer than you think."

"Like how long?"

"Years, possibly decades. And these recent attacks—"

"Elliot, you need to get to DC—I can send an escort."

"No. I'll reach out when the time is right," Elliot said as he ended the call.

The three of them stared at the phone on the table.

"Uh, you just hang up on the FBI?" Jake asked.

Elliot nodded. "Yeah, that was probably not a good idea." He looked at LiLo.

"Don't look at me. I'm not on speaking terms with them."

"Well, they say no idea is bad, but we all know when they're stupid," Jake said. "So now what?"

"I'm not sure," Elliot said.

Chapter 28

LiLo sat in silence with Elliot and Jake, the three focused again on the news. The blackout had begun to spread west, to Louisiana, Mississippi, and Arkansas. There was no information about the cause, but that didn't stop commentators from discussing possibilities, including hacking.

"I can't watch this anymore," LiLo said, standing up. "I'm going to get something to eat. Either of you hungry?"

Jake and Elliot shook their heads without turning away from the TV. LiLo closed up her laptop and dropped it in her bag. *Never leave anything behind.* Another lesson burned into muscle memory. She walked out the lab door and headed out of the building toward a collection of food trucks she'd seen in an area of campus that intersected with the surrounding neighborhood.

She stood in front of the few trucks—decision time. *Fancy grilled cheese or poke bowl?* Fancy grilled cheese it was. She paid with cash and started back toward the lab, taking a few bites of her cheesy sandwich as she walked. The grassy lawn in front of the lab was crisscrossed with walkways. Foot traffic was light, with more tourists and families than students on the clear summer weekend.

As she got closer she spotted two black SUVs parked along the side of the building, both with drivers still in them. *Those are new.*

She slowed her pace, her eyes darting from face to face, entrance to entrance. Something wasn't right. She sat down on a bench close to the entrance of the building and ate her sandwich like she was any other student taking a break from a long day of studying. She glanced at the SUVs and the side of the building she could see clearly. A few minutes passed before two men, both casually dressed, walked around to the main entrance. Their heads were on swivels, not bothering to disguise their actions. Not that it mattered—anyone in the area either had their head buried in their phone or were busy chit-chatting. LiLo didn't blame anyone—they weren't trained to notice these things.

She continued to sit on the bench, taking slow bites of her sandwich. She watched the two men make their way into the lab. As they did, two more came around the other side of the building, walking quickly past a side entrance. She took out her phone and texted Elliot.

LILO: *you and jake need to leave the building now*

There was a pause before a response came through.

ELLIOT: *everything ok?*
LILO: *no. Walk out the lab, front door, act like students*
ELLIOT: *ok*

LiLo finished her sandwich, then walked toward a trash bin and dumped her wrapper. She had her phone out, pretending to be another student lost in their screen. Her eyes bounced from her phone to the men and their movements. She sent a message to Elliot.

LILO: *I'm out front, ten yards or so*

She waited, glancing at her phone every few seconds for a response. *If they don't come out within three minutes, what's my backup plan?* She could pull a fire alarm. Call 911 with some made-up emergency. She had options but waited. *Come on, come on.*

The moments continued to tick by as she held her breath—she'd have to make a move. Then, the front door opened. Elliot and Jake walked out, doing their best to look like students, having a conversation with each other. Jake had an extra skip in his step, which didn't help, but they were in the clear. Two of the men eyed them as they crossed the grassy courtyard. As Elliot approached, LiLo looked up. Playing the part, she smiled and gave Elliot a hug.

"When I let go, smile and let's keep walking," she whispered in his ear.

They let go and the three of them continued walking across the courtyard.

"Who the hell is that?" Jake said as nonchalantly as possible.

"FBI probably," Elliot said.

"It wasn't," LiLo said.

"Then who?" Jake asked.

LiLo shook her head.

The three of them held on to that question and kept walking further from the lab. "What now?" Jake asked as he glanced over at Elliot.

"DC," Elliot said after a moment's pause.

LiLo held back from making a suggestion, beginning to understand her own motives might compromise her advice. There was the slightest possibility she might be able to clear her name. It was a stretch, but she was home and wanted to stay. She was done running. She wanted a normal life without having to look over her shoulder every step. Gemini was a brief glimpse into that world. She wanted to trust people enough to let her guard down.

"I should stop home and grab a change of clothes and my backup laptop," Jake said.

"Bad idea," LiLo said as Elliot and Jake looked at her. "If they're here, they've already been to your apartments. Most likely another team waiting."

"At least I have an extra shirt in my backpack," Jake said under his breath.

"Maybe we take Blackwell up on his offer and head to DC?" Elliot asked as he panned back between Jake and LiLo.

"Hell with it. Why not? Anyways, I'm curious to see what he'll do to you after you hung up on him," Jake said as he shrugged his shoulders.

LiLo nodded with a hint of hesitation. She was about to take a big risk, and a pang of guilt settled in her stomach, knowing she might be pulling these two into deeper trouble than they could understand. One step at a time.

#

Jake's car wasn't the prettiest of the lot, but it could get them to DC without much issue. Thankfully, Jake had parked it down the street from his apartment—the problem with street parking in a city with more cars than street. LiLo sat in the backseat, plugged into her laptop via a secure hotspot on her phone. The first few hours of the drive were silent. Elliot stared out the window, watching the world pass by, each car with clueless passengers heading to their next destination. They'd likely seen the headlines about the power grid in the Southeast but carried on with life. A problem that wasn't theirs but would be.

Elliot zoned out to the steady sounds of the highway until a voice penetrated his wandering mind.

"Hey, you check in with your mother?" Jake said.

Elliot snapped out of his fog and grabbed his phone. "Not yet. How about your parents? They okay? Weren't they in Florida?"

"Yeah, my father already packed the Winnie and headed out of town. Said he didn't like Florida anyways. They're probably halfway to Texas, knowing my mom."

The *Winnie*. The self-sufficient mobile time capsule Jake's parents had been using for road trips since he and Jake were kids. Jake's father prided himself on keeping that thing forever. "It runs better than any of those computer chipped machines they make today, and you don't need people tracking where you drive," he'd always preach. A constant reminder their youthful reliance on technology would get the better of them.

Elliot took a moment to think. "What if they're watching my mother?"

"Who?" Jake asked.

"The FBI, or whoever that was back at MIT."

"If it makes you feel any better, I don't think she's being watched," LiLo said from the backseat.

"How would you know?" Elliot said as he looked back at her.

"I'm not seeing any messages between either group about her or about Princeton, New Jersey."

"How the hell do you know that? Wait, do I want to know?" Jake said, glancing at her through the rearview mirror.

"And how do you know where I grew up?" Elliot said.

LiLo ignored Elliot's question but answered Jake's. "I dropped a sniffer on your Wi-Fi network."

"Jesus, when this shit is over, we need to talk boundaries," Jake said.

"Then I just needed one of them to connect to your open guest network via their phone. Which most phones will do automatically. There's always one loose cannon who doesn't check those settings," LiLo said. "But now we have access to the 'secure' chats"—she mimed air quotes— "of whoever that was back there."

Elliot faced forward. "I'll tell her to go to the cabin."

"That doesn't sound like a good idea," Jake said.

"Why not?"

"If they aren't watching her yet, they will be, and you're going to send her to a remote location by herself? Also, no way your mom is buying any of this shit."

"Good point."

"What does your mom do for work?" LiLo asked.

"She's a nurse at the Princeton Emergency Center."

"Tell her to stay at work."

"What?" Elliot asked.

"Tell her to stay at work. Don't get her more concerned for no reason. The hospital will have security plus backup power, and if this blackout reaches the area, they're going to need her. Right now, she's in the safest place she can be. Plus, she's a nurse—she's not going to run from an emergency."

Elliot couldn't argue with that logic. He called his mother, who was already heading into work to review the hospital's emergency protocols. He knew full well that getting her to leave at that point would be impossible. They talked about the power outage, and he hinted that she should be prepared for it to reach the Northeast, without telling her what he knew. He assured her he was fine, and they ended the call.

Elliot didn't think it was enough, but it was all he could do.

Chapter 29

Exhaustion had set in for Elliot and judging by the looks of Jake and LiLo they were equally as tired. Not able to sleep, he leaned his head against the passenger window, contemplating if heading to DC was the right move. Could he trust Blackwell? His first thought was no, but what options did he have? Was he putting his friends in further danger? They had crossed a line and the only option was forward.

After a brief stop for gas and a stretch an hour outside New York, they got back on the road. Elliot turned on the radio and tuned to NPR, looking for updates on the blackouts. The Southeast was still in darkness, as were portions of the Midwest now. The grid had been down for hours now in some locations and people were getting nervous, heading to gas stations with generators to fill up and leave town or preparing for the worst. Most stayed in their homes. Crews were spread thin trying to address what had happened. Reports of system failures due to lockouts started to come in. There was speculation about hacker groups, but no concrete information. No messages or ransoms mentioned. Everyone was in the dark.

"Alright. As the driver of this mobile shit show, I'm changing the station," Jake said as he tuned the radio to a '90s alt-rock station that was playing "Black Hole Sun" by Soundgarden. "Okay, not my favorite song by them, but seems fitting." The mood eased for a moment as the three traded smiles.

Elliot glanced back at LiLo as she stared out the window like she was seeing something for the first time. Elliot figured it'd been years since she'd seen the landscape of her former home. What had changed? What else had she left behind?

"What do you remember?" Elliot asked as he watched the world pass by through his passenger window.

"Road trips with my family. We used to go to Rehoboth Beach every year," LiLo said.

Elliot leaned his forehead against his window.

"I miss the beach. I miss not having to worry," LiLo said. Elliot could hear the longing in her voice like she broke character and let her guard down. "I miss my brother . . . my family."

"Well, you're back in the States now—can't you find them?" Jake asked.

"I, uh, can't." She shifted in her seat like she was snapping out of a dream. "They died when was I young."

Elliot and Jake exchanged a look.

"My dad and I used to do this road trip to DC every couple of years. The Air and Space Museum. Every trip he'd have a new lesson for me as we drove down," Elliot said, letting out a chuckle. Jake looked over at his friend with a smile.

"Even now I feel like he's teaching me something . . ."

A heavy silence sat in the middle of the car like an unwelcome passenger.

"I miss . . . my lab," Jake said, breaking the silence.

Elliot eyed his friend. "Really?"

"What? I do."

LiLo let out a soft laugh. "Jerk," she whispered.

"She's right," Elliot said as he looked back at LiLo then at Jake. "As smart as you are, you're an idiot."

Again, for a moment, the weight of the ride, their circumstance, lifted.

Elliot turned on his phone to check if he'd received any messages. Once booted up it buzzed with a voice mail. It was Liu.

"Liu left me a message," he said.

Jake and LiLo perked up with interest.

"She says she may have something for us, something about frequency matching?" Elliot looked over at Jake.

Jake nodded. "Hell yes! I had a theory but wasn't a hundred percent on it. What else did she say?"

"She asked if we could get to GBO."

The group shared a look.

"GBO is a radio silent area and fairly remote—could be a good place for us to hide out for a bit," LiLo said.

"Liu and I could bounce some ideas around, and there might be something there we could use," Jake said.

"And it buys us some time to think about Blackwell, and maybe figure out what that group back at MIT is up to," Elliot finished.

There was a moment of silence before Jake exclaimed, "I love this plan! Next stop, off the grid."

Chapter 30

Even with Elliot and Jake sharing the driving, they didn't arrive at GBO until the following morning. The radio droned on in the background about the blackouts, which hadn't reached the Virginias or DC yet. They seemed to be moving west now, reaching the eastern edge of Oklahoma. As they neared the facility, Elliot appreciated strangely calming effect of driving right through nature. Nothing but trees, hills, then patches of open fields. Repeat.

"Jesus, there's nothing out here," Jake said.

"Think that's the point," Elliot replied.

"Off the grid right in the backyard," LiLo added.

"Thinking of relocating?" Jake smirked at LiLo in the rearview mirror. She returned the look.

Elliot pointed out the window. "It's coming up on the right."

"I have a feeling it won't be hard to spot," Jake said.

A moment later they spotted the GBO entrance, featuring a small replica of the top of the 'Great Big Thing' telescope. In the distance they could see the tip of the real telescope against a backdrop of mountain ranges.

"Anyone else just get a shiver?" Jake said.

They parked in the visitor lot with a few other cars. No one was around that they could see. Elliot hopped out first and took in the scene. LiLo and Jake followed.

"This isn't creepy at all," Jake said.

"Must still be closed to the public." Elliot started toward the Science Center.

"Brought the family back, I see," Karl the security guard said as Elliot entered.

Elliot smiled. "Good to see you too, Karl."

Karl waved them on. "Dr. Liu is waiting for you, she's in the labs in the back. Follow the hallway to the left to the end—you'll see her back there."

"No guided tour?" Elliot said.

"Only guided tour I offer is of the front door leading outside, if you give me a headache. And tell them not to touch anything and no Wi-Fi." Karl pointed at LiLo and Jake as the three walked by.

A short walk down the hallway led them to a few rooms; only one had the door open. Elliot poked his head in to see Liu sitting at a shared table in the middle of the room. She was focused on a laptop screen. The rest of the room was broken into cubicle-style office spaces, each with its own computer station and set of monitors. The far wall had a floor-to-ceiling bookshelf loaded with binders.

As Elliot moved into the room, Liu glanced up to welcome him with a smile and stood to meet the others. "You made it."

"A quick stop for some rest, but yeah, not a bad ride," Elliot said. "These are my friends Jake and LiLo." They all exchanged handshakes.

"Nice to meet you, and welcome," Liu said.

An awkward pause sat between them.

"Please, grab a seat or stand, whichever," she said, like this was the first time she was hosting guests.

Elliot and Jake each took a seat, while LiLo remained standing and eased her way around the room.

"So where do we start?" Elliot said.

"Well, when we last spoke I mentioned we didn't have anything here related to the signal because the FBI basically cleaned everything out," Liu started, "but that doesn't mean another telescope doesn't."

"What do you mean?" Elliot said.

"There's probably a hundred and fifty or more observatories around the world," Jake chimed in. "They may have captured the same data but may not know it."

"Exactly. What we do know is the date and time an instance of the signal appeared in the data we captured here," Liu said.

"We could reach out to other observatories and pull their data for those dates," Elliot said.

"Most of the larger observatories do archive their data for the public to access," Liu said.

"Still, that leaves us having to dig through data from hundreds of observatories. That could take a long time—time we may not have," Elliot said.

"It could, except I already did some digging and found our signal," Liu said.

Jake and Elliot sat up. LiLo, too, was listening intently from her position, leaning against one of the workstations.

"CHIME, also captured it," Liu said.

"Makes sense—they've been a leader in finding and tracking the sources of FRBs since they started in 2018," Jake said.

"CHIME?" LiLo asked from the back of the room.

Jake started, "The Canadian Hydrogen . . . something or other."

"Intensity Mapping Experiment," Liu finished as she rolled her eyes at Jake.

"Do they know what they have?" Elliot said.

"When I reached out, they told me that they'd spotted it but are still investigating. It was such a hit they figured it was a calibration issue," Liu said. "Either way, it gave me a chance to really take a look at it and think about how we can track it further."

"It seemed Keating thought this signal wasn't the first of its kind," Elliot said.

"No, and I started to spin up a profile of it so we can use that to get started and search historical data for other instances," Liu said.

"Using frequency and dispersion measurement, I assume?" Jake said.

"Yup, we could add more parameters to narrow the field, but this should get us a quick glimpse of how often this signal has been around," Liu said.

"Does it seem odd no one else has figured this out or even stumbled on it?" Jake said.

"Well, they could think it's a technical issue like CHIME did," Liu said. "There's a lot of data out there."

"Or everyone is looking in the wrong place and has no idea this exists," Elliot said.

"Or someone is doing a really good job of covering things up," LiLo said. The comment caught everyone's attention.

"Sorry, that's our government paranoia expert," Jake said to Liu.

"So, what now?" Elliot said.

Liu adjusted her glasses. "Well, I'd like to further analyze the most recent signal we received—there might be more it can tell us."

"I can help with that and digging through historical data," Jake said.

LiLo pushed off the cubicle table she'd been leaning against. "I need to get out of here."

Elliot turned to her. "But we're making progress—"

"Just for a walk. Some fresh air."

"Oh," Elliot said with relief, "want company?"

LiLo looked confused.

Jake moved to a station to start working. "You say 'yes' because that's what humans do, weirdo."

"Sure," LiLo said.

"There are some great trails that will take you down to the telescopes and loop back," Liu said.

Elliot nodded. "Perfect."

                              #

The afternoon sun beat down on Elliot as he and LiLo walked one of the many trails on the observatory premises. The trail, just over a mile, led out to the 'Great Big Thing' telescope.

"Pretty wild, isn't it?" Elliot said as he eyed the large telescope in the distance.

"For a giant listening device spying on our galactic neighbors, sure," LiLo said.

Elliot couldn't tell if she was joking or not, but left it alone. They continued down the dirt path in silence for a few moments.

"You don't say much, do you?" Elliot said.

LiLo shook her head, then smirked.

"Funny," Elliot said. After a moment, he asked, "So who do you think those guys at MIT were?"

"People we don't want to get mixed up with," she said.

"Okay, you need to give me a bit more than that." Elliot glanced at her, waiting for a response. She ignored his comment. He shook his head and looked in the opposite direction.

"I think they're my former employers," LiLo said.

Elliot turned back to her, waiting for more.

"I was recruited, you could say, at a young age. By the time I turned eighteen I was a full-time employee in their cyber division," she said.

"Doing what?"

"Changing the world for the better, as they put it," she continued. "They're a powerful group embedded in every aspect of how this world works. They can move mountains if they wanted."

"Why are they after you?"

"I ran away. I stopped drinking their Kool-Aid, so to speak, and realized they shouldn't have that much power. No one should," she said.

Elliot listened as he glanced over at the first of eight telescopes visible on the trail. A forty-five-foot portable radio telescope sat, pointing at the sky, in an open field to their left. Flags along the way marked a scale model of the solar system. Saturn was next.

"I've spent most of my life running, hiding, and doing what I can to cause them headaches. When I came across the script, and then you two, I started to suspect they may have a hand in this."

"They're chasing this too, aren't they?"

LiLo nodded.

"Whatever this is, they'll want to know and control it."

"Guess that means we need to get there first," Elliot said.

"Easier said than done."

They stopped walking just before the marker for Neptune and gazed at the Great Big Thing telescope. The size was overwhelming even from a distance. A slight summer haze made it look like a painting. It sat peacefully among nature and stood out against the rolling green mountains in the backdrop. As if someone dropped it there.

"You think there's anything out there? Any little green men?" LiLo asked with a smirk as she looked to the sky.

"Anything other than space rocks, no. We're pretty lucky to be here. If there is any life out there, it's not intelligent," Elliot said.

"Isn't that what gets you excited about space? That possibility."

"Definitely, but there's so much we still have to learn about our own space backyard. The idea of anything else is—"

"Overwhelming?"

Elliot glanced at LiLo. "Yeah."

LiLo nodded her head in agreement. "The world wouldn't be able to handle it."

#

Elliot and LiLo walked back to the lab, hoping Jake and Liu had found something—anything. When they entered Liu was at a workstation with a screen full of data, Jake sitting next to her like a passenger in a car, both glued to the screen in front of them.

"Tell us you found something," Elliot said as he walked over to them. LiLo headed for a side table and took a seat, watching from a distance.

"Oh, we found something alright," Jake said as he leaned back in his swivel chair and spun to face Elliot.

"Oh yeah?" Elliot crossed his arms, at full attention.

"Yeah, well, it seems our signal has a pattern," Jake said.

Elliot looked on with anticipation.

"So first we analyzed the signal's signature. What it's made up of—the intensity, wavelength, and timing. Something, it seems, no one has had time to do without being chased," Jake said. "We also built a basic profile to match against historical data and help us pinpoint it over time."

Liu turned around in her chair. "We then pulled historical data from other observatories—Mauna Kea Observatory in Hawaii, Parkes

Telescope in Australia, VLT in Chile, and a few others—to fill the gaps that CHIME or GBO didn't capture."

"Then we did a needle and haystack search," Jake said.

Liu eyed Jake. "We just did a match search of our signal's signature over the last five years of data we pulled," Liu explained.

"Way to kill the drama," Jake said.

"And?" Elliot said.

"And we had a few matches—actually, many matches over the last five years," Liu said.

"So we can prove it's been around for awhile?" Elliot said.

"Oh yes, it's a full-fledged repeating signal," Jake said.

"Anything else?"

"Oh sure, yes, you want the scary news next?" Jake shared a look with Liu and took a deep breath. "So a few things. First, we found the signal has some type of sub-structure to it."

"Sub-structure?" LiLo asked, standing and moving closer to the group.

"Yeah, a sub-structure typically points at distinct peaks of noise with regularity, or something hidden within an FRB pulse. It's not seen often, but helps rule out sources," Jake said.

"And our signal's sub-structure?" Elliot said.

"Well, ours has something embedded in it, like code." Jake shook his head slightly like he couldn't believe what he'd said.

"Code?" LiLo repeated.

"Yup. Code that I have never seen and can't understand," Jake said. Silence filled the room.

"Cool, now for the scary part," Jake continued as he clapped his hands together. "Our signal, uh, to put it neatly, is, umm, somehow pinging specific IP addresses."

Elliot shook his head in disbelief. "What?"

"Do you have the IPs?" LiLo asked.

"Yup," Jake said.

"Show me a few." LiLo moved over to the workstation and glanced over Liu's shoulder as she pulled up a few they had connected to the signal.

"Holy shit."

"What is it?" Elliot asked.

"These are the same IPs where I found the scripts," LiLo said.

"You have them memorized?" Jake said.

"Yeah," LiLo said, like it wasn't a big deal.

"Remind me to invite you to trivia night," Jake muttered.

"So the signal is pinging various IPs dropping scripts onto whatever server is associated?" Elliot said.

"From what we can see here, yes," Jake said, "but the super scary part is that over the last five years it's been hitting, let's just say, more important IPs."

"Like?" Elliot said.

"Military installations, for starters, and government sites," Liu said.

"Five years is a long time," Elliot said.

"Yeah, and it could have been more than five years, when we first saw the correlation it was hitting observatories, weather services, libraries—"

"Libraries?" Elliot asked.

LiLo, still looking at the screen over Liu's shoulder, glanced back at Elliot. "Libraries have information. What better way to learn about your enemy?"

"No one would notice those hits or care, and the bigger hits would look like more noise getting blocked," Elliot said.

"Problem is, I don't think this is getting blocked," LiLo said as she turned back to Liu. "Mind showing me this sub-structure?"

Liu nodded and began typing on the keyboard.

"The scripts look for weak points. Might explain why whoever you're looking for is interested in this signal and the data Keating had," Elliot said to LiLo then to Jake, "this signal is supposed to look like an FRB, an anomaly."

"That's possible, and it's just hiding in space trying to pass as radio noise, and no one would think a satellite is hacked," Jake said.

Elliot's mind started moving faster than he could speak. Who was controlling this signal and where did it come from? It was too powerful for any one person or group to control.

"Who would have the tech and resources to pull something like this off?" Elliot leaned back on a table.

Jake adjusted his glasses and crossed his arms. "China, Russia . . ."

"North Korea? Iran?" Elliot added.

"Five years ago, probably not," Jake said.

"But we just named the top four—how about some rogue hacker group?" Elliot turned to LiLo.

"It's possible, since our friend over there could probably do it in her sleep with a few GPUs strung together," Jake said. "The operating systems on most sats are old, or aren't designed with security in mind because, well, money and why would anyone hack a satellite?"

"Us," LiLo said as she continued to view the screen with Liu.

The comment cut through the air and stopped the group in their tracks. A cold shiver rolled through the room. It was easy to point fingers from your own soil. A hard but realistic pill to swallow.

"I feel like you're hanging on to something else here," Elliot said looking at his friend.

"I know, I'm a terrible poker player," Jake said. "Your comment about this *looking* like an FRB is pretty accurate."

"What do you mean?"

"Well, we know it's an FRB and some portion of it matches our signal, but even with it repeating over the five years it seems to just . . . appear, then disappear in space."

"Not that strange for an FRB, right?"

"True, not totally weird and we're still learning about FRBs, but typically they can be traced to a region of space, then connected to a supernova explosion, a pulsar, or a magnetar in another galaxy. This one there's nothing."

Elliot held his friend's look; he'd never seen him stumped before.

"This code, it looks like it's rooted in Python, but I've never seen it before," LiLo said, finally pulling away from Liu's workstation.

"Aren't there hundreds of languages out there?" Jake said.

"Sure, but I feel I would've seen it if it's doing anything this complex. In theory."

"We need to figure out how far back this signal goes," Jake said. "There's more here to research."

"I think I need to get in touch with Blackwell and share this with him," Elliot said.

"We're going to DC, aren't we?" Jake said.

Elliot shared a look with Jake and LiLo. He was unsure if this was the right move. The pressure of the situation weighed on him. He'd take a chance trusting Blackwell, but what other play did he have? For a split second he thought what advice his father would have for him.

Elliot nodded to his friends. "Yeah, we are."

"If you head to DC, I have some friends that can help you," Liu said.

Chapter 31

NASA's headquarters was south of the National Mall by a few blocks, a low-rise building tucked in the corner of the two main interstates that passed through DC. The blackouts seemed to have stopped spreading, for the time being, at least. Elliot thought it strange that life continued to move along while a few hours away towns, homes, and communities were in the dark. No concern until it was a problem.

Thanks to Dr. Liu, Elliot and Jake were meeting with a team from NASA's Space Technology and Human Exploration departments. LiLo had decided to skip the meeting in order to "sight see" the FBI, as she put it. Elliot had a feeling that meant she was going to poke around the FBI's network, but he didn't want to know.

The outside of NASA headquarters looked like any ordinary office building, but the inside was a different story. Considering the situation Elliot felt he shouldn't be so excited, but it was hard to contain. The open lobby was full of NASA memorabilia; space suits from various space missions were displayed in glass cases, and small rovers and satellites hung from the ceiling.

Soon after giving their names at reception, they were greeted by an older man with a welcoming smile. He was casually dressed in a button-down shirt and khaki pants. His brown hair was salted with white; Elliot figured he was in his early fifties but could pass for younger.

"Elliot?" he said, extending a hand. "I'm Robert Watkins, the Director of Space Technology here at NASA."

Elliot shook his hand and introduced Jake.

Guiding them through the security checkpoint, Watkins said, "Our mutual friend, Dr. Liu, told me you two have some interesting things to share."

Jake and Elliot both nodded. "I think we do," Elliot said.

Watkins led them down a corridor to a set of elevators. Turning to Elliot, he said, "Your father was John Bishop, correct?"

Elliot, caught off guard, responded, "Yes, he was."

"I heard of his passing, my condolences. He and I knew each other from our university days. Stayed in touch here and there. The last we chatted he was tracking something in LEO but couldn't quite pinpoint it. I'd told him we should get together to discuss but, well, time had other plans."

"Well, whatever he was tracking might be why I'm here. At first I thought he'd turned into just a crazy old man in his basement, but it feels real now," Elliot said.

"Your father had some eccentric ideas, but nothing he couldn't convince you of," Watkins said.

Elliot smiled and nodded at the comment that rang true.

They exited the elevator on the top floor, then made their way to a sizable conference room, with a large projection monitor at one end and windows lining the outside wall to allow for plenty of natural light. A room built to impress guests. On the shorter wall, at the opposite end from the monitor, was a spread of snacks and drinks. As they entered, Jake snagged a water.

There was one person at the conference table in front of a laptop; he stood as they entered the room. He was on the shorter side, dressed casually with a button-down, short-sleeved shirt with little astronauts on it, a shirt one would wear on casual Friday. His receding hairline made his forehead look big, his hair pushed back like he was in an '80s action film. His round cheeks expanded with his smile.

"Gentlemen, make yourselves comfortable," Watkins said. "This is my colleague, Dr. Aiden Young, a lead engineer on our team."

Young met Elliot and Jake halfway and shook each of their hands. "Nice to meet you both. If you're friends of Dr. Liu's then you're friends of ours."

"Thank you," Elliot said.

The group settled at the table.

Watkins kicked things off. "So Dr. Liu mentioned you found something of interest relating to a fast radio burst the Green Bank Observatory captured? Can you walk us through it?"

Elliot readjusted his seat, took a sip of water, and thought for a moment about where to begin. "I apologize if I start to explain something, a concept, everyone in this room already knows—I just want to get all that we know out in front so we can discuss it."

Everyone nodded, so he continued. "A few weeks ago, a signal was picked up at Green Bank. At the time it looked like another FRB, except this one came in a cluster of bursts, stronger than usual but just as fast, and all with the same pattern."

Watkins and Young shifted in their seats and glanced at each other. Elliot noticed the change, unsure of what to think yet.

"Green Bank was shut down shortly after this, correct?" Young leaned back in his chair, flipping a pen between his fingers.

"Yes, and closed because what they found weren't FRBs," Elliot said.

Young's pen fidgeting stopped. He looked over at Watkins again. Watkins leaned forward, his elbows resting on the table, listening.

"Dr. Keating, the director from Green Bank and Dr. Liu's colleague, had captured the last large burst and recorded it, analyzed a portion of the data, and dropped the rest on an SD card. In addition, Jake and Dr. Liu have been digging through historical data from CHIME."

He nodded to Jake, who picked up the thread. "What we found within it is surprising. For one, the signal has the ability to pull and, it seems, potentially push massive amounts of data."

Elliot could sense Young and Watkins' disbelief. These two were leaders in this field, and here were Elliot and Jake telling them their physics was closer to home than expected.

Jake continued, "The signal also has a sub-structure that we can't quite figure out. Something Liu thought you might be able to help with."

"This all sounds . . . intriguing. And we can certainly help. You mentioned historical data. What did you find there?" Watkins asked.

Jake leaned back. "We matched the signal going back five years. We believe, based on Keating's data and theories, that it goes even further back. Liu mentioned you fellas might be able to help put some processing power behind that search."

"We can do that. Is there anything else?" Watkins said.

"Yeeaaah," Jake said.

Watkins, wide-eyed, looked at Elliot then at Jake, who straightened up again in his chair. "This signal is coming from a satellite."

"Uh, how is that possible?" Young said.

"We think a satellite was hacked with this signal and is spreading it to others," Elliot said.

Watkins and Young shared a look of disbelief.

"Think we need you to be more specific. You talking GPS . . . emergency distress array or . . ." Watkins said, aiming for the worst.

"Communications satellite but don't think any others are off the table," Elliot said.

"We think the answer to where this came from is in the historical data," Jake said.

"Okay. This is a lot to process," Young said.

"I don't think you meant it, but I see what you did there," Jake muttered, with a side glance to Elliot.

"But that's the only source, a satellite?" Watkins said.

"Yes, one my father was tracking," Elliot said. "He'd found and tracked this signal but hadn't gotten any further with his research before he passed away."

"This is what he reached out to me about . . ." Watkins said, his words weighted with sadness like he'd let someone down.

Elliot nodded.

"Now for the interesting part," Jake said.

"Jesus, there's more?" Young said, perking up.

"Remember when we said it looked like an FRB?"

The group nodded.

"Well, that's because we matched the signal's profile to what looks like an *actual* FRB. But here's the real fun part," Jake said with a smile that made him look like he was leaning into being a wild professor. "If this really *is* an FRB, we can't track it to a single patch of our known sky, or even another galaxy. We have no idea where it's coming from."

Watkins leaned back in his chair and let out a sigh. "This . . . this is—"

"Crazy," Young finished. "When do we start?"

Chapter 32

LiLo sat in a sterile, generic coffee shop not far from NASA HQ. She wasn't happy about it. The coffee sucked and all the suits made her nervous, but it had Wi-Fi and enough people around that she wouldn't be noticed as she worked. For a moment she missed the disconnected life at Green Bank. Here she was thrust back into a connected world she couldn't escape. There'd been no sign they were followed to or from Green Bank, but that didn't ease the tension that simmered inside her.

It'd been over ten years since she was last in the US. She'd spent those years bouncing from country to country on the run from the agency that had created her and seemed intent on finding her again. Thoughts of home—the last home she'd had with her family—spun in her mind. She was so close, but she knew it'd be impossible. There wasn't anything to return to anyways.

When they'd arrived in DC she'd separated from Elliot and Jake for her own purposes. Being at NASA was a level of exposure that'd be like playing with fire with her eyes closed. Plus, she thought it better that Elliot and Jake didn't know what she was up to. Her concentration would break every so often, wondering if she was making a mistake trusting them. They knew more than most people did about her. A break in the chain of trust she couldn't afford. Especially if what she was about to attempt didn't work. Information was her currency and she decided to use it to get information. That was the plan at least.

The risk of being here was high, but she needed to figure out what YellowJacket and her former employers were up to. Unfortunately, YellowJacket had been completely off the grid since the attacks. If Yellow-Jacket was an agent tracking her, he was a ghost now. Leaving her at a dead end, with no leads. She was still spinning on why her former agency would have an agent pull together these attacks. *A position play? But for what?* All signs were pointing toward them, at least that was obvious to her. She knew why they sent an agent after her, and they would keep sending them until she was dead or handcuffed in one of their interrogation rooms, or 'suites' as they called them. But what do they gain by causing a disruption on US soil?

She took a moment, moved the thought process to the background, and focused on the next task. Maybe she could figure out what Black-well and his team were up to with the signal. Why did they close down the observatory? And who was this mole within his team?

It didn't take her long to form a plan, but it involved Agent Blackwell himself. She'd done enough recon on him to know he was clean—at least on the surface. Convincing him to listen to anything she in particular had to say would be tough, if not impossible. She knew what she needed to do. She needed to reach out to Blackwell. Even though her face was plastered across their most-wanted list. *What could go wrong?*

Maybe blunt force was the way to go. She was running out of time. While the progression of the blackouts had slowed, power hadn't been restored and there were reports that gas pipelines had been shut down, slowing gas delivery to southern states. The longer they were locked out, the longer it'd take to get deliveries up to speed. Being without gas and draped in darkness started to make people nervous. The US government had blamed the failures on a cyberattack. No mention of who was responsible, but that didn't stop the talking heads on various news networks inferring it was a superpower that didn't like the US. *Pick one.*

Enough news. She glanced up over her laptop at the customers coming in and out. Two states away the world was in darkness, but no one here seemed to care. Not their problem.

She focused on the short line forming at the counter. Five customers: two women, three men. Third in line, a tall, athletic man waited with strict patience. He was the only one not on his phone. His tight crew cut made the angles of his face sharper. He had on business casual attire: tie, crisp button-down shirt with the sleeves rolled up neatly and evenly. *The Boy Scout.*

Chapter 33

Elliot wiped at his eyes. He'd been staring at a computer screen for hours without a break. By now, he and Jake had moved to another room at NASA HQ with Watkins and Young, a lab with cubicle-style workstations and an open conference space.

Jake and Aiden Young had spent hours drawing diagrams and politely disagreeing about how to refine matching the signal's signature to older datasets. Typically, this wouldn't be a difficult task, but since the signal was unique they wanted to make sure they didn't collect any noise or unwanted matches. After much back and forth they'd finally come to an agreement.

Having NASA resources made the process easier than Jake or Elliot reaching out to get data from observatories or poking at archived datasets. Based on their first pass, Jake noted Australia had picked up an increase in fast radio burst activity right around the same time as Green Bank did. The team reached out to the Commonwealth Scientific and Industrial Research Organization, also known as CSIRO, in Australia; NASDA in Japan; and the ESA, the European Space Agency. Given the time difference, some responses would take a while to arrive, but it was an easy first step. With some help from colleagues at CHIME in Canada, Jake and Young were able to start their search.

Elliot liked to think he understood it all, but this was a level of knowledge much deeper than he had. He'd spent most of his time reading about the blackouts, which still plagued at least a dozen states. By now some people were evacuating, heading west to states that still had power. There were concerns about a next big hit occurring in the Northeast, from DC to New York. If this was an attack, that would be the logical next step. The fear was spreading even to those areas not yet impacted.

"How's the world holding together?" Jake asked from across the conference table.

"Barely," Elliot said.

"Sounds about right."

"How's the search going?"

"Well, we have our top men on it," Jake said in a mock military voice. He added, "It'll take a bit to start pulling matches if there are any. We have data going back over fifty years, so only time will tell."

Elliot rolled his eyes. "Funny."

"Dr. Young over there is digging into the signal sub-structure we found."

Young stood at a whiteboard, focused.

"Dr. Young, have you found anything yet?" Jake said.

"Every time you interrupt me I gain the knowledge we need, so please, keep doing so," Young retorted.

Elliot and Jake shared a look.

Watkins walked back in the room with a tray of food. "Figured everyone would be hungry."

"If there's a genius in this room, it's you, sir," Jake said.

Watkins paused. "I am, actually."

Elliot, Jake, and Watkins grabbed seats and started divvying up the standard cafeteria food.

"I give up," Young said as he tossed a whiteboard marker on the table. "I don't understand it."

Jake waved him over. "Come, sit, eat an overcooked dehydrated burger with sad lettuce—it'll give you the power you need."

The group ate in silence for a moment, only the wrappers making noise.

"You hear from, uh, *Emma*?" Jake asked Elliot mid-bite.

Elliot shook his head, not wanting to discuss what she might be doing in front of the group.

"Power," Young said, seemingly out of nowhere.

Elliot glanced up to see Young's face covered in revelation.

"Some have it, most use it incorrectly. What about it?" Jake asked.

"Energy! How does this signal that is coming from a satellite match an FRB? The energy output doesn't make sense."

"Why does it need that much juice?" Jake said.

"You mentioned the script that it dropped on various servers had the ability to pull data. Do we know how much and how fast?" Young asked.

The group shared a look, not sure how to answer.

"We know it's a lot but not how fast," Jake said.

Watkins stepped over to his laptop while the group continued to eat. "We got a response from CHIME. They did the matching against the historical data we pulled together for FRBs."

"Jesus, man, the anticipation," Jake said.

"They have, uh, a few matches."

"A few?" Elliot said.

"By few I mean, right now, hundreds," Watkins said.

"How far back?" Young asked.

"They found matches going back as far as forty years so far," Watkins said with a smile plastered across his face.

Jake let out a whistle.

"Holy shit," Young said like his mouth couldn't contain the words.

"Keating was right," Elliot said. "It's been around a lot longer than we thought."

#

Elliot, Jake, Young, and Watkins sat spread out in the conference room, the table covered in notepads and crushed paper with forgotten ideas. Elliot leaned back in his chair, his head hanging back, staring up at the ceiling. Thoughts and exhaustion collided as he tossed the baseball he'd gotten from Keating in the air. Playing catch with gravity. Jake picked at his leftover french fries from hours before. Aiden Young hunched over his laptop while Watkins scribbled ideas and doodles on a notepad.

"So," Watkins started, "we don't know the data rate, but we can surmise a little based on the power output of the signal and the distance from the source. What's the current fastest data transfer we know of?"

"Connected cloud server infrastructure, probably thirty-five terabits per second, give or take. The world record for fastest known data transfer is 178 terabits per second. Done by researchers at UCL in London. Of course that'll change by tomorrow," Young said, barely looking up from this laptop.

"And," he added, "that record was set with optical communication, which converts an electrical signal to light and passes it down an optic fiber into a converter that flips it back to an electrical signal."

"Optic fiber is still a physical, albeit transparent, material," Watkins said.

"Even our TBIRD system is capped at around two hundred gigabits per second," Young said.

"TBIRD?" Elliot asked.

"Terabyte Infrared Delivery system. It's a direct-to-Earth optical communications link we launched recently with Space Force that can transmit data from LEO to a ground station on Earth."

"So, given the power this signal generates, and no physical restraints, this signal, theoretically, blows this TBIRD out of the sky and any known data transfers we can perform on Earth. In terms of data it can transfer in fractions of a second, and completely via a wavelength. Today we can do six gigabytes per second over radio waves," Jake said as he tossed a sad french fry back on his plate.

Young leaned toward Jake and whispered, "I see what you did there with our TBIRD—not sure I like it."

Jake shrugged. "Maybe don't name your toys after things that can be shot out of the sky."

"It's possible it could do more," Elliot said, leaning forward in his chair.

The group paused on his comment.

He continued, "This signal is on other satellites—"

"It's networking. It's crowdsourcing power from other devices, but it's also connected to them and what data they send," Jake said.

"Satellite data, Wi-Fi, cellular, radio. Any bandwidth of frequencies it can jump on," Elliot said.

"If it can ride any frequency, in theory it could read or pick up any data passed on that frequency," Young said as he started flipping a pen between his fingers.

"Theoretically speaking, of course," Jake said.

Watkins stood up and walked to the window. "The implications of this technology . . ."

Elliot joined him, gazing out over DC. "People would kill for this."

Chapter 34

LiLo tracked the Boy Scout, Blackwell, only as far as his office. Predictable. Tailing the lions in the den was not what she had in mind, but she'd wanted to get a closer look. Her plan to flush out the mole in his team would involve reaching out to him, and she'd just wanted to see him first—get a gut check.

Once she'd stopped tailing Blackwell, she found herself in a quiet library about a ten-minute walk south from NASA HQ. At a small table tucked in a corner on the first floor, close to a rear exit, she pulled up Blackwell's team records. Cycling through them, skimming through for any threads she could pull on. *Who's hiding something?*

She focused on Evans and Hansen. These two she couldn't shake. Evans was pretty much a kid, even if LiLo was on the older end of the same decade as him. She had everything she needed about each of them, but no motivation. Blackwell and Hansen were in Seattle when Keating was murdered. Elliot mentioned one of Blackwell's guys was following him. Hansen would've been the one. It didn't make him a killer or a mole. *MICE: Money, Ideology, Coercion, Extortion. Primary reasons for any act of treason.* Or any act when it came down to it. Another lesson learned in her time with the agency.

Follow the money. Always a good start. She had enough personal information about Evans and Hansen to gain access to their financial statements. Most people will change their tune about anything if the amount is right.

Nothing stood out in Hansen's accounts. No large sum deposits, nothing out of the ordinary. No new cars, boats, or houses. She jumped to Evans's. The first account, again, nothing. But he had a crypto account, one that she'd found later, and that's where she spotted what she needed. A capped-sum deposit from a peer-to-peer payment app. She kept scrolling, spotting recurring, daily transactions that capped the payment app limit. It continued for the last six months, hundreds of thousands of dollars. *Bingo. Where is this money coming from?* In her experience, money was usually the root cause for any choice against one's own country. If the signal was as powerful as her and the boys thought it was, who wouldn't want access to it?

She focused her monitoring on Evans's communications and habits. She could pull his GPS trail for the last week to see where he was going and was already in his FBI-appointed phone. He most likely had another for communicating with whoever was making these large payments. But, more importantly, she needed to get this to Blackwell. She spun up an account on the messaging app Blackwell's team was using, an internal FBI messaging service that connected agents by team. She used her name of choice, Emma Smith, and pinged Blackwell directly. *This should be interesting.*

ESMITH: *Agent Blackwell?*
ABLACKWELL: *Yes?*
ESMITH: *I have reason to believe you have a mole on your team.*
ABLACKWELL: *Who is this?*
ESMITH: *I have information that could point to Agent Evans as a mole.*
ABLACKWELL: *Can you give me this information in person?*

ESMITH: *Check his financial records over the past two years. His crypto account and his personal communications. You'll spot dead-drop tracks.*

ABLACKWELL: *And what department are you from?*

ESMITH: *I also believe Elliot Bishop's life is in danger. You ever figure out who killed Keating?*

ABLACKWELL: *How do you know about Elliot Bishop?*

ESMITH: ...

LiLo waited a moment then disconnected. She could only hope Blackwell would look into what she gave him. But, if she guessed correctly, he was already alerting security breach teams and figuring out who ESMITH was. He wouldn't find anything.

Chapter 35

Evening arrived, leaving the building in silence. The night-shift security guards clocked in and a cleaning crew began their daily routine throughout the building.

Elliot stretched out on a small sofa, attempting to get some rest. Young and Watkins sat at the table, heads resting on their fists.

"Want to hear my theory?" Jake said as he crunched on a fresh bag of chips he'd gotten from a vending machine. He paused between crunches, seemingly still working through his own thoughts, or at least organizing them for presentation. The group didn't budge.

"It's a learning computer," he said and crunched into another chip.

Elliot rolled his eyes and pulled his hoodie over his head.

Young said as he shifted in his chair. "Yeah, yeah, with a neural-net processor . . ."

"I'm serious. How is it on multiple satellites and potentially riding digital wavelengths full of data? Yet it has the same structure in every instance? It's like an amoeba, absorbing what it needs to move on."

Jake wiped crumbs from his hands. "Stay with me on this. Maybe we're overthinking it. Over-engineering it. If this signal has been around for forty or fifty years, tech was limited back then. Maybe it hung out, pinged what it could within range, and as our satellite network grew, it grew. We still don't know what this embedded code is doing or how it works. And we've got what, about four thousand plus pieces of hardware active and inactive in the orbit now? What a great breeding ground."

Restless, Elliot turned on his back on the sofa and started tossing the baseball in the air again. Up and down. Up and down.

"That's a fun theory but pushing it, even for the tech we have today," Watkins said.

"Given everything we've seen so far, the possibilities are endless," Jake said.

Elliot caught the ball and sat up at Jake's comment, then stood as his words shook something loose in his head. He moved to his backpack, which was sitting on the table, and rifled through it.

"Hey, we're finally getting some responses from other observatories," Young chimed in.

"What are they saying?" Watkins said.

"A team in Australia and Japan picked out the FRB with the same signature as ours and the signal."

"Anything else?" Watkins said.

"Australia says the FRB they see just appears but leaves nothing to trace. Very strange."

"So nothing new," Watkins said.

"Well, get this, Australia also said they can connect the same signature to a couple satellites," Young said.

Watkins shook his head.

Elliot stood at the table with an excited energy, a second wind. After a few moments of digging through his bag, he'd finally located his father's star map and one of his notebooks.

"I have an idea." He spread the map out on an open table. He dropped the notebook next to the map and began scanning through pages. "My father was tracking an AeroTech satellite, or many of them, before he passed away. At least one with the signal on it."

The rest of the group closed in on him, getting a glimpse of what he was working through. He tapped the map and stepped away. "These other coordinates aren't satellites, they're where the FRB is located. He was mapping the FRB to the satellites."

"Sooo what does that mean?" Young said.

"I'm . . . not sure." Elliot squeezed the baseball in his hand. "Wait, we know this signal is on other satellites, the team in Australia just confirmed that—"

"And now that we know what the signal signature is," Watkins said, picking up on Elliot's excitement, "we can map its activity to any active satellites, which will help us identify exactly which ones it's coming from."

"That might help us figure out how it works," Young said.

"Let's reach out to key space agencies and observatories, get as many eyes as possible on this," Watkins said to Young.

Jake clapped his hands together, drawing the eyes of everyone in the room. "I love it when a plan comes together!"

#

Midnight showed up like an uninvited guest. Yet a renewed energy filled the room. The table was a mess, with scattered pages of notes covered in ideas, thoughts, and half-baked diagrams. Elliot paced back and forth, Keating's baseball in hand. Watkins was on video calls with various agencies, walking through their notes. Young sat at his laptop.

"How we looking?" Jake asked.

"We've heard back from a majority of teams across the globe. We're still waiting on the EU space agency, but that'll fill the gaps and map a good percentage of the active satellites in the sky with our signal," Young said.

Jake nodded and turned back to his laptop, propped up on his lap as his feet took rest on the edge of the table. "What's on the brain, Elliot?"

Elliot continued to pace as he traced his fingers along the seams of the baseball, his mind drifting.

"Talk to me, Goose. Your pace is inhuman."

"So we find out what satellites the signal is on, but what then?"

"We'll confirm it's spreading and have a better idea of how far, which might give us a clue as to how it works," Jake said.

Elliot, still pacing, tossed the ball in the air and watched it gently spin as it dropped back into his hand.

"How did it get there?" he whispered to himself.

Suddenly, Jake pulled his feet off the table and focused on his screen. "Uh, so looks like someone is claiming responsibility for the power grid attacks. It was ransomware, and they're asking for a ton of money," Jake said.

Young perked up. "Jesus, who?"

"Some hacker group with a funny name they got from a name generator probably. *Honey* something or other. They even sent a message—'A line has been crossed, no more surveillance.' Ethically, I don't disagree with them, but morally, sending civilians into the dark ages ain't cool," Jake said.

"The future of warfare on display," Young said.

Jake nodded. "Got that right."

"Jake, I think I have an idea," Elliot said breaking the moment.

Jake looked over as Elliot tossed the baseball in the air to him. The ball landed in Jake's hand with a smack.

"Why does your old man keep the Winnie around?"

"Partly because my mother hates it, but also because it's simple. He can fix it himself. He knows every bolt in that damn thing."

"It's simple. Easy to hack."

"Hmmm, I'd like to think I know where you're going with this," Jake said.

"We need to see this signal in action, how it interacts with satellites, to learn what it is," Elliot said.

Jake looked at the baseball then tossed it back to Elliot.

"What if we had an old, easy-to-hack satellite to play with?"

Elliot smiled, then glanced at Young, whose attention had been pulled into their conversation.

"We could reactivate an older satellite to see if the same signature is present. If it's not, we could use it as a dummy to see if the signal pings it," Young said.

"How long would that take?" Elliot said.

"Active satellite identification with signal on board, probably a couple hours. If we get our friends on the other side of the world involved we could do it much quicker and do a wider analysis," Young said.

"How about actually activating an older satellite?"

"Depends on how old, but I can pull a list fairly quickly," Young said.

The three looked at each other, then at Watkins as he entered the room. "What? What now?"

Young and Watkins pulled a list of inactive potential test satellites. Earth's orbit was becoming a floating landfill of space debris from dead satellites. When a satellite went quiet or inactive, it was supposed to be dragged down into the atmosphere to burn up, but that practice wasn't always followed. The increase in debris increased the risk of collisions and orbital traffic jams. Both the debris and the influx of new equipment created noise, wreaking havoc for listening stations and amateur astronomers.

"We have a pretty good list to work from," Watkins said as he shared what they had on a projected screen.

"Looks like we *could* flip on an old military satellite that dates back as far as the early '70s. Anything earlier is dead dead," Young said after glancing at the list.

"Could we do that from here?" Elliot said.

Young shared a look with Watkins, checking that the director was still in the foxhole with the group.

"Not exactly. We'll need to run it by some folks in the Air Force as they own that, umm, space. From a military perspective," Young said as he retreated a bit after his pun.

"In other news, active signal satellite mapping is mostly done," Jake said. He was off in his own world, leaning back in his chair, legs crossed up on the table like he was home but with better resources.

"And . . . uh . . . this *thing* is everywhere," he said.

"Everywhere?" Watkins repeated.

"Not just AeroTech sats?" Elliot said.

"Nope. If there's approximately four thousand satellites in the air, it's connected to at least twenty-five percent of those that are active. That's just from our data," Jake said.

The room shared a look.

"Australia and Japan are still doing analysis on their side. We can assume that number will jump to fifty with their data," Young said.

"That's quite the blanket," Watkins said under his breath.

"A scratchy one at that," Jake said to no one in particular.

"This all still doesn't answer the question of how it got there," Elliot said. "Maybe we could check for anomalies that would've impacted these satellites—anything in the sky, any type of electromagnetic wave or electrical burst when they were launched. If we can detect a similar signature coming from Earth that interacts with these satellites, then we should be able to pinpoint where it came from. My theory is this signal gets loaded the same way it spreads."

"If they were just hacked that would raise alarms, but using its own technology to load itself is, well, genius. Its own work hidden by a trail we simply see as another blip. Masked as an anomaly because that's all we know how to chalk it up as," Jake said.

"We should loop in other agencies on this," Young said.

"We'll need to coordinate with the Air Force if we plan to turn on one of their old birds anyways," Watkins said. "I can pull in General Conrad and others. We run through this with his team and go from there."

Jake glanced at Elliot with a smile. "Well, shit, there's hope for you yet, Bishop."

Chapter 36

Elliot and Jake had gotten a few hours of sleep before heading back to NASA HQ the next morning. Elliot checked if LiLo was around, but she was nowhere to be found. He wasn't sure how much that concerned him. She'd helped them get this far. There was no obligation for either of them.

When Elliot and Jake arrived at NASA HQ, they got through security with the passes Watkins had arranged for them before they left. The conference room where they'd spent most of the previous day had a few new faces today. Young and Watkins were seated at the front of the large table, across from what looked like a NASA team. Looking further down the table, Elliot was startled to see Agent Blackwell. A woman he didn't recognize was sitting next to him.

Elliot tensed as he and Jake took their seats. He didn't realize Blackwell would be involved, but guessed they got wind when the general was notified.

Blackwell nodded to him. "Mr. Bishop, last time we spoke you ended our chat early."

"Had other things come up," Elliot said.

"It happens," Blackwell said simply.

Elliot wasn't sure what to think of Blackwell. *Did he order Keating's death? It didn't make sense. And what if LiLo was right about a mole in Blackwell's team?*

Everyone was still getting settled when the door opened and an entourage of Air Force personnel entered, led by General Conrad, who had the kind of intimidating presence that could scare even the hardest of people. He had a narrow bald head, with sharp features that could cut through any defense. He was tall enough that, even seated, he was slightly above everyone else. Elliot guessed, given his rank, he must be in his late fifties, but he was in better shape than anyone else in the room.

Jake seemed to not want to be the focus of the table, somehow making himself seem hidden in plain sight. The group was working on little to no sleep, each of their faces showed it.

Watkins started the conversation. "Thank you, everyone, for joining. General Conrad, in particular, thanks for taking the time."

"Let's hope not too much time. We have a lot to do in the coming days," Conrad said, reminding everyone how important his time was.

"Of course," Watkins said, then continued, "we have new information regarding the signal that we believe is important for any op being planned based on the recent attacks. Along with new theories we're working through with other agencies in the EU, Australia, and Japan."

"We've already pulled in other agencies?" Blackwell said. His question made the decision sound like a bad one.

"Yes, we wanted to confirm signal spread and get more eyes on this. Given the situation and that the signal is not contained, understanding what other agencies know or don't know could help us piece this all together. Right now, with their help we've mapped approximately fifty percent of the satellites in orbit that have the signal associated with it. Without their help we wouldn't have gotten here. What we want to avoid is making an assumption of what the puzzle looks like with only one piece," Watkins said.

"Fifty percent? You're saying that signal is coming from over half of the satellites in space?" Conrad looked around the room in surprise.

"Yes, sir. From what we can tell, the signal could be on any active satellite. We're still mapping this with the help of the other agencies, so we're expecting the number to increase significantly," Watkins said.

"The team also discovered this signal has been around a lot longer than we'd first thought," Watkins said, then looked to Young to continue.

Young stirred in his seat like a nervous kid about to give a presentation. Today he'd opted for a more subtle button-down shirt, in a solid color with no floating astronauts.

"How long?" Conrad said before Young could utter a word.

"We can map it back at least forty years, but we suspect it goes further back," Young said. "Any satellite past that point we don't have communication with or is dead. But we think it could go as far back as Vanguard 1."

"You're kidding me?" Conrad said, his face washed over with a *what the hell are you telling me* look.

"No joke here, uh, sir," Young responded, deadpan.

"So what are we getting at here?" Conrad asked.

There was a silent pause across the room, then Elliot said, "Are we planning a retaliation for this attack?"

The room was silent again. Conrad focused on Elliot with eyes that could burn through him, like he was part of the set dressing. "And who are you?" Conrad asked, as polite as he would get today.

"This is Elliot Bishop, sir," Watkins answered. "He and Jakob Fischer are the ones who discovered the signal."

"Well, Mr. Bishop, I applaud your direct nature, but that's classified. But, since we're all being direct, I can assure you the US government won't take this lying down. Whether this a well-organized state-backed group or not. US soil has been penetrated by enemies. No doubt we'll coordinate an effort to neutralize the threat." Conrad let his comment hang for a moment in the silence. "You wouldn't be a very good boxer, Mr. Bishop."

That's fair, I wouldn't, Elliot silently agreed.

The general shifted forward with his hands on the table, panning around the table making eye contact with each person. "Look, folks, this is good intel, but let's have Blackwell's team vet it first. We're keeping tabs on satellite activity, and I can't speak for other agencies involved yet, but I don't see us letting this recent attack on our infrastructure, or satellite operations, go unchecked."

"General, if we retaliate it will kick off a chain reaction. Are you ready for World War III to start on your watch?" Elliot said. The question pulled the air out of the room. The general was silent. *Of course he was ready for World War III,* Elliot thought, *it's what he was built for.*

"There is nothing here that states this signal isn't from a hacker group or another superpower," Blackwell said, breaking the silence.

"And there isn't data saying it is," Watkins responded.

"That's the problem," Elliot said. "Right now, everyone is using the signal as a means to justify their own goals, when in fact no one knows what it is. Yes, we were attacked but that was an assumption out of fear. I'm getting more and more skeptical that the signal is related to the attacks. I think this is a well-timed advantage someone is taking. We shouldn't make the same decision. We have the power to stop this now and we should."

"Right now, we have half a country in the dark, and panic running rampant. Other organizations and parts of this government are making plans based on what we know." Elliot could see the General linger on his own thoughts. "Folks, you realize at some point I'll have to inform the Joint Chiefs, who will inform the president. So, who here wants to visit the oval office with your career at stake?" The room held silent. "Thought so. Don't make me regret this, but I'll bite. What are your next steps? What do you need to prove we shouldn't retaliate for an attack on our soil?" The General asked, his tone unwavering.

Elliot knew he was asking for facts, not theories. "We need to understand how the signal got on to a satellite to begin with," Elliot said.

"And how do you propose we do that?" Blackwell asked.

"We want to turn on an old military satellite and see if it connects."

"That could take time we don't have. If the infrastructure attacks are going to stop, we need to make a statement sooner rather than later," Blackwell said.

Surprisingly, Blackwell's reaction seemed to make the general more open to considering their request. "You fellas have one in mind?" The general asked.

"Sir, you're not actually believing this, are you?" Blackwell asked.

The general glared at him. "I'm not believing anything yet. But this seems to be a rapidly evolving situation. I want all the facts before we go ahead with any operation, or before this moves up the chain, and it seems there are still more to be found."

He turned his focus from Blackwell to the rest of the table. "I can give you a little more time and a bird to flip on, but the moment this doesn't work, we go ahead with our plan A and bring in the cavalry. Blackwell, let's coordinate with key intel agencies, CISA, and inform the Chief of Staff."

"That's all we can ask for, General," Elliot said.

Chapter 37

A sliver of early afternoon sunlight pierced through the closed blackout curtains of LiLo's hotel room. She'd been up most of the night attempting to track Agent Evans and find out what she could about the infrastructure attacks, which seemed to have stopped spreading. Nothing new came to light. The situation was troubling and getting further out of control.

LiLo opened the curtains and let the room fill with sunlight. Her mind swirled, unsure what to make of her brief interaction with Blackwell. She hoped he'd look into Evans. Blackwell was by the book enough he couldn't look the other way with such information. She lit the path for him to walk, he just needed to take the first step.

She moved to the bathroom and splashed water on her face to wake up. Looking back at herself in the mirror, one thought hung in her mind—Elliot was in trouble. The men who showed up at MIT weren't FBI, and if this signal is what it seems, they all were in deeper than they should be. She had focused her monitoring on Evans, but needed to get closer. Access to his personal phone was the key, but it would take more time than she felt she had. A hunch is what she was working with. She didn't like it. She packed up her things and sent Elliot a text but there was no response.

She waited. Her instincts told her to run. She couldn't. She needed to find Elliot and at least make sure he was okay. Then she could run, again. The idea of clearing her name, a stretch to begin with, was slipping from thought.

She knocked on Elliot's hotel room door. No answer. She waited a few minutes and knocked again. No response. She went to Jake's room and knocked on his door. She could hear him yell, "Coming" and a second later the door opened.

"Oh, it's you," he said.

"Where's Elliot?"

Jake wiped his tired face; he looked like he'd just woken up.

"He went for a walk on the National Mall."

"A walk? What's he thinking? Those guys back at MIT aren't going to just give up," she said.

"It's a busy area—what could happen?"

LiLo shook her head, agitated. "What happened at NASA?"

"Classified," Jake said.

If her eyes could burn through him they would.

"Fine. They helped us analyze the data—it's wild shit. We presented it to an Air Force General, and his team is informing the *cavalry*, as he put it. He wanted more details so we broke for the day."

LiLo stared off for a brief moment in thought.

"What's up?" Jake asked.

"He's not responding to my texts."

Jake shrugged. "I can try him."

"If you hear from him tell him to head to the hotel or the nearest police station. Did he say he was going anywhere in particular?"

"Yeah, he mentioned the Capitol Building. Hey, is everything okay?"

"I don't think so," she said as she turned and headed down the hallway.

"I'll come."

"No. Stay here. If he comes back, get in touch with Agent Blackwell. And only him."

Jake's eyes were wide now but he nodded. "Okay."

LiLo left the hotel and headed toward the National Mall. It would be like finding a needle in a haystack. But if he was heading toward the Capitol she might be able to cut him off. It was a shot in the dark. A thought crossed her mind—she took out her phone and opened a GPS tracking app, the same she'd installed on Elliot's phone. Nothing. She could only hope he'd turn it on even for a moment. If it connected she'd be able to narrow down where he was.

She didn't like how much she was starting to give a shit about these two, but, in a way, she felt responsible. Guilt burned a hole in her, an emotion considered a weakness to the people who made her. The same who buried her. The same who kept her running. More and more of this was starting to feel like her past running up behind her.

Chapter 38

When they'd finally decided to break at NASA HQ, Jake headed back to the hotel to take a much-needed nap, and Elliot had decided to split off to clear his head. They walked together as far as the edge of the National Mall, then Elliot turned down Independence Ave, which put him right by the Smithsonian and the Hirshhorn museums. The weather was nice—a sunny, warm summer day without the humidity that often swamped the city. Tourists flooded the park area, as well as families or government workers having lunch in the park, enjoying the day. Elliot kept walking and headed toward the Capitol.

On his way, he stopped outside the Air and Space Museum, watching the tourists take photos. Elliot scanned the crowd of people, doing his best to track faces. His eyes scanned across the horizon of people's heads; as more and more faces passed by, they became a blur of motion. But across the way from Elliot, a face stood out. Not moving, just staring back at Elliot.

Elliot's stomach sank as he made eye contact. The man had a shaved head, black jeans, and T-shirt. He was bulky and older. Elliot recognized him—he was one of the guys raiding Jake's lab back in Boston. The man glanced to his left and nodded to another man, who had a tight buzzed haircut, a military look, and sunglasses.

Elliot forced himself to turn his back on them and tried to stay cool as he headed toward the Capitol. Staying in a busy public area was his best move. *Then again, it didn't work for Keating.* He didn't want them knowing he'd spotted them. He fumbled in his pocket for his phone, pulled it out and checked the lock screen. Messages from LiLo and Jake.

As he continued to walk, he called LiLo. "Come on. Pick up," Elliot said under his breath as his pace picked up, even though he had nowhere to go.

No answer. He ended the call and continued walking. He did a quick check over his shoulder and stopped on the sidewalk, turned and scanned groups of people. Checking faces in the crowd to see if he could spot the two men. Sure enough, one was strolling up Elliot's side of the street. The other was parallel on the other side. They were closing the gap. Elliot snapped a picture of each of them, put his phone away, and started back toward the Capitol Building, which was about a half mile away. But what would he do once he got there? He could try and lose them in the crowds, but the space was too open. With two of them it was much more difficult.

Suddenly, his phone started vibrating. He scrambled to answer. "LiLo?"

"Elliot!" she answered.

"I think I'm being followed," he said.

"Where are you?"

"I'm on the National Mall, just past the Smithsonian, heading to the Capitol."

"Stay on that path, and in the open. I'll meet you around the reflecting pool."

"Okay," Elliot said as they both disconnected.

Elliot looked back. The goon with the shaved head and T-shirt had closed the gap between them. Elliot picked up his speed, a panicked walk at this point. All three men maintained pace through the park, each aware of the other.

Elliot came up alongside the reflecting pool that stretched in front of the Capitol, where the Ulysses S. Grant memorial came to a point. He checked over his shoulder; the tall lanky one wearing sunglasses had slowed and dropped back. Widening his position, creating a triangle between the three of them. Elliot's heart raced. His breath was tight.

The shaved-head goon closest to Elliot spoke first.

"Elliot, we're friends of Agent Evans of the FBI. Come with us and we'll figure this all out." He ran his hand over his shaved head, as he closed the remaining distance between himself and Elliot. His lanky teammate swung out wide to the edge of the reflecting pool, his head turning between his partner and Elliot. Tracking which move to make next. His sunglasses hiding his intention.

"It's okay, just come with us," the man repeated, his hands out as if to calm the situation.

Elliot was skittish like a deer in the woods, his eyes bouncing between them. He looked around—the crowds had migrated away, fewer people stood in the vicinity. Elliot realized the second lanky man was closing the distance like they were herding a lost cow.

"I think I'm good. I'll catch up with Evans later," Elliot said, knowing it didn't change the situation.

Elliot was now standing in front of the Grant monument. The shaved-head goon glanced around, casing options. Even with the thin crowds, they wouldn't do anything here. Elliot hoped.

"We just need that SD card you have," the taller man finally said.

Elliot paused on the comment. "Bad enough to kill for it?"

The man shrugged off the comment and moved closer. Elliot's options were dwindling as each moment passed. He could turn and run, find a busier area, to a museum. *I could make it.*

Suddenly, the lanky man dropped to his knees.

"Elliot! Run!" LiLo yelled.

The shaved-head man looked over to see his partner was downed, and Elliot took the opportunity to sprint away back to the main park area of the National Mall, LiLo catching up to him as he ran.

Chapter 39

After the meeting at NASA, Blackwell and Agent Klein returned to the FBI headquarters to start coordinating with other agencies and teams. Much to Blackwell's dismay. Red tape was in their future. They strode through the lobby, passing through security, as they came up with a plan. Blackwell rattled off contacts at various agencies who'd help move the process along.

"I'll start pulling these together," Agent Klein said as they reached a row of elevators.

Blackwell hit the elevator call button, a thought lingering on his mind. "We ever find anything on the Keating death?"

Klein shook her head. "No. It went to a local team in Seattle. Haven't heard anything since."

"Add it to the list," Blackwell muttered as he slapped the call button again.

"Everything okay?"

"My gut is saying no."

The elevator arrived. As they entered, Blackwell turned to Klein. "You hear from Evans today?"

"He mentioned working from the field office earlier, but that was it."

Blackwell gently shook his head as he watched the floor numbers tick by.

Klein turned to him. "Okay, what's going on?"

Blackwell glanced at her with a raised eyebrow.

"We've been on a team long enough, and friends long enough, that I know when you're stewing about something," she said.

Blackwell let out a light sigh. He wanted—needed—more details about Evans before pulling in other team members, but he'd reached a tipping point and some backup was better than none. "Whatever we do from this point on, Evans stays out of communication. For now."

"Okay," Klein dragged out. "The anticipation is killing me."

Blackwell eyed her. "There's been a breach to our internal system. I was contacted directly from someone on the outside. They passed along some concerning details about Evans and mentioned Elliot Bishop." Blackwell paused before going any further. The breach and the info about Evans had him on edge. *A mole? On my team?* He couldn't shake the mysterious message. He knew he could trust Klein. More importantly, he needed to.

"Jesus. Any thoughts on who messaged you?" Klein asked.

Blackwell shook his head. "No, but I think Elliot might. I need to find him."

The elevator opened and they headed for Blackwell's office.

"Who else knows about this?" Klein asked with a lowered voice.

"No one yet. And let's keep it that way. I need you to do some digging on Evans. Financial records. Since he joined and anything before if possible."

They reached Blackwell's office. Klein closed the door behind her.

"What about the breach?" Klein asked.

"I'm going to wait." Blackwell sat behind his desk, gripping the arms of his chair. He didn't need to bring in other agents or departments just to have them tell him ESMITH wasn't real or an agent. And if the mysterious guest had planned something malicious it would've happened already. No reason to fire a flare at someone then take a shot at them.

Klein tilted her head. "*Wait?* That's not like you."

"Yeah, well, nothing about this is like me. I can't be locked down in a room explaining what happened for the next twenty-four hours. Something isn't right."

Blackwell popped a piece of gum in his mouth. "Find what you can about Evans. I'll find Elliot and we'll go from there. Then we'll bring in who we need. I want facts before we raise an alarm on another agent, especially from our team."

"And Hansen?" Klein asked.

"I'll talk to him."

Klein nodded and headed out.

Blackwell went about trying to contact Elliot. He knew where he was staying but he wouldn't be able to get guest details from the hotel. He reached out to Director Watkins at NASA, who had Jake's number. A burner number, which surprised Blackwell. *What are these boys hiding from?* He dialed Jake's number.

"Hello?" Jake answered.

Blackwell could hear Jake's rushed answer like he'd run to the phone in anticipation. "Jake. This is Agent Aaron Blackwell."

"Is Elliot okay?"

"That's what I'm checking on. Have you heard from him?"

"No, but a friend of ours said he might be in trouble. She went looking for him, said that if anything weird happened or if Elliot showed up to call you, in fact."

Blackwell paused. *She?*

"Wait, a friend of yours told you this?"

"Well, I shouldn't say a friend—we just met her a few days ago in Boston."

"What's her name?"

"Emma."

The connection landed like a punch on Blackwell. *ESMITH.* "Do you know where they headed?"

"Yeah, the Capitol."

"Can you give me Elliot's number and Emma's?"

"Don't know Emma's, but Elliot's sure," Jake said and rattled off Elliot's burner number from memory.

"Stay at the hotel. I'm going to send a couple agents over. Agents Porter and Scott. If anyone knocks, ask for ID and their last names. Okay?"

"Yeah, sure. I'm not leaving this room," Jake said.

Blackwell was already standing and walking out the door as they disconnected. In a hurry, he called the agents and sent them to the hotel, then contacted Agent Hansen to meet him out front.

#

Blackwell brought Hansen up to speed on the situation as they drove toward the Capitol Building. Keating, the breach, the anonymous tip, and more importantly, Evans.

"I never liked that kid anyways. Too smug," Hansen said.

"You know, you could've told me earlier," Blackwell said, eyeing his gruff team member as they weaved through light traffic.

"Figured you knew what you were doing. Maybe I should be running things."

Blackwell smirked. "That'd be the day." He did his best to brush off the thought for later, but deep down it was his fault Evans slipped through. It ate at him to think he'd made a mistake. He dialed Elliot's number and put it on speaker.

After a short ring Elliot answered.

"Hello?"

"Elliot. This is Agent Blackwell. Where are you?"

"I'm heading into the National Gallery of Art, East building," Elliot said, his voice strained and breathless like he'd run a quick mile. "I was chased by some guys, said Evans wanted to speak with me."

Blackwell set his jaw. "Elliot, listen to me. Hold tight in the lobby area. I'll be right there."

Meanwhile, Hansen called in for backup as they cruised down Pennsylvania Avenue. The museum was within view. Blackwell's phone rang. Caller ID showed Agent Klein.

"Klein, what's up?" Blackwell said.

"Got some details from the Seattle team about Keating. They were able to pull camera footage in the area at the time of death. I'm sending you a photo and profile of their only lead. Long story short, whoever killed Keating was also dead."

"What?" Blackwell said as he and Hansen exchanged looks.

"Kaleb Lind. Ex-military. Died in a car accident a few years ago, according to his records. Before his death he was spotted with an Anton Yates, photo and profile included. Also ex-military, has been pretty quiet lately. Last known location for Yates was Belgium."

"Jesus, okay—thanks, Klein. Send those photos to DC Police and Agent Hansen," Blackwell said.

"No problem," Klein said, then continued, "there's more. I did some digging on Evans—looks like he's got a very lucrative side hustle that's hard to track. We can talk more when you're back."

Blackwell and Hansen shared a look. Hansen shrugged then said under his breath, "Told you I didn't like him."

"Thanks, Klein," Blackwell said as he disconnected the call.

Hansen pulled up the photos Klein sent on his phone, rattled off the details he could.

"Lind. Approximately five foot ten. Bulky fella. Shaved head down to gray stubble. Yates. Over six feet. Lanky bastard. Scruffy brown hair."

"This doesn't feel good," Blackwell said.

#

Blackwell and Hansen pulled into the emergency lane of the National Gallery of Art. They entered the building; glass windows lined the walls from floor to ceiling, allowing natural light to reflect off the marble floor. Abstract metal art installations adorned the walls and sat in seemingly random places throughout the space. Further in, the walls were a cool, smoothed concrete that gave a sense of lightness—a perfect palette for the art to stand out against.

They each flashed their badges to security. Blackwell continued into the museum while Hansen informed the guards of the situation. Past the information desk, the space opened up. The ceiling was three-dimensional, with interconnected triangular glass structures, allowing more light to fill in below. Trees in one corner with circular bases added a sense of nature within the futuristic structure. The building was its own abstract layout with purpose. Corners of walls jutted out, angled walkways above gave a sense of depth, staircases zig-zagged and seamlessly blended into the walls from a distance. Blackwell stood at the center of the ground level and glanced around. No sign of Elliot.

Hansen came up next to Blackwell. "Security says they haven't noticed anyone from the descriptions we have."

Blackwell shook his head as he continued scanning faces. "Did you add they look like ex-military, special-ops, professional stone-cold killers?"

"Sorry, left that detail out."

"You take downstairs, I'll head up. If you run into them, remember who you're dealing with. And don't get distracted by the art," Blackwell said.

"No promises. My first time here," Hansen said as he sauntered to the first set of stairs.

Blackwell watched his partner from above as he made his way up a set of stairs, then glanced around as he reached the top. Another set of windows from floor to ceiling greeted him along with a piece of abstract art he thought contained a face, maybe. A small tour group passed by as he stood at the glass railing overlooking the ground floor. People stood staring at museum maps, their phones, deciding if they'd gotten enough culture for the day. A low hum of indistinguishable chatter from multiple groups filled the gaps of silence the space encouraged. He continued to search for Elliot. Nothing.

He moved to the modern art collection gallery that branched off from the main area. He wasn't much of an art person, but a small statue of a person hunched over with their head sagging to their chest stood out to him. He knew the feeling.

He continued through the gallery, which broke into smaller rooms with benches to take a rest and view the art. A hushed quiet filled the rooms. Blackwell continued, room by room. Each one filtered out to the next. He circled back to the main area, which connected the upper and lower levels. Museum staff were setting up rows of chairs and folding tables for an event. Security guards lingered above on the next floor, arms resting on the glass railings. He took out his phone and texted Hansen.

BLACKWELL: *Anything?*
HANSEN: *Nothing*
BLACKWELL: *Moving to the upper levels*

HANSEN: *k*

Blackwell made his way to the upper level, a room with close-up, high-detail photographs of faces lined one wall, opposite was a large mural of squares of what looked like skin tones. He strolled through each room scanning faces and art trying to blend in. It didn't do much to hide his frustration. He came back out to a walkway that connected to the terrace café. Still, nothing.

Suddenly, his phone buzzed.

UNKNOWN: *Ground level. Near a set of trees. Lost him. Shaved head.*

Blackwell texted Hansen.

BLACKWELL: *circle back up to the ground level entrance with caution*

HANSEN: *you got it*

Blackwell put his phone away and took an escalator down to the second floor. The same abstract art piece he first saw stared back at him. He glanced around the area—at least he had something to look for now. He got to the glass railing and looked down at the trees in the main lobby. It took him a second, but he spotted Elliot sitting on a circular base surrounding one of the trees. His head was down; a woman sitting next to him glanced up every so often.

Blackwell slowly moved down the stairs—he was at a vantage point with the high ground. He could see everyone in the area. The tour group stood in the center. His eyes jumped from corner to corner, face to face, as he made his way to the top of the stairs, never losing sight of Elliot. Another glance over the edge of the staircase and then up behind him. With each step he paused and surveyed the space. Elliot glanced up and spotted him. Blackwell looked to the far left of the museum and saw a man with a shaved head, Kaleb Lind, making a direct line to Elliot.

Blackwell hurried down the stairs, careful not to draw attention to himself. He had surprise on his side for the moment, and knew he'd need it when taking on a special-ops type like Lind. The woman sitting next to Elliot tapped him on the shoulder. Elliot turned and spotted Lind; they stood and started to make their way toward a back exit.

Lind was focused on Elliot entirely, not seeing Blackwell coming from his right side down the stairs. Elliot glanced at Blackwell. Blackwell raised his right hand waist high, signaling for him to stay where he was.

Lind was moving fast, but Blackwell was faster. Lind reached into his jacket. Blackwell couldn't see his hand but assumed he was pulling out a weapon. *Bold move.*

Lind was within fifteen feet of Elliot and the woman next to him. Blackwell inched closer to Lind, moving swiftly, wanting to cut him off. He could see now that the man had a short-bladed knife in his hand.

Before Lind could do anything, Blackwell sideswiped and tackled him in the middle of the room.

Everyone in the vicinity turned, unsure of what was happening. Surprised gasps and screams echoed throughout the open space. Some bystanders moved away, while others stood by, mouths agape, not sure what to do.

The knife hit the ground and slid a few feet from Blackwell and Lind. Blackwell tried to reorient himself and get a grip on Lind. Before he could, Lind threw his elbow up and caught Blackwell across the face.

Blackwell was stunned for a moment, both still on the ground. Before Lind could make a move for the knife, Blackwell hammered his fist into Lind's lower back twice. His kidneys wouldn't be too happy.

Lind let out a grunt and continued to scramble for the knife. Blackwell, now on his feet, tripped him up. Before he could bring his arms up, Lind's face hit the floor with a hollow thud, blood squirting from his nose.

A few security guards not ready for any action other than locking doors started to move closer. Hansen darted up the stairs and immediately pulled his badge for the security officers.

Lind lay on the ground, stunned. Blackwell grabbed his arms and put them behind his back, his knee between Lind's shoulder blades—he wasn't going anywhere. Security came over and helped Blackwell cuff Lind. Moments later, DC police along with other FBI agents showed up to lock down the scene and take Lind into custody.

Wiping the sweat from his face, Blackwell walked over to Elliot and the woman who was with him. Elliot was visibly shaken up. The woman making nervous movements was clearly on edge. Blackwell sensed it wasn't due to what had just happened. She eyed Blackwell and the other FBI agents with caution.

"You okay?" Blackwell asked, directing the question to Elliot.

"Yeah, shaky but fine," Elliot said.

"Nice friends you have." Blackwell turned to the young woman next to him with an exhausted smirk. "Emma Smith, I assume?"

Chapter 40

Elliot opened and closed his hands into fists, trying to remove the slight shake that now occupied them. He sat on a small love seat in his hotel room. Jake was in the office chair across the room, arms crossed, nibbling at his thumb nail as he processed the events Elliot had gone through. LiLo placed a glass of water in front of Elliot. He nodded thanks. She offered a quick smile as she glided to the window and stared out over the nighttime DC skyline.

After the incident at the museum, Blackwell had Elliot and LiLo escorted back to the hotel to get some rest. A pair of agents remained at the hotel in case of emergency. LiLo did her best to distract Elliot's thoughts in the aftermath. It helped but the adrenaline still pumped through his veins even hours later.

"How are you not terrified right now?" Elliot said, his question directed at LiLo.

"Who says I'm not?"

She turned and propped herself up on the short window ledge as a seat and leaned against the glass. "Like muscle memory, you learn to control it."

"Trained to control it?" Jake said.

LiLo nodded.

"You took a big risk coming here," Elliot said.

"Yeah. Kinda past the point of no return now."

Jake shook his head like he'd been stuck on a thought. "So wait, you just . . . dropped this lanky dude like a sack of potatoes in the middle of the National Mall, all Chuck Norris style?"

LiLo smirked. "Don't give me too much credit. If someone isn't expecting it, it's not hard."

"Is that what they taught you? Your former employers?" Elliot said.

"Even those of us behind a keyboard still got field training. Like any other agency, you learn the basics."

"Well, you're on my Christmas card list now," Jake said as he stood and stretched.

They each shared a smile.

"Those guys. They were from Antwerp. Before I came here. Probably at MIT too," LiLo said.

"You think they were in Seattle?" Elliot asked.

"I'd say it was them or some associates that caught up to Keating, but your guy, with the scar on his face. Agent Hansen. It wasn't him."

Elliot felt a little reassurance with that. After seeing him at the museum, he was flooded with emotions and memories of Keating's body. That now seemed a distant memory given all that had happened.

\#

Elliot sat in the back of a black SUV with tinted windows, squeezing his armrest every few seconds until his knuckles turned white. A pit formed in his stomach like he was about to give a presentation he wasn't prepared for. His free hand tapped at his knee.

"Hey, with the tapping already," Jake said as he glanced over.

"Sorry," Elliot said.

"It's okay. Just your nervousness is making me nervous and I'm not nervous. I think."

Elliot gazed out the window as the SUV continued toward its destination—NASA headquarters. After the events of the previous day, Blackwell thought it best if Jake and Elliot were escorted by agents from the hotel. They didn't disagree.

"Did LiLo say where she'd be?" Jake asked.

"No. Just that she'd be *around*. Do we even want to know?"

Jake nodded. "Good point."

Moments later they pulled up to NASA HQ and were greeted by Director Watkins, who wore a nervous smile on his face. "Welcome back, fellas. I heard about yesterday—you okay?"

"Uh, we're swell," Jake said with a big grin.

"Well, follow me. We have everything set up and ready to go."

The excitement Elliot had felt entering the building the last time was now enclosed in a claustrophobic cage. He didn't know how to sort through what was happening. He carried on in hope this would ease in time.

Everyone met in a large conference room that resembled the situation rooms Elliot had seen on TV. The front of the room had a few monitors with video feeds to teams in various parts of the world. A projector hung from the ceiling, and the side walls had multiple whiteboards. Blackwell, along with Agents Hansen and Klein, stood at the far end of the room.

The plan, in its simplest form, was to flip on an old satellite and monitor how the signal worked. The hope was that the signal would identify the newly active satellite, so they could see it in action. There was no telling how long it might take—it could be minutes, hours, or days. All that mattered was they had a direction.

As the group hurried around and planned the operation, Elliot zoned out for a moment, thinking of Keating's note and the nature of the signal. Thanks to their contacts at observatories around the world, they'd discovered that the signal was pulling data in other countries as well. Similarly, it pulled basic sociological data then moved to more complex concepts, suggesting it had a purpose. *But what is it?*

Once General Conrad arrived, leading a much larger Air Force team this time around, the conference room was full. As the senior officials and scientists settled in their seats, Elliot and Jake took up positions leaning against a side wall.

Director Watkins kicked things off. "Welcome, everyone. Everything we know so far about the signal is in the folders in front of you. Our current goals are to, one, understand how the signal moves from one host to another. With the help of the Air Force we can work through our plan for the operation to be completed today. Two, we need to understand how it got there to begin with. It's a complex bit of technology, but each day we're learning more and more. These first two goals are huge steps in that direction."

Young took over. "We've identified a satellite we'd like to test with. An old military communications relay that launched in 1970 and has been offline since 1971. We can still communicate with it and have the ability to analyze the onboard framework, which is why it's a top choice for us. We've written an algorithm we'd like to upload to it. It'll help us monitor and analyze the signal once it makes its jump. You can find the details of this portion on page five."

Everyone in the room shuffled through the folders in front of them. Jake and Elliot waited for things to happen.

The general looked over at his team for any questions or objections. A young officer chimed in, "I don't see this as a problem. That particular satellite can be flipped on within a few hours. We have the clearance in this room to do so." The rest of the group nodded in agreement.

Working remotely with a team at the Pentagon and an off-site Air Force base, they started the process of activating the old satellite. At this point the old hardware was space debris, but they wanted to confirm it wouldn't cause any issues for any surrounding technology.

Everyone watched and waited patiently over video conferencing as the Air Force teams did their jobs. Young was hunched over his laptop preparing to upload the algorithm once the satellite was flipped on.

An Air Force engineer chimed in on the video call. "Old bird has been identified and activated. ID and sat details sent to you. Ready to receive upload. Confirm."

Young nodded. "Confirmed. Identified and starting upload."

"Riveting stuff," Jake whispered to Elliot.

The upload didn't take as long as Elliot thought it might.

"Upload complete. Reboot sequence can begin," Young said.

"Confirmed. Rebooting."

"Now we wait," Young said to the rest of the room as he leaned back in his chair.

"What's our fail-safe?" General Conrad asked.

"If anything goes wrong we have a kill switch that would put the satellite back in sleep mode," Young said, fidgeting with his pen. "It'd allow us to uninstall the patch and return it to its default state or golden image. Just in case the new patch doesn't take or causes a fatal error."

The room waited in hushed silence. Watkins paced in the background, softly biting his thumbnail. Blackwell and his team had a hushed discussion Elliot couldn't hear. The room was filled with a balloon of anticipation ready to pop at any moment. Elliot couldn't help but tap his fingers against his leg. Jake took up a seat at the end of the table in front of Elliot. He seemed to be the only one not focused on the monitor.

Elliot watched as his friend shuffled through the prepared folder and documents, then opened his laptop; his fingers glided over the keys in a frenzy of typing. Elliot knew his friend well enough to know.

He was onto something.

Elliot stepped over to Jake to see what he was up to and pulled up a seat at the table next to him.

"What're you looking at?" Elliot asked, his voice low.

"Well, I'm trying to figure out how the signal got onto the host satellite by mapping the signal's signature to a time before a satellite started showing the same activity." After a moment, Jake continued, "It's odd but I keep seeing the FRB pulse near a few satellites before the signal started from them."

"The FRB my father was tracking," Elliot said.

"Yeah, the same one," Jake said.

"Could they come from another satellite?"

"I thought about that but not like this. The original signatures are millisecond blasts, but slightly more intense and they hit these few satellites"—he pointed at a list on his laptop—"just before the signal is readable from them. I'll tell you, without those two guys,"—he pointed at Young and Watkins—"and the hardware here, we never would've spotted this."

"So this isn't coming from any specific country is what you're saying?" Elliot asked.

Jake glanced at Elliot, his expression serious. "No, it's not."

Suddenly, from the front of the room, Young called out, "We're live!"

Jake and Elliot both shifted their focus to the monitor and the rest of the room.

"Reboot complete. Test bird back online. Please verify, NASA," the same Air Force engineer called out.

Young responded, "Confirmed, back online. And the patch has successfully updated."

There was a short burst of cheering from everyone in the room and on the call. A wave of relief cascaded across the room and tension dipped.

"Monitoring response rolling in," Young said. "All quiet, wait . . . Whoa, what the hell . . . just . . ."

"What happened?" Watkins said.

"Not sure. But we're getting a ton of data responses."

A collective silence rolled over the room.

"I see a quick burst activity coming from another satellite," Young said. "The signal made the jump!"

The room held on to his last statement with bated breath.

"That explains the influx of data responses. But I can't keep up with this," Young said.

"Is it doing anything else?" the general asked. His tie was loose and the top button of his collared shirt was undone.

"Not that I can tell—seems like it's cycling through something," Young said.

"Maybe it's doing a diagnostic check?" Watkins said.

The room settled a bit, everyone thinking through the implications.

"So what's our next step?" the general asked the room.

"We wait, and listen. Monitor anything and everything. Spend some time looking at these data responses in the meantime," Watkins said. "We hear anything from the other global teams?"

"Not yet," Young said.

Elliot decided this might be a good time to raise Jake's theory.

"What if the signal isn't coming from another country?" Elliot asked from the back of the room. Everyone paused and turned to look at him, most with confused looks.

"What do you mean?" Young asked.

Jake stepped in. "I was doing analysis of activity on satellites before they showed signs of generating the signal. Most, I'd bet, would match what we just saw. Short, high-powered bursts from another satellite. But I've mapped a few where the activity was higher and looked more like an actual FRB."

The group focused on Jake.

"An actual FRB, generated from space?" Young asked, as he leaned back in his chair.

"What the hell are you saying?" the general blurted.

Elliot looked directly at him. "We're saying maybe this isn't coming from another country—or even Earth."

The general waved his hand, like he was shooing a pesky animal. "I'm not sure I want to head down the path you're trying to send me."

"Well, if it makes you feel any better, I doubt they're little green men—it'd probably be an AI of some sort or a probe—but this path could be very real," Jake said.

The general, exasperated, looked to Watkins for a response. "Okay, let's look at the data," Watkins said, nodding to Jake.

Jake shared his screen to the large monitor. "Here's what I found. These were the satellites I identified having been around some higher wavelength activity before the signal started. There are just a handful and they're all old communication relays. I'm not sure if those were targeted specifically, but the activity and timing are too much of a coincidence. This activity was found in the SD card data too. Keating wanted this to be found. The activity hitting these satellites isn't coming from any source on Earth. They look exactly like an FRB, a fast burst, but stop at the satellite. Then . . . the signal starts."

"Can we confirm this with other stations?" Watkins asked.

"Already on it" Young said. "Also getting some responses from them for new satellite data and mappings. Our fifty percent number is going to jump."

"So, say you're right, do we just wait until they decide to eliminate us?" the general asked.

"Who says they're going to eliminate us? Why is that the first thought?" Elliot said.

"Because it's my job to think of the worst-case scenario and plan for it," the general snapped. "I gave you more time, we're at the brink here with countermeasures against an attack on our soil. We have intel and targets ready to go. An entire initiative is on hold, hinging on you all finding me an answer to *who*. Right now, I still have no answers and now you're telling me, basically, it's aliens."

The room was silent. Elliot realized that he'd brought it up, now it was on him to continue. "Right now, this is what we have," Elliot said.

"Getting some responses from Australia and Japan," Young reported. "They're saying they see the same activity around the birds we identified. No clue what it is either, but it's definitely not of this Earth."

The general and Elliot traded a look. If *screw you* weren't written on Elliot's face, the general could at least hear Elliot think it.

"Look at the data that's been pulled so far," Jake said. "It's historical, cultural, financial, weather patterns, and so on. It's learning, but why? If we explored a new planet, we wouldn't send humans. We'd send rovers, machines, or a satellite-hacking AI to learn for us. It has the capability, from what we can tell, to connect to any device and the ability to push data. Why hasn't it thrown our world into chaos by simply shutting down everything, or crashing the market, or telling military intel the wrong thing? It's scouting, exploring, collecting, but to what end? Who knows. Maybe they're just snooping like we do."

"We did that ourselves," Klein said.

The General glared at her, taking the hint.

"The signal isn't what attacked us, sir," Elliot said. "The attack was orchestrated based on the same knowledge we have—we think this is a surveillance tool from another country."

"The signal on the test satellite stopped cycling. Maybe performing a diagnostics check, but it just pinged a range of satellites," Young said.

"It's looking for another host to jump to," Elliot said.

"Is the data response making any sense?" Watkins asked.

"Not yet, it's also coming in too fast," Young said. "It looks like it's communicating with other signal-hosted satellites. Creating a network. There's a repeating activity bouncing back and forth. Like it's probing, almost."

"Are they doing anything? We'd need to coordinate with other agencies and fast if we think this is another attack," Blackwell said.

"Unclear," Young said.

"Wait, there's a bunch of activity happening from our test bird," Watkins pointed out.

"I see it too," Young said. "Whoa, what is this?" His hands were off the keyboard like his laptop had been taken over and he couldn't do anything. Watkins moved to look over Young's shoulder.

"What is it?" Elliot asked.

"The data feed just stopped and is sitting at a command prompt," Young said. He grabbed an HDMI cable and plugged it into his laptop to share his screen to the monitor. His screen popped up on the monitor, showing a terminal window, with a stream of data responses collected by the algorithm, then just stops at a command prompt and a blinking cursor.

"Well, I guess we proved it can take over a device," Jake whispered to Elliot.

"Can you type anything?" Klein asked.

"No, I'm locked out," Young said.

Then a response came through on the prompt:

Hello. World.

"What the hell is going on?" the General asked; his voice had a tickle of fear behind it.

"It's the first thing you print when you learn a new language," Young said to the room.

Another message started to come through:

Signal. Response. Beyond what's possible.

Jake and Elliot looked at each other.

Suddenly the terminal window was blasted with data output so fast they couldn't keep up with what was showing on the screen. Line after line of responses poured in.

"Holy shit," Young said.

"Seeing some serious activity across known host birds," another engineer said.

"Are we capturing all of this?" Watkins asked.

"Sure are, but this is a crazy amount of data," Young said.

After a couple minutes of this chaotic flurry of responses—it stopped. The terminal window closed and Young had control of his laptop again.

The room was silent.

"What the hell just happened?" General Conrad asked.

"I'm not seeing any activity from any satellite now—they're all quiet," Young said.

"Let's confirm with Japan and Australia," Watkins said, as Young turned back to his laptop to relay the message.

"Can we confirm nothing outside this room was impacted?" Blackwell said.

Air Force engineers who were still on the call jumped on the task immediately.

"Japan, Australia, and EU all not seeing activity anymore on their side. Asking what happened?" Young said.

"Tell them we'll coordinate a debriefing once we parse through the data," Watkins said.

An Air Force engineer on the call chimed in. "No impact to any known systems, infrastructure, or the like. All is quiet."

Elliot turned to look at Conrad.

"So, General, that theory I had . . ."

Chapter 41

Agent Blackwell waited in line at a coffee shop that was steps away from Elliot's hotel. It wasn't his usual stop; he wasn't sure what to expect but hoped it was at least hot and in a cup. Right now, that's all he wanted.

After the discovery with the NASA team, Blackwell spent most of his day coordinating with other agencies on what the next steps were. He spent more time moving from meeting to meeting and filing reports than he was typically used to. Satellite security was top of the list. The same questions surfaced over and over again: How did this happen, and could it happen again? He provided his findings and moved on. Each bureaucratic meeting after the other held promises he didn't believe they could keep.

Details from the discovery, the signal, filtered all the way to the top at the White House. For a short period, it was a scramble for information. In the end, the decision to abort any cyber counterattack was made. Lights were slowly coming back on in the impacted southern states with a promise of Federal support going forward. *More promises.* A sense of relief sat in Blackwell, even if he didn't fully understand the signal or what might happen next with it.

He'd spent the rest of the previous day working with an internal investigation team within the FBI. Once it was discovered Agent Evans was selling classified intel, his team was under scrutiny. An investigation that wouldn't end any time soon, but Blackwell was happy to help in any way possible. Or at least, so he could get back to work. By the book.

There were no leads as to who Evans was selling intel to, but loose connections to Lind and Yates started to show themselves—shared dead drops and contacts that, unfortunately, led nowhere. What they did know was that Yates and Lind were in Seattle at the time of Dr. Keating's death, and strong evidence was coming together that put one of them at the scene of the murder. But Yates turned into a ghost after his encounter with LiLo on the National Mall, and Lind wasn't talking. Another lost trail. He didn't have much to go on and this investigation was being taken from him. The CIA had come in to "handle" the situation. They thanked Blackwell for his efforts, but it still felt like a slap in the face.

He arrived at Elliot's hotel and took a deep breath. The weight of exhaustion lingered throughout his body. His hot cup of coffee was now lukewarm. He took a sip, contemplating his next move. His team shorthanded, and under investigation, pushed him to the brink of uncertainty. An unsettling feeling for the *by-the-book* agent. Maybe by the book wasn't the right approach anymore.

#

LiLo met Elliot, as they'd arranged, in the lobby of their hotel. Her eyes bounced around, checking faces and exits.

"It'll be okay," Elliot said.

A moment later Agent Blackwell entered the hotel and approached them. He was alone as he said he would be.

"No Jake?" Blackwell asked.

"He's busy working with the NASA team," Elliot said. "They had plenty more to do with the signal."

"I bet," Blackwell said. "What's next for you?"

"Heading back to Boston tomorrow."

Blackwell nodded then turned to LiLo. "And what about you?"

There was a thick pause between them.

Before she could speak Blackwell said, "You know, at first glance you don't look like the photo that's splashed across our website."

Adrenaline rushed through LiLo—she knew how to control it but this was not a space she wanted to be trapped in. Her eyes glanced around for options.

"Look, if I was going to take you in, it would've already happened." Blackwell glanced around the sparse lobby. "I did a little digging on you—no surprise there isn't much. You don't leave anything behind, do you?"

LiLo held his look for a moment, waiting to see if this was going somewhere. She peered over his shoulder then her eyes bounced left to right. Confirming he was alone.

"Don't say much either. Well, I was curious why you're on our most-wanted list and, frankly, it wasn't very clear. Nothing added up. So I reopened your very lean file to have that listing reevaluated."

LiLo glanced at Elliot.

"Thanks for those tips," Blackwell said to LiLo. "I'm assuming it was you, and because of them, we were able to get through the ransomware locks. That will make it easier to get access back to areas still affected by the blackouts. Also, we traced another round of planned attacks back to a for-hire hacker group working abroad. Saved lives."

Relief washed over LiLo as she let out a tight smile, happy she was able to do something to prevent any further disaster.

"Yeah, thought so," Blackwell said. "Does the word TELOS mean anything to you?"

LiLo shook her head. *How did he know?* Either way, she wasn't ready to reconnect herself. She had more to solve before inviting the FBI in.

She could tell Blackwell didn't buy it but he played along. "How about YellowJacket?"

LiLo glanced at Elliot then back at Blackwell. She nodded. "They leveraged a friend of mine to help build the scripts used in the attacks."

"Gemini?" Blackwell said.

LiLo did her best to hold back a reaction but realized it was too late—she'd given herself away. She nodded.

"I'm sorry to have to tell you this. But she was found dead in her apartment."

Her eyes dropped to the floor for a lost moment then snapped back to Blackwell. A burning feeling welled inside her, reaching to escape. Her jaw tightened. She wanted to scream at the top of her lungs. She let out a short tight breath and bottled what was left inside. Her composure was intact.

"Some friends of ours working with Interpol found her in London. There's some connection to Lind and Yates, the gentlemen you both encountered here in DC. Who seemed to have a connection to YellowJacket. And the YellowJacket handle, we discovered with your help, is tied to former Agent Evans. Not quite sure how they connect to the signal but clearly they wanted something if they were willing to kill Dr. Keating. And of course, their connection to you," Blackwell said, letting the last comment linger.

LiLo remained unmoved. She wasn't sure of his intentions other than him poking and prying for her to slip up. She closed off that connection, unwilling to reveal herself. They didn't trust each other, which didn't bother LiLo. It's how she lived.

Blackwell bounced a glance between Elliot and LiLo. "Look, I know you've been running for a long time. There's only so much I can do right now, but I think reopening your file and reviewing your status will get it reduced. At the very least get you off our damn website. There's more to this situation and, well," Blackwell took out a pack of gum, "gum?"

Elliot and LiLo shook their heads.

Blackwell popped a piece in his mouth. "Well, what I could use is some unofficial help."

"Unofficial help?" LiLo said.

"Well, since you took out my tech lead, I'm in need of someone. Unofficial. Less by the book."

LiLo smirked. "Maybe."

Blackwell slowly nodded. "Okay. Maybe works."

Blackwell was smart, he knew more about LiLo than she expected. But she already knew everything about him, and he could be useful.

They nodded at each other. Blackwell turned to Elliot. "Well, Mr. Bishop, good luck."

LiLo watched as he turned and walked out of the hotel. No police, no FBI agents storming the hotel to put her in cuffs and lock her away. She was close to escaping the life she was living. She could see a path forward. A path she didn't need to hide from. A path she didn't need to run from. The bottled heat dissipated within her. She was almost home.

Chapter 42

Two weeks had passed since the moment at NASA HQ when the signal sent a message then went quiet. Elliot had returned to Boston for a few days to meet with Trevor, his editor, to review his story. Then he planned to head to Maine to finish cleaning out his father's office, a final goodbye to another lesson. A task that felt like he started an eternity ago.

After his story was reviewed and dissected by the FBI and other government agencies, and promises were made to Chris Burns at AeroTech to leave key names out, there was nothing left to print. The truth was buried under a classified label.

So he wrote a different story. One focused on something he wasn't sure he believed in—that there was something or someone else out there in the depths of the universe. A concept, a thought, he could hold on to when he was younger, but escaped him as he grew older. His only reference in the story to any facts, people, or events that happened was his final line, a cryptic message of hope that found its way to him: *Think beyond what's possible.*

Before his story even printed, news about the signal leaked and the world spun feverishly with conspiracy theories flooding forums, local news, and message boards alike. Twenty-four hours a day, talking heads on news networks offered their opinions as facts. Alien theorists were in their heyday. Even if they didn't know exactly who, or what, sent the signal, they knew it wasn't from here. That's all they needed. For a short period, protests spread across the world, people seeking answers their governments didn't have. UFO sightings were at an all-time high, everyone claiming to have seen the creators of the signal. Social media feeds were buried in fake videos of UFOs, commentary from both sides with *answers*. The signal became a political talking point to swing votes and divide sides.

The signal had left the world with many questions, and no one had answers. Elliot's story would become a slice of this news cycle that would be lost in the daily feed of life.

Jake remained in DC to continue research on the signal with NASA and various teams around the globe. They still didn't understand it or know if it could be replicated. Data was being shared between countries. The signal was a sign of technology at a scale no one could imagine. An unprecedented infiltration of the Earth. In the coming weeks, NATO and world military leaders would begin holding regular conferences to understand and plan for a global threat. On the surface, it was a time of peace, but a layer below, each still protected their own. New regulations about space and how we, as a global community, should use and interact with it were being debated. Most were still generic enough that they could be manipulated, but it was a start.

Elliot had hope that whoever sent the signal wasn't a threat. It was an idea not held by many.

Elliot arrived in Maine on a clear summer afternoon. He took his laptop outside to work on a new story beside the lake, its waters smooth and calm.

His chat client lit up.

JAKE: *Hey. How's ME?*

ELLIOT: *Quiet. You going to visit?*

JAKE: *In a couple days. Wrapping up some new findings we have.*

ELLIOT: *Oh, yeah?*

JAKE: *Our friend that can't be named, but is probably reading this right now because she doesn't have boundaries, figured out what some of the embedded code was doing in the signal. Explains how it works, how it taps power sources to replicate, and it has some algorithm buried within it. It's wild stuff.*

ELLIOT: *Sounds like it.*

JAKE: *Don't worry, I'll share allllll the classified knowledge I have when I visit.*

ELLIOT: *Can't wait.*

#

Elliot spent the next day cleaning and packing his father's remaining things. That night he made a fire by the lake, like he'd done many times before with his father, and let himself get lost in his memories.

"Do you see it?" he recalled his father asking, a smile splashed across his face like he was in on the trick, waiting for the big revelation. He sat close to his temporary, eager-to-learn student. Watching his eyes as if he could track them.

"You're not seeing it, are you?"

The young student, Elliot, shook his head.

"Okay. Start at the Big Dipper." He pointed toward the wide open, clear sky. It blanketed the two in a tapestry of celestial light. The mesmerizing sight invoked awe, inspiration, and reflected the smallness of the human species and their hope. The stillness of the night presented a peacefulness that didn't exist anywhere else in this moment. The light from the moon was crisp, bright, and skimmed the tops of the surrounding trees. The moonlight landed and reflected off the still lake, which sat in front of them like an old friend. All of it overshadowed the crackling fire they'd built, which provided some warmth on the cool summer night.

"Okay. Big Dipper," Elliot said, as he fidgeted in his seat, ready to restart the lesson with fresh eyes. A lesson they could spend all night doing, no matter how many times it took.

"Alright, now follow the tip of my finger," John said, as he guided it along the sky like he was touching each star he came across. The student sat patiently with a beaming smile, enjoying the show. He followed his father's hand as he pointed out each star, one at a time.

"Now, the Big Dipper *technically* isn't a constellation. It's an asterism, a group of stars that make up a portion of the constellation Ursa Major, the Great Bear," his father continued in a low voice, happy to share and teach what he knew, like he was running a show at a planetarium. "The Big Dipper is the head, neck, and chest of the bear. Now, follow along the topside of the dipper, and down . . ." He named each star of the Great Bear. The stars, almost hidden within each other, created something larger.

"I see it," Elliot said, with soft, contained excitement. The trick revealed. The stars burned into his memory like they burned in the sky.

Elliot sat by the same fire pit from so many years ago, then as a young student, now with only memories. The fire crackled in the cool summer night; the sky was as clear as the night he learned his first constellation. A distant memory that revisited him as he looked up to the stars.

But he'd traced his own path now—he no longer needed a guide. His mind was distant, light-years farther away than any of the stars over his head. Wondering if there was a beginning to it all, or did it always exist.

He remained under the night's cover until the fire calmed to embers, soaking in the quiet moment before it vanished.

* * *

Acknowledgements

If you made it this far, thank you. I hope you enjoyed reading HOST as much as I enjoyed writing it.

Writing is an isolating process and can be that way, unless or until you want to share your words with the world. Then it becomes a group effort. This book would not have happened without the support of my friends and family.

First and foremost I want to thank my old man aka *The Captain* aka Dad aka Dad-dad-daddio for the daily inspiration, motivation, ideas, and research. At times my inbox was so flooded with articles and ideas for dialogue that I couldn't keep up.

To my mother for the marketing ideas and talking through my progress every week. For the push to take a risk on myself and get the damn thing done!

To my super talented cousin, Kasey Regan, for the kickass cover art and variants. You took what I had in my head and turned it into reality.

To my first reader, Kav, for being brave enough to read an early draft (yikes it was bad), and for being honest about what was good, bad, and terrible.

To my weekly writing chat buddy, podcasting partner, Tim Letteney, for the pep talks, ideas, therapy(?), and dropping everything (even his own project) to read later drafts and help refine the ideas I had.

To my beta readers; Dad, Mom, Jared, Thais, Morgan, Elizabeth, Rob L., Max, Brit, Will, and Stephanie. Thank you for taking the time to read a draft, provide feedback, and help refine the story and characters (and catch all my terrible mistakes). Any mistakes found are my own.

To my editor, Kristen Tate, for helping me shape this story and build my toolset for future stories.

And finally, to all my friends, family, and readers that took the time to pick up and read a copy, thank you.

About the Author

Russ Capasso writes and sleeps in Somerville, MA.

When he's not writing or sleeping he's gaming (video or the dice kind), nerding out about movies, playing hockey, homebrewing, or biking around the city.

HOST is his first novel.

For more information visit: www.russcapasso.com

Made in the USA
Middletown, DE
10 October 2024

62411637R00168